THE IMPERFECTIONISTS

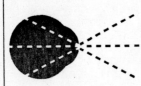
This Large Print Book carries the
Seal of Approval of N.A.V.H.

THE IMPERFECTIONISTS

TOM RACHMAN

THORNDIKE PRESS
A part of Gale, Cengage Learning

GALE
CENGAGE Learning

Detroit • New York • San Francisco • New Haven, Conn • Waterville, Maine • London

GALE
CENGAGE Learning

LIBRARY OF CONGRESS CATALOGING-IN-PUBLICATION DATA

Rachman, Tom.
    The imperfectionists / by Tom Rachman.
      p. cm. — (Thorndike Press large print reviewers' choice)
    ISBN-13: 978-1-4104-3065-6
    ISBN-10: 1-4104-3065-0
    1. Reporters and reporting—Fiction. 2. Newspaper publishing—Fiction. 3. Newspaper editors—Fiction. 4. Large type books. I. Title.
    PR9199.4.R323I57 2010b
    813'.6—dc22   2010024166

Published in 2010 by arrangement with Dial Press, a division of Random House, Inc.

Printed in Mexico
5 6 7 14 13 12 11

For Clare and Jack

CONTENTS

■ ■ ■ ■ ■

"Bush Slumps to New Low in Polls"

• • •

PARIS CORRESPONDENT — LLOYD BURKO

■ ■ ■ ■ ■

Lloyd shoves off the bedcovers and hurries to the front door in white underwear and black socks. He steadies himself on the knob and shuts his eyes. Chill air rushes under the door; he curls his toes. But the hallway is silent. Only high-heeled clicks from the floor above. A shutter squeaking on the other side of the courtyard. His own breath, whistling in his nostrils, whistling out.

Faintly, a woman's voice drifts in. He clenches his eyelids tighter, as if to drive up the volume, but makes out only murmurs, a breakfast exchange between the woman and the man in the apartment across the hall. Until, abruptly, their door opens: her voice grows louder, the hallway floorboards creak — she is approaching. Lloyd hustles back, unlatches the window above the courtyard, and takes up a position there, gazing out over his corner of Paris.

She taps on his front door.

11

"Come in," he says. "No need to knock." And his wife enters their apartment for the first time since the night before.

He does not turn from the window to face Eileen, only presses his bald knees harder into the iron guardrail. She smoothes down the back of his gray hair. He flinches, surprised to be touched.

"Only me," she says.

He smiles, eyes crinkling, lips parting, inhaling as if to speak. But he has no reply. She lets go.

He turns finally to find her seated before the drawer where they keep old photographs. A kitchen towel hangs from her shoulder and she wipes off her fingers, damp from peeled potatoes, dishwashing liquid, diced onions, scented from moth-balled blankets, soil from the window boxes — Eileen is a woman who touches everything, tastes all, digs in. She slips on her reading glasses.

"What are you hunting for in there?" he asks.

"Just a picture of me in Vermont when I was little. To show Didier." She rises, taking a photo album with her, and stands by the front door. "You have plans for dinner, right?"

"Mm." He nods at the album. "Bit by

12

bit," he says.

"What's that mean?"

"You're shifting across the hall."

"No."

"You're allowed to."

He hasn't resisted her friendship with Didier, the man across the hall. She is not finished with that part of her life, with sex, as Lloyd is. She is eighteen years younger, a gap that incited him once but that, now he is seventy, separates them like a lake. He blows her a kiss and returns to the window.

The floorboards in the hallway creak. Didier's front door opens and shuts — Eileen doesn't knock over there, just goes in.

Lloyd glances at the phone. It has been weeks since he sold an article and he needs money. He dials the paper in Rome.

An intern transfers him to the news editor, Craig Menzies, a balding worrier who decides much of what appears in each edition. No matter the time of day, Menzies is at his desk. The man has nothing in his life but news.

"Good time for a pitch?" Lloyd asks.

"I'm a tad busy, actually. Could you zing me an email?"

"Can't. Problem with my computer." The problem is that he doesn't own one; Lloyd still uses a word processor, vintage 1993. "I

13

can print something and fax it over."

"Tell me by phone. But please, if possible, could you get your computer working?"

"Yes: get computer fixed. Duly noted." He scratches his finger across the notepad, as if to tease out a better idea than the one scrawled there. "You folks interested in a feature on the ortolan? It's this French delicacy, a bird — a sort of finch, I think — that's illegal to sell here. They stick it in a cage, poke out its eyes so it can't tell day from night, then feed it round the clock. When it's full up, they drown it in Cognac and cook it. Mitterrand ate one for his last meal."

"Uh-huh," Menzies responds circumspectly. "But sorry, where's the news?"

"No news. Just a feature."

"You have anything else?"

Lloyd scratches at his pad again. "How about a business piece on wine: sales of rosé outstripping white for the first time in France."

"Is that true?"

"I think so. I still have to double-check."

"Do you have anything more timely?"

"You don't want the ortolan?"

"I don't think we have space for it. It's a tight day — four pages in news."

All the other publications Lloyd freelanced

14

for have dumped him. Now he suspects that the paper — his final string, his last employer — is looking to send him away, too.

"You know our money problems, Lloyd. We're only buying freelance stuff that's jaw-dropping these days. Which isn't saying yours isn't good. I just mean Kathleen only wants enterprise now. Terrorism, nuclear Iran, resurgent Russia — that kind of thing. Anything else we basically take from the wires. It's a money thing, not about you."

Lloyd hangs up and returns to the window, gazing out at Sixth Arrondissement apartment buildings, white walls dirtied where rain drizzled and drainpipes leaked, the paint peeling, shutters closed tight, courtyards below where residents' bicycles huddle, handlebars and pedals and spokes jammed into each other, zinc roofs overhead, capped chimney pipes streaking white smoke across white sky.

He walks over to the closed front door and stands still, listening. She might come back from Didier's unbidden. This *is* their home, for Christ's sake.

When the dinner hour arrives, he bangs about as clamorously as possible, crashing the door into the coatrack, simulating a coughing fit on his way out, all to ensure that Eileen across the hall hears him leaving for his supposed dinner plans, although no such plans exist. He simply will not sit down for another charity meal with her and Didier.

He wanders down Boulevard du Montparnasse to kill time, buys a box of *calissons* to give to his daughter Charlotte, and returns home, as stealthy now as he was noisy before. When he enters the apartment, he raises the front door on its hinges to dull the squeak, clicks it gently shut. He doesn't turn on the main light — Eileen might see it under the door — and fumbles in the kitchen, leaving the fridge ajar for illumination. He opens a can of chickpeas and digs straight in with a fork, catching sight of his right hand, which is mottled with age spots. He switches the fork to his left hand, the decrepit right thrust deep in his trouser pocket, hugging a thin leather wallet.

Been broke plenty of times. Always spent better than he saved. On tailored shirts from Jermyn Street. Cases of Château Gloria 1971. Shares in a racehorse that almost landed in the money. Impromptu vacations to Brazil with impromptu women. Taxis everywhere. He takes another fork of chickpeas. Salt. Needs salt. He drops a pinch into the can.

At dawn, he lies under layers of blankets

and bedcovers — he doesn't use the heating anymore unless Eileen is here. He'll visit Charlotte today, but doesn't relish it. He turns on his other side, as if to flip from her to his son, Jérôme. Sweet kid. Lloyd flips again. So awake, so weary. Lazy — he's become lazy. How did that happen?

He forces off the covers and, shivering in his underwear and socks, makes for his desk. He pores over old phone numbers — hundreds of scraps of paper, stapled, taped, glued in place. Too early to call anyone. He grins at names of former colleagues: the editor who cursed him out for missing the first Paris riots in '68 because he had been drunk in the bathtub with a lady friend. Or the bureau chief who flew him to Lisbon to cover the coup in '74, even though he couldn't speak a word of Portuguese. Or the reporter who got the giggles with Lloyd at a Giscard d'Estaing presser until they were flung out and upbraided by the press secretary. How many of these ancient numbers still work?

The living-room curtains brighten gradually from behind. He parts them. The sun is not visible, nor clouds — only buildings. At least Eileen doesn't realize his money situation. If she found out, she'd try to help. And then what would he have left?

He opens the window, breathes in, presses his knees into the guardrail. The grandeur of Paris — its tallness and broadness and hardness and softness, its perfect symmetry, human will imposed on stone, on razored lawns, on the disobedient rosebushes — that Paris resides elsewhere. His own is smaller, containing himself, this window, the floorboards that creak across the hall.

By 9 A.M., he is trooping north through the Luxembourg Gardens. By the Palais de Justice, he rests. Flagging already? Lazy bastard. He forces himself onward, over the Seine, up Rue Montorgueil, past the Grands Boulevards.

Charlotte's shop is on Rue Rochechouart — not too high up the hill, thankfully. The store isn't open yet, so he wanders toward a café, then changes his mind at the door — no money to waste on luxuries. He gazes in the window of his daughter's shop, which is full of handmade hats, designed by Charlotte and produced by a team of young women in high-waisted linen aprons and mobcaps, like eighteenth-century maids.

She arrives later than the posted opening time. *"Oui?"* she says upon seeing her father — she only talks to him in French.

"I was admiring your window," he says. "It's beautifully arranged."

She unlocks the shop and enters. "Why are you wearing a tie? Do you have somewhere to go?"

"Here — I was coming here to see you." He hands her the box of candies. "Some *calissons.*"

"I don't eat those."

"I thought you loved them."

"Not me. Brigitte does." This is her mother, the second of Lloyd's ex-wives.

"Could you give them to her?"

"She won't want anything from you."

"You're so angry with me, Charlie."

She marches to the other side of the shop, tidying as if it were combat. A customer enters and Charlotte puts on a smile. Lloyd removes himself to a corner. The customer leaves and Charlotte resumes her pugilistic dusting.

"Did I do something wrong?" he asks.

"My God — you are so egocentric."

He peers into the back of the shop.

"They're not here yet," she snaps.

"Who aren't?"

"The girls."

"Your workers? Why are you telling me that?"

"You got here too early. Bad timing." Charlotte claims that Lloyd has pursued every woman she ever introduced him to,

19

starting with her best friend at lycée, Nathalie, who came along for a vacation to Antibes once and lost her bikini top in the waves. Charlotte caught Lloyd watching. Thankfully, she never learned that matters eventually went much further between her father and Nathalie.

But all that is over. Finished, finally. So senseless in retrospect — such effort wasted. Libido: it has been the tyrant of his times, hurling him from comfortable America all those years ago to sinful Europe for adventure and conquest, marrying him four times, tripping him up a hundred more, distracting and degrading and nearly ruining him. Yet now it is mercifully done with, desire having dwindled these past years, as mysterious in departure as it was on arrival. For the first time since age twelve, Lloyd witnesses the world without motive. And he is quite lost.

"You really don't like the candies?" he says.

"I didn't ask for them."

"No, you didn't." He smiles sadly. "Is there something I could do for you, though?"

"What for?"

"To help."

"I don't want your help."

"All right," he says. "All right, then." He nods, sighs, and turns for the door.

She comes out after him. He reaches to touch her arm, but she pulls away. She hands back the box of *calissons*. "I'm not going to use these."

Back home, he runs through his contact numbers and ends up calling an old reporter buddy, Ken Lazzarino, now working at a magazine in Manhattan. They exchange news and get nostalgic for a few minutes, but an undercurrent runs through the conversation: both men know that Lloyd needs a favor, but he can't bring himself to ask. Finally, he forces it out. "What if I wanted to pitch something?"

"You never wrote for us, Lloyd."

"I know, I'm just wondering if."

"I do online strategy now — I don't have a say in content anymore."

"Is there someone you could get me in touch with?"

After listening to several variations of no, Lloyd puts down the phone.

He eats another can of chickpeas and tries Menzies again at the paper. "What about me doing the European business roundup today?"

"Hardy Benjamin handles that now."

"I know it's a pain for you guys that I

don't have this email stuff working. I can fax it, though. It won't make a difference."

"It does, actually. But look, I'll call if we need something out of Paris. Or give me a ring if you have something newsy."

Lloyd opens a French current-affairs magazine in hopes of stealing a story idea. He flips the pages impatiently — he doesn't recognize half the names. Who the hell is that guy in the photo? He used to know everything going on in this country. At press conferences, he was front-row, arm raised, rushing up afterward to pitch questions from the sidelines. At embassy cocktail parties, he sidled up to the ambassadors with a grin, notebook emerging from his hip pocket. Nowadays, if he attends press conferences at all, he's back-row, doodling, dozing. Embossed invitations pile up on his coffee table. Scoops, big and little, pass him by. He still has smarts enough to produce the obvious pieces — those he can do drunk, eyelids closed, in his underwear at the word processor.

He tosses the current-affairs magazine onto a chair. What's the point in trying? He calls his son's mobile. "Am I waking you?" he asks in French, the language they use together.

Jérôme covers the phone and coughs.

"I was hoping to buy you lunch later," Lloyd says. "Shouldn't you be down at the ministry at this hour?"

But Jérôme has the day off, so they agree to meet at a bistro around Place de Clichy, which is near where the young man lives, though the precise location of Jérôme's home is as much a mystery to Lloyd as are the details of the young man's job at the French foreign ministry. The boy is secretive.

Lloyd arrives at the bistro early to check the prices on the menu. He opens his wallet to count the cash, then takes a table.

When Jérôme walks in, Lloyd stands and smiles. "I'd almost forgotten how fond I am of you."

Jérôme sits quickly, as if caught out in musical chairs. "You're strange."

"Yes. It's true."

Jérôme flaps out the napkin and runs a hand through his floppy locks, leaving tangled tents of hair. His mother, Françoise, a tobacco-fingered stage actress, had the same hair-mussing habit and it made her even more attractive until years later, when she had no work, and it made her disheveled. Jérôme, at twenty-eight, is tattered already, dressed as if by a vintage shop, in a velvet blazer whose sleeves stop halfway up

23

his forearms and an over-tight pin-striped shirt, cigarette rolling papers visible through a rip in the breast pocket.

"Let me buy you a shirt," Lloyd says impulsively. "You need a proper shirt. We'll go down to Hilditch & Key, down on Rivoli. We'll take a taxi. Come on." He speaks rashly — he couldn't afford a new shirt. But Jérôme declines.

Lloyd reaches across the table and grips his boy's thumb. "It's been ages — we live in the same city, for God's sake."

Jérôme takes his thumb back and studies the menu. He settles on the salad with goat cheese and walnuts.

"Have something proper," Lloyd protests. "Have a steak!" He grins, though his gaze runs down the menu to the price of steak. He clenches his toes.

"Salad is fine," Jérôme says.

Lloyd orders the salad himself since it's the cheapest item. He offers his son a bottle of wine and is relieved that this, too, is declined. Lloyd wolfs down his food and all the bread in the basket. Too many chickpeas, too little meat. Jérôme, meanwhile, pecks at his goat cheese and ignores the lettuce.

Teasingly, Lloyd tells him in English, "Eat your greens, boy!" Jérôme's face creases with incomprehension, and Lloyd must translate into French. Jérôme could speak English at one stage, but Lloyd moved out when the boy was six, and he had limited chances to practice after that. How peculiar, then, for Lloyd to see in this French kid's face the features of his own long-gone Ohio father. Ignore the hair and otherwise the resemblance is striking — the flat nose and the foggy brown eyes. Even Jérôme's habit of using three words where twenty would do. Except, of course, that Jérôme's words are in the wrong language. An unsettling thought crosses Lloyd's mind: one day, his son will die. It's a plain fact, but it had never occurred to him before.

"Come on," Lloyd says. "Let's get that pretty waitress over here." He raises his arm for her attention. "She's cute, no? Let me get you her number," he says. "You want it?"

Jérôme pulls his father's arm down. "It's fine," he says, hurriedly rolling a cigarette.

It has been months since their last meeting, and the reason is soon clear: they are fond of each other, but there is little to say. What does Lloyd know of Jérôme? Most of his knowledge derives from the boy's first few years — that he was timid, always reading Lucky Luke comic books, wanted to be a cartoonist. Lloyd told him to be a journalist. Best job in the world, he said.

"So," Lloyd asks, "you still drawing?"

"Drawing?"

"Your cartoons."

"Haven't done that for years."

"Sketch me now. On a napkin."

Jérôme, looking down, shakes his head.

This lunch will end soon. Lloyd must ask the question for which he arranged the encounter. He snatches the bill, rebuffing his son's outstretched hand. "Absolutely not. This is mine."

Outside the café, he could still ask Jérôme the question. The last moment arrives. Instead, he says, "Where are you living now?"

"I'm moving to a new place. I'll give you the details then."

"Care to walk for a bit?"

"I'm headed the other way."

They shake hands.

"Thank you," Lloyd says, "for meeting me."

All the way home, he curses himself. Around Les Halles, he stops on the sidewalk to count the money in his wallet. A teenager on a motor scooter drives down the sidewalk toward him, beeping maniacally.

"Where am I supposed to go?" Lloyd

shouts. "Where do you want me to go?"

The boy slows, swearing, his machine scraping Lloyd's leg.

"Fucking prick," Lloyd says. He never asked Jérôme the question.

At the apartment, Eileen says, "I wish you'd bring him by. I'd love to cook him a meal. Wouldn't it be lovely if he just dropped in sometimes?"

"He has his own things going on."

"At the ministry?"

"I imagine. I don't know. I ask him questions and I get these vague —" Lloyd opens his hand searchingly, looks into his palm, unable to find the word. "I don't know what. You ask him."

"Okay, but you have to get him over here first. Does he have a girlfriend?"

"I don't know."

"No need to snap at me."

"I'm not. But how am I supposed to know, Eileen?"

"Must be interesting working at the ministry."

"He might be making photocopies, for all I know."

"No, I'm sure not."

"But I have to say, I find it pretty odd."

"Find what odd?"

He hesitates. "Just that he — knowing

what I do for a living, what helped bring him up, what paid for his childhood — he knows that I'm a reporter, yet he's never once given me any sort of tidbit, any scrap from the ministry. It's no big tragedy. Just, you'd think he would have."

"Maybe he doesn't have anything to give you."

"I'm aware of how those places work. He has stuff I could use."

"He's probably not allowed to talk to reporters."

"Nobody is. But they do. It's called leaking."

"I know what it's called."

"I don't mean it that way. Sorry." He touches her arm. "It's okay," he says. "I'm okay now."

The next morning, he wakes up furious. Something in his sleep enraged him, but he can't recall what. When Eileen comes over for breakfast, he tells her to go back and eat at Didier's. She leaves, and he wishes she had not, that she'd slept there last night. He opens his wallet. He knows how much is there but checks anyway. If he doesn't earn something soon, he can't stay in this apartment. If he moves out, Eileen won't come with him.

Without her, where does he go? He needs

money; he needs a story.

"I'm waking you for the second day running. What time do you normally get up?" he asks Jérôme over the phone. "Listen, I need to meet again."

Jérôme arrives at the café and shakes his father's hand. As rehearsed, Lloyd says, "I'm sorry to bother you again. But there's something important I need to check for work."

"With me?"

"A small thing. I'm doing a piece relating to French foreign policy. It's urgent. Deadline's today. This afternoon."

Jérôme leans back in his chair. "I don't know anything useful."

"You haven't even heard my question yet."

"I really don't know anything."

"What do you do there?" Lloyd says, then reels in his temper. "I mean, you haven't even heard what I'm asking. You must have been there three years now. You won't let me visit, you won't tell me about it. So are you a janitor and you're afraid to admit it?" He laughs. "They do give you a desk, right?"

"Yes."

"All right, a guessing game. You keep giving me one-word answers. I'll get there eventually. Is your desk close to where the minister sits? Or far?"

Jérôme shifts uncomfortably. "I don't know. A medium distance."

"Medium is close."

"Not that close."

"For God's sake, this is like pulling teeth. Listen, I need a story. Just let me pick your brains for a minute."

"I thought you had a specific question."

"But do you have any ideas? I did buy you lunch yesterday." He adds, "I'm kidding."

"I can't."

"I'm not going to cite you. And I'm not asking you to go in there and steal documents or anything."

"What sort of thing do you want?"

"Not sure. Something terrorism-related maybe. Or to do with Iraq. Or Israel."

"I don't know," Jérôme says softly to his knees.

Lloyd's other children would have dismissed him by now. Only Jérôme is loyal. All three daughters are like Lloyd — always striving, always driving at something. Jérôme, though, doesn't push back. He alone is loyal. He proves it by saying, "If anything, it'd be this thing about a Gaza force."

"What Gaza force?" Lloyd perks up.

"I don't know all the details."

"But wait, hang on. The ministry is talking about a force in Gaza?"

"I think I heard that."

"You think?"

"I think so."

Lloyd gleams. "We might have something here. We might, we might." He pulls out a notebook and jots this down. He teases out the nugget, tugs, tweaks, yanks at it. A shiver passes through Lloyd: this is what he's good at. But Jérôme is clamming up. Too late — he's been opened. Out it comes. Come on.

"You can't use any of that."

"You're not going to get in trouble."

"It's my information," Jérôme says.

"It's not yours. It's just information. Doesn't belong to anybody. It exists independent of you. I can't *not* know it now. You want me to grovel? I asked for a bit of help. I don't see what's so difficult. I'm sorry," Lloyd concludes, "but you gave it to me."

He rushes home — he might still make deadline. He phones Menzies. Ha-goddamn-ha, Lloyd thinks, as he is transferred. "Well, my friend," he says, "I've got you a story."

Menzies hears him out. "But wait — France proposing a U.N. peacekeeping force in Gaza? Israel would never go for that. It's a nonstarter."

"Do you know that for a fact? Anyhow,

I'm reporting that the French are floating the idea. What happens next is another matter."

"We'd need this firmed up."

"I can do that."

"You've got four hours till cutoff. Look, report the hell out of it and check back in ninety minutes."

Lloyd puts down the phone. He glances at his contact numbers. He doesn't even have up-to-date background on Gaza. He dials Jérôme's cellphone, but it rings and rings. He finds a number for the foreign ministry. Maybe he can get details without revealing Jérôme as his source. Of course he can. He has done this sort of thing a million times. He phones the ministry press office, thankful for the first time that crazy Françoise changed their son's last name to hers — no one will tie the name Lloyd Burko to Jérôme.

Lloyd poses a few introductory questions to the duty officer. But she's more intent on extracting information than on giving it, so he cuts the conversation short. The moment he hangs up, his phone rings: it's Menzies.

"You're phoning *me* now," Lloyd says with a hint of triumph.

"I mentioned your story at the afternoon meeting and Kathleen is excited about it," he says, referring to the editor-in-chief. "As you know, you don't want to get Kathleen excited."

"So you're taking it?"

"We'll need to see it first. Personally, I'd like to run it."

"How many words you looking for?"

"As long as you need. Provided it holds up. As I say, we'll have to see the copy first. You think this could be frontable?"

If the story runs on the front page, it has to jump to the inside pages, too, which means it must be longer. And longer means more money. "Page one," Lloyd says. "Definitely page one."

"You're hammering this, right?"

"Just got off the phone with the foreign ministry."

"And?"

"More of the same."

"But you're getting this confirmed — that's amazing. I haven't seen this anywhere."

After they hang up, Lloyd paces around his apartment, stares out the window, scratching the pane, searching his memory for any useful source. No time. All he can do is work with what he has — finesse a single-source story, plump it up with background material, and pray that it slips through. He sits at his word processor and types out a story that, when he yanks the paper from the machine, is easily the flimsiest he has ever tried to flog. He places the sheet to one side. No quotes, nothing.

He feeds in a fresh sheet and starts anew, writing the piece as it ought to have been: full quotations, dates, troop numbers, disputes within the cabinet, transatlantic hostilities. He knows his craft — all is couched in terms of possibilities, proposals, balloons floated. All the fabricated sources are "on condition of anonymity," or "officials close to," or "experts familiar with." No one is cited by name. Fourteen hundred words. He calculates how much that will earn him. Enough to pay the rent — a reprieve. Enough to buy Jérôme a decent shirt. To take Eileen out for drinks.

He reads the article, using a red pen to slice away what might be contested. This shortens the text, so he concocts a couple of repetitive quotes from "an administration official in Washington." He retypes it, makes amendments, and faxes it from a phone center down the street. He bounds back up to his apartment, pausing on the landing, out of breath, trying to smile. "Lazy bastard!" he tells himself. He bangs on Didier's door. "Eileen? You there?" He enters his place and locates a dusty quart of Tanqueray, pours himself a shot and swirls the liquor in his mouth, letting it burn inside his cheeks. He has never falsified a story before. "Feels all right," he says. "Shoulda done this years ago! Saved myself a whole lot of work!" He pours another splash of gin, waits for the inevitable call.

The phone rings.

"We need to tighten the sourcing," Menzies says.

"Tighten how?"

"That's Kathleen's say-so. Incidentally, this faxing stuff is a nightmare on deadline. We had to retype everything here. You really need to get your email working."

This is a good sign: Menzies is counting on pieces in the future.

"You're right. I'll get the computer fixed right away."

"And sourcing. We have to be clearer. Like in the third graf, the quote reads weird. We can't identify the person as 'familiar with the report' when we haven't mentioned any report."

"Did I leave that in? I meant to cut that."

They make tweaks, work their way down the story, hang up in accord. Lloyd takes another sip of gin. The phone rings again. Menzies is still not happy. "This isn't sourced directly to any person or institution. Could we just say the 'French foreign ministry'?"

"I don't see why 'an official' isn't good enough."

"On the meat of the story, you have a single unnamed source. It's too vague for page one."

"How is it vague? You run this sort of stuff all the time."

"I thought you said the foreign ministry confirmed it."

"They did."

"Can't we say that?"

"I'm not gonna burn my source."

"We're near deadline here."

"I don't even want you writing 'French' anything. Just say 'an official.' "

"If you can't agree to more exact wording, we won't be able to run it. I'm sorry — I've got Kathleen right here telling me so. And that'd mean tearing up page one. Which means hell on earth this close to deadline, as you know. We need to decide now. Can you budge on this?" He waits. "Lloyd?"

"A source at the foreign ministry. Say that."

"And it's solid?"

"Yes."

"Good enough for me."

But not for Kathleen, it turns out. She calls a contact in Paris who scoffs at the piece. Menzies phones back. "Kathleen's source is some top ministry flack. Is yours better than that?"

"Yes."

"How much better?"

"They just are. I can't get into who."

"I'm battling Kathleen on this. I don't doubt your source. But for my state of mind, give me a clue. Not for publication."

"I can't."

"Then that's it. I'm sorry."

Lloyd pauses. "Someone in the Mideast directorate, okay? My source is good: policy side, not press side."

Menzies conveys this to Kathleen, who puts Lloyd on speakerphone. "And this guy is bankable?" she asks.

"Very."

"So you've used him before?"

"No."

"But we can trust him?"

"Yes."

"Off the record, who is it?"

He hesitates. "I don't see why you need to know." But he does see, of course. "It's my son."

Their chuckles are audible over the speakerphone. "Are you serious?"

"He works at the ministry."

"I'm not too enthused about quoting your family members," Kathleen says. "Though at this hour it's either that or we run wire copy on Bush's plunging approval ratings, which frankly is no longer page-one material at this stage."

Menzies suggests, "We could plug in the Five-Years-After-9/11 setup, which is pretty much done."

"No, the anniversary is Monday, so I want to save that for the weekend." She pauses. "Okay, let's go with Lloyd."

He's drunk by the time Eileen returns home. She left Didier with his friends at a jazz club and knocks at the front door. Why doesn't she just walk in? But he won't bring that up now. He hurries for another tumbler and pours her a gin before she can decline.

"Make sure you buy the paper tomorrow," he says. "Page one."

She rubs his knee. "Congrats, babe. When was your last of those?"

"The Roosevelt administration, probably."

"Franklin or Teddy Roosevelt?"

"Definitely Teddy." He pulls her closer, a little roughly, and kisses her — not one of their normal soft pecks but an ardent embrace.

She shifts back. "Enough."

"Right — what if your husband turned up."

"Don't make me feel lousy."

"I'm only kidding. Don't feel bad — I don't." He pinches her cheek. "I love you."

Without a word, she returns across the hall. He flops onto his bed, mumbling drunkenly — "Goddamn page fucking one!"

Eileen wakes him gently the next morning and places the paper on the bed. "It's freezing in here," she says. "I put the coffee on."

He sits up in bed.

"I didn't see your story, babe," she says. "Not running today?"

He scans the page-one headlines: "Blair to Step Down in 12 Months"; "Pentagon Forbids Cruelty in Terror Interrogations"; "Gay Marriages Roil America"; "Australia Mourns 'Crocodile Hunter' "; and finally, "Bush Slumps to New Low in Polls."

His Gaza story didn't make the front. He flips through the inside pages. It's nowhere. Cursing, he dials Rome. It's early, but Menzies is already at his desk. "What happened to my piece?" Lloyd demands.

"I'm sorry. We couldn't use it. That French flack friend of Kathleen's called back and denied it all. Said we'd be screwed if we

went with it. They'd issue an official pro-
test."

"A flack friend of Kathleen's pisses on my
piece and you guys buy that? Anyhow, why
is Kathleen re-reporting my work? I told
you, my son works at the ministry."

"Well, that's kind of weird, too. Kathleen
mentioned your son's name to her friend."

"She identified him as the source? Are you
out of your mind?"

"No, no — hang on. She never said he
was your source."

"It's not going to be hard to figure out.
Jesus Christ!"

"Let me finish, Lloyd. Let me finish here.
No one called Jérôme Burko works there."

"You morons. He goes by his mother's
maiden name."

"Oh."

Lloyd must warn his son, give him time to
come up with an excuse. He calls Jérôme's
cellphone, but he isn't picking up. Maybe
he's at work early for a change. Jesus, what
a disaster. Lloyd rings the ministry switch-
board.

The operator says, "I'm looking at a list of
all the people in this building. That name is
not on it."

Lloyd hurries down to Boulevard du
Montparnasse, raises his arm for a taxi, then

40

drops it. He hesitates at the curb, squeezing his wallet, which is thinner than ever. Then again, if he's going to go bankrupt this is how he should do it. He waves down a cab.

At the ministry building, the security guards won't let him inside. He repeats his son's name, insists that it's a family emergency. This gets him nowhere. He shows his press accreditation, but it expired on December 31, 2005. He waits outside, phoning Jérôme's mobile. Functionaries stroll out for cigarette breaks. He searches among them for his son, asking if anyone here works in the North African and Middle Eastern directorate.

"I remember that guy," a woman says. "He was an intern here."

"I know, but what section is he in now?"

"He's not in any section. We never hired him. I think he wrote the exams, but he couldn't pass the languages part." She narrows her eyes and smiles. "I always thought he was lying about having an American father."

"How do you mean?"

"Just that his English was so hopeless."

She dredges up an old address for Jérôme and gives it to Lloyd. He takes the Métro to the Château Rouge stop and finds the building, a decaying chunk of plaster whose main

41

gate is broken. He scans the list of residents at each inner courtyard, hunting for Jérôme's last name. He can't find it. Then he spots an unexpected last name, his own. The buzzer reads, "Jérôme Burko."

Lloyd presses it, but there is no response. Residents come and go. He sits at the edge of the courtyard and gazes up at the shuttered windows.

After an hour, Jérôme appears through the main gate but does not immediately see his father. He opens his mailbox and, flipping through junk, weaves down the passage.

Lloyd says his son's name, and Jérôme starts. "What are you doing?"

"Sorry," Lloyd says, standing sorely. "Sorry to appear like this." He has never spoken to his son in this manner, with deference. "I just turned up — is that okay?"

"About your article?"

"No, no. Nothing to do with that."

"What, then?"

"Can we go upstairs? I'm cold. I've been out here a while." He laughs. "I'm old, you know! I might not look it, but —"

"You're not old."

"I am old. I am." He reaches out his hand, smiles. Jérôme moves no closer. "I've been thinking about my family lately."

"Which family?"

42

"Can I come inside, Jérôme? If you don't mind. My hands are ice-cold." He rubs them together, blows on them. "I had an idea. I hope you don't take offense at this. I was thinking maybe — only if you wanted — maybe I could help you with your English. If we practice regularly, you'll pick it up, I guarantee."

Jérôme flushes. "What do you mean? My English is fine. I learned it from you."

"You didn't have that many opportunities to hear it."

"I don't need lessons. Anyway, when would I do them? The ministry would never give me time off."

To make a point, Lloyd switches to English, speaking intentionally fast: "I'm tempted to tell you what I know, son. I don't want to make you feel lousy, though. But what are you doing in this dump? My God, it's incredible how much you look like my father. So strange to see him again. And I know you don't work. Four kids I've produced, and you're the only one who wants to talk to me anymore."

Jérôme hasn't understood a word. Trembling with humiliation, he responds in French: "How am I supposed to know what you're saying? You're speaking so fast. This is ridiculous."

43

Lloyd reverts to French himself. "I wanted to tell you something. Ask you something. You know, I'm thinking of retiring," he says. "I must have done, what, an article a day since I was twenty-two. And now I can't rustle up a single new idea. Not a one. I don't know what in hell's going on anymore. Even the paper won't publish me. It was my last — my last string. Did you know that? No one prints my stuff anymore. I think I'm leaving my apartment, Jérôme. I can't pay for it. I shouldn't be there. But I don't know. Nothing's settled yet. I'm asking, I guess — I'm trying to figure it out. Quite what's the thing to do. What would you say? What's your opinion on the matter?" He struggles to ask this. "What would you advise that I should do? Son?"

Jérôme opens the door to the building. "Come in," he says. "You're staying with me."

1953. Caffè Greco, Rome

Betty rattled her highball glass and peered inside, seeking a last dribble of Campari under the ice cubes. Her husband, Leo, sat across the marble café tabletop, hidden behind an Italian newspaper. She reached over and knocked on his page, like the door to his study.

"Yaaahs, m'dear," he bellowed, the great wall of newsprint having rendered him insensible to the fact that he was in public and that shouted marital chitchat could be heard by all; after years in Rome, he still assumed no one overseas understood English.

"No sign of Ott," she said.

"True, true."

"Another drink?"

"Yaaahs, m'dear." In his cupped hand, he planted a kiss and lobbed it at her like a grenade, tracing with his eyes the parabola up and over the table, down onto her cheek. "Direct hit," he declared, and disappeared behind the newspaper pages. "Everyone's so stupid!" he said, giddy at all the wonderful reports of chaos. "So amazingly stupid!"

Betty raised her arm to hail a waiter, then caught sight of Ott, just sitting there at the bar, watching them. Her hand drooped at the wrist and she cocked her head, mouthing "What are you doing over there?," small muscles tugging at the sides of her mouth,

45

smile rising, then falling, then rising.

Ott observed Betty and Leo an instant longer, stood from his bar stool, and made for the seating area at the back.

He had last seen her twenty years earlier in New York. She was in her early forties now, a married woman, her black hair a little shorter, her green eyes softened. Still, Ott glimpsed in the tilt of her head, in her hesitant smile, the woman he had known. By fading, the past seemed only to sharpen before him. He had an impulse to reach across the table and touch her.

Instead, he took the extended hand of Betty's husband and gripped the man's shoulder, expressing toward Leo — whom Ott was meeting for the first time — the warmth he could not appropriately express toward his wife.

Ott sat beside Betty on the velvet banquette, tapped her arm by way of greeting, and slid athletically behind the adjacent table, agile still at fifty-four. He squeezed the back of his thick neck, ran a hand over his buzz-cut scalp, touched his wrinkled brow, from under which he considered them, his pale blue eyes shifting expressions, as if threatening to fight the whole room, to laugh, to give up altogether. He patted Leo's cheek. "I'm pleased to be here."

With these few words, Ott flooded them with gratification — Betty had forgotten what it was like to be around him.

Cyrus Ott had traveled here from his headquarters in Atlanta, leaving his businesses plus his wife and young son, solely for this meeting. On the passenger ship over, he had read their articles. Leo, the Rome correspondent for a Chicago newspaper, had mastered every cliché, his pieces unfolding in that journalese realm where refugees are endlessly flooding across borders, cities bracing for storms, voters heading for polls. Betty was a freelancer for U.S. women's magazines, specializing in light humor pieces about life abroad and cautionary tales about American girls seduced by Italian skunks. In the old days, she'd had ambitions. Ott was sorry to see they had availed so little.

"So," Leo said, "what was it you wanted to see us about exactly, if I may ask?"

"I want to talk about a newspaper."

"Which one?"

"My own," Ott answered. "I intend to start one. An international English-language newspaper. Based in Rome and sold around the world."

"Oh yeah?" Leo said, leaning forward and releasing his brown knit tie, which he'd been pinning against his chest to cover a missing

47

shirt button. "Pretty interesting," he said, tie swinging like a clock pendulum, revealing a thread blossom where the button had been. "Could work," he said. "Definitely could. Uhm, you looking for people?"

"You two. You'll run it."

Betty wriggled up higher on the banquette. "Why would you start a newspaper?"

"The more I think about it," Leo interrupted, "the more I like it. Nobody's done it right yet. Nobody's making real money out of something like this."

Ott alone was sober when they parted that night. He shook their hands, patted Leo's shoulder, and walked up the Spanish Steps to the Hotel Hassler, where he was staying. Betty and Leo stumbled down Via del Babuino for home.

Leo took her ear and whispered into it. "Was he serious?"

"He always used to be."

But Leo hardly heard. "That's the richest guy I ever got loaded with," he said.

They arrived at their building and dragged themselves up to the fourth floor as if the stairwell banisters were rope. Theirs was a decent-sized apartment for a childless couple, high ceilings and bared wooden rafters, but only one window, which wasn't a bad thing when it came to the hangovers. She

48

made coffee.

Suddenly serious, she said, "Be sweet to me." She touched the point of Leo's cheekbone, where he had missed a patch of stubble — Betty had been noticing it all evening.

A few blocks away, Ott sat on his hotel bed. Perhaps, he thought, I should go no further with this. Perhaps I should leave everything as it was. Perhaps I should not start this paper.

■ ■ ■ ■

"World's Oldest
Liar Dies at 126"

• • •

OBITUARY WRITER — ARTHUR GOPAL

■ ■ ■ ■

Arthur's cubicle used to be near the water-cooler, but the bosses tired of having to chat with him each time they got thirsty. So the watercooler stayed and he was moved. Now his desk is in a distant corner, as far from the locus of power as possible but nearer the cupboard of pens, which is a consolation.

He arrives at work, flops into his rolling chair, and remains still. This persists until inertia and continued employment cease to be mutually tenable, at which point he wriggles off his overcoat, flicks on the computer, and checks the latest news reports.

No one has died. Or, rather, 107 people have in the previous minute, 154,000 in the past day, and 1,078,000 in the past week. But no one who matters. That's good — it has been nine days since his last obit, and he hopes to extend the streak. His overarching goal at the paper is indolence, to publish as infrequently as possible, and to sneak away when no one is looking. He is realizing these professional ambitions spectacularly.

He opens a manila folder so that, if anyone happens past, he can flutter sheets, peer up irascibly, and mutter "Preparedness!" which seems to put most people off. Not all people, sadly.

Clint Oakley appears behind him, and Arthur swivels around in his chair as if twisted by a garrote. "Clint. Hi. Morning. I've been over the wires. Nothing obvious. To me, at least. Not so far." He despises this tendency to justify himself so abjectly to his superiors. He should shut up.

"Didn't you see it?"

"See what?"

"Are you serious?" Clint is a specialist in queries that are at once hectoring and incomprehensible. "Don't you read email? Wake up, faggot." He raps Arthur's monitor as if it were a skull. "Anybody home?" Clint Oakley, Arthur's boss, is a dandruff-raining, baseball-obsessed, sexually resentful Alabamian with a toilet-brush mustache and an inability to maintain eye contact. He is also the culture editor, an ironic posting if considered. "Rectum," he says, apparently meaning Arthur, and struts back to his office.

If history has taught us anything, Arthur muses, it is that men with mustaches must never achieve positions of power. Sadly, the paper has not heeded this truism, because Clint has authority over all special sections, including obituaries. Lately, he has heaped endless chores upon Arthur, ordering him to collate This Day in History, Brain Teasers, Puzzle-Wuzzle, the Daily Ha-Ha, and World Weather, in addition to his regular necrological duties.

Arthur finds the e-mail Clint was referring to. It's from the editor-in-chief, Kathleen Solson, who wants preparedness — that is, an obituary prepared before the subject dies — on Gerda Erzberger. Who on earth is that? He checks the Internet. She turns out to be an Austrian intellectual, once lauded by feminists, then decried by them, then forgotten. Why should the paper care that she's about to die? Well, because Kathleen happens to have read Erzberger's memoirs while at college. And, as Arthur knows, "news" is often a polite way of saying "editor's whim."

Kathleen arrives to discuss the piece.

"I'm working on it right now," he says preemptively.

"On Gerda?"

"Gerda? Do you know her personally?" If the answer is yes, his assignment assumes fresh peril.

"Not well. Met her a couple of times at events."

"Not a friend, then," he suggests hopefully. "How urgent would you say this is?" Which is to say, When's she planning to die?

"Unclear," Kathleen responds. "She's not having treatment."

"Is that good or bad?"

"Well, it's not typically good with cancer. Listen, I'd like us to do this properly for once — give you enough time to get an interview with her, go up there and so on, rather than just working from clips."

"Go up where?"

"She lives outside Geneva. Have the secretaries work out travel arrangements."

Travel means effort and a night away from home. Bleak. And nothing is worse than obit interviews. He must never disclose to his subjects what he's researching because they tend to become distressed. So he claims to be working on "a profile." He draws out the moribund interviewee, confirms the facts he needs, then sits there, pretending to jot notes, stewing in guilt, remarking, "Extraordinary!" and "Did you really?" All the while, he knows how little will make it into print — decades of a person's life condensed into a few paragraphs, with a final resting place at the bottom of page nine, between Puzzle-Wuzzle and World Weather.

At this disheartening thought, he sneaks out of the office to fetch his daughter. Pickle, who is eight, emerges from the school gate, satchel strap around her throat, arms flat at her sides, potbelly distended, glasses scanning nothing in particular, her untied shoelaces flailing with each step. "Antiques?" he asks, and she slips her hand into his, squeezing it in affirmation. To Via dei Coronari they amble hand in hand. He observes her from above, her tangled black hair, tiny ears, the thick lenses that bend and swell the cobblestones. She babbles softly and snorts with amusement. She is a wonderful nerd, and he hopes this won't change. He'd be distressed if she were cool — it'd be as if his flesh and blood had grown up to be purple.

"Your aspect," he says, "recalls that of a chimpanzee."

She is humming softly and offers no response. After a minute, she says, "And you remind me of an orangutan."

"I can't argue with that. Nope, I cannot argue with that. By the way," he adds, "I

57

have a new one for you: Tina Pachootnik."

"Say it again?"

"Pachootnik. Tina."

She shakes her head. "Impossible to say."

"Do you like Tina at least?"

"I'm willing to consider it."

She has been looking for a pseudonym, not for any purpose but because it took her fancy. "What about Zeus?" she asks.

"Taken, I'm afraid. Though he's been gone long enough that there'd be little room for confusion. Would you use it like that — Zeus, on its own — or would it be Zeus something?"

She opens her pudgy hand within his cool dry palm and he releases her. She drifts, stepping over her own feet, beside him but abstracted, apart. Then she swoops back, plunges her fingers into his, and looks up, nostrils swelling with mischief.

"What?"

"Frog."

"I forbid it," he says. "Frog is a boy's name."

She shrugs, an oddly adult gesture in such a little girl.

They enter one of the opulent antiques shops on Via dei Coronari. The clerks watch Arthur and Pickle closely. The two of them come here often, never buying, except once, when she knocked over a mantel clock and Arthur had to pay for it.

She prods a 1920s telephone.

"You hold that part to your ear," Arthur explains, "and you talk into the other bit."

"But how do you make a call?"

He sticks his fingers into the dial and cranks a rotation. "You've never seen a phone like this before? My God, when I was growing up this was all we had. Imagine the strife! Hard times, my dear, hard times."

She purses her lips and pivots to investigate a bust of Marcus Aurelius.

Back home, Arthur prepares her a Nutella sandwich. She eats one every afternoon, legs dangling from the kitchen chair, smudges of chocolate accruing on the underside of her nose.

He tears off the crust and pops it into his mouth. "Father tax," he explains, chewing. She does not object.

When Visantha's car pulls up outside, Pickle hurriedly swallows her last bite and Arthur hastens to rinse off the sticky plate — it is as if a teacher approached.

"How was work?" he asks his wife.

"Okay. What are you guys up to?"

"Nothing much."

Pickle ambles off to the television room, and Arthur absentmindedly follows. They chat in there and laugh at their TV show.

Visantha trails in. "What are you watching?"

"Just some junk," he replies.

Pickle hands him the remote and wanders off to her room. He watches her go down the hall, then turns to Visantha. "You know what she told me today? She doesn't remember the twentieth century. Isn't that terrifying?"

"Not particularly. What are we doing for dinner?"

"Pickle," he calls down the hall. "Any thoughts on dinner?"

The secretaries book Arthur from Rome to Geneva by rail, a ten-hour journey with connections in Milan and Brig. Supposedly this saves money on a short-notice flight but is a colossal nuisance for him. He boards the early train at Stazione Termini, buys pastries in the cafeteria carriage, and, squashed amid the second-class rabble, settles into the first volume of Erzberger's memoirs, which is called, modestly, *In the Beginning.* From the author photo, Erzberger is, or was, in her early thirties, pretty and gaunt, with shoulder-length dark hair and twisted, ironic lips. The picture is from 1965, when the book came out. She must be in her seventies by now.

As his train pulls into Geneva in the early evening, he lifts his nose from the book and stares at the seat-back before him. From the blurbs on the Internet, he had expected a weary, politically dated autobiography. Instead, her prose communicates courage and humanity. He studies her photo again and feels scandalously unprepared.

He passes customs, obtains Swiss francs, and finds a cabbie who will take him to her house, which is just across the French border. The taxi drops him on a wet country road; the red taillights disappear down the hill. He is sweaty, uncertain, late. He dislikes being late, yet invariably is. He rubs his hands together, huffs a breath cloud onto them. This is the place: the right number, the pines, as she described. After a little searching, he finds a gate within the pleached fence and enters. Her home is built of sturdy timber beams, with icicles hanging from the eaves like wizards' caps. He snaps one off — he can never resist — and turns around to survey the twilight sky. A crust of clouds overlays the Alps. The icicle drips down his wrist.

She opens the door behind him.

"Hi, hi, sorry I'm late," he says, then switches to German. "Sorry, I was just admiring the view."

"Come in," she says. "You can leave the icicle outside, please."

The living room is illuminated by potted lights that pick out columns of dust in the air. An ebony coffee table bears an overflowing ashtray and a moonscape of stain rings from hot mugs that spilled. On the walls, African war masks leer. The bookshelves are perfectly stocked from wing to wing, like a residence whose management has ceased accepting new applicants. The room smells of strong tobacco and of hospital, too.

Erzberger's hair is short and white, and when she passes under the lights her scalp is visible. A tall woman, she wears a hand-knitted sweater that hangs loosely around her throat, like a sock that has lost its elastic. For trousers, she has flannel pajama bottoms, and on her feet, sheepskin slippers. The sight reminds him that it is cold; he shivers.

"What would you like to drink? I'm having tea."

"Tea would be perfect."

"So can I assume," she asks, half turned toward the kitchen, "that you're writing my obituary?"

He is caught out. "Oh," he says. "Why? Why do you ask?"

"What *are* you writing, then? You said on

the phone it was a profile." She disappears into the kitchen, returning a minute later with his steaming mug. She places it on the coffee table, motions him to a black leather armchair, and sits on the matching couch, which does not sink to accommodate her as he expects but holds its shape as if bearing her upon its palm. She reaches to the table for her cigarette pack and lighter.

"I mean, yes," he admits. "It is for that. For an obituary. Is that awful to hear?"

"No, no. I rather like it. This way, I'll know it's accurate — I won't have a chance to send a letter of complaint afterward, will I." She coughs, covering her mouth with the cigarette pack. She lights one. "You?"

He declines.

A lick of smoke slithers from her mouth, her chest rises, and the thread is yanked back inside. "Your German is excellent."

"I lived in Berlin for six years as a teenager. My father was a correspondent there."

"Yes, right — you're the son of R. P. Gopal, aren't you."

"I am."

"And you write obituaries?"

"Primarily, yes."

"Claw your way to the bottom, did you?"

He responds with a polite smile. Writing for an international newspaper in Rome

normally earns him a degree of respect —
until, that is, people learn of his beat.

She continues: "I liked your father's
books. What was that one with 'Elephant' in
the title?" She glances at her bookshelf.

"Yes," Arthur says. "He was an excellent
writer."

"And do you write as well as he did?"

"Alas, no." He sips his tea and pulls out a
notepad and a tape recorder.

She crushes her cigarette in the ashtray,
picks at the stitches on her slippers. "More
tea?"

"No, I'm fine, thank you." He turns on
his tape recorder and inquires about the
start of her career.

She answers impatiently, adding, "You
should ask me other things."

"I know this is basic. I just need to confirm
a few facts."

"It's all in my books."

"I know. I'm just —"

"Ask what you want."

He holds up his copy of her memoirs. "I
enjoyed this, by the way."

"Really?" Her face lights up and she takes
a quick drag of her cigarette. "I'm sorry you
had to suffer through the boring thing."

"It wasn't boring."

"I'm bored by it. That's the problem, I

suppose, with writing a book about your life. Once you're done, you never want to hear about it again. But it's hard to stop talking about your own life — especially if you're me!" She leans forward solicitously. "Parenthetically, Mr. Gopal, I do like obituaries. I didn't mean to sound as if I was denigrating your work. You didn't take it that way?"

"No, no."

"Good. That makes me feel better. Now listen, when do I get to read this piece?"

"You don't, I'm afraid. It's against our rules. Otherwise everyone would demand to edit this bit or that. I'm sorry."

"Pity. How entertaining it would be to know how I'll be remembered. The single article I'd most like to read is the one I never can! Ah, well." She weighs the cigarette pack in her hand. "People must grow terribly upset when you turn up with a notepad. No? Like the undertaker arriving to measure the dowager."

"I hope I'm not that bad. Although in truth, most people don't realize what I'm researching. Anyway, I'm relieved that I don't have to pretend tonight," he says. "It makes life a great deal easier for me."

"But does it make death a great deal easier for me?"

He attempts a laugh.

"Ignore me," she says. "I'm only playing with words. In any case, I'm not afraid of it. Not in the least. You can't dread what you can't experience. The only death we experience is that of other people. That's as bad as it gets. And that's bad enough, surely. I remember when for the first time a dear friend of mine died. Must have been, what, 1947? It was Walter — he's in the book, the one who's always wearing his waistcoat to bed, if you remember. He got sick, and I abandoned him in Vienna and he died. I had a terror of illness. I was petrified by — by what? Not of getting sick and dying. Even then, in an elementary way, I understood what death was at its worst: something that happens to other people. And that is hard to bear; that is what I couldn't face back then with Walter, what I've never been good at.

"But my point, you see, is that death is misunderstood. The loss of one's life is not the greatest loss. It is no loss at all. To others, perhaps, but not to oneself. From one's own perspective, experience simply halts. From one's own perspective, there is no loss. You see? Yet maybe this is a game of words, too, because it doesn't make it any less frightening, does it." She sips her tea.

"What I really fear is time. That's the devil: whipping us on when we'd rather loll, so the present sprints by, impossible to grasp, and all is suddenly past, a past that won't hold still, that slides into these inauthentic tales. My past — it doesn't feel real in the slightest. The person who inhabited it is not me. It's as if the present me is constantly dissolving. There's that line of Heraclitus: 'No man steps in the same river twice, for it is not the same river and he is not the same man.' That's quite right. We enjoy this illusion of continuity, and we call it memory. Which explains, perhaps, why our worst fear isn't the end of life but the end of memories." She considers him searchingly. "Do I make sense? Does that seem reasonable? Mad?"

"I hadn't thought of it that way before," he says. "You probably have a point."

She reclines. "It's an extraordinary fact!" She leans forward again. "Don't you find it striking? The personality is constantly dying and it feels like continuity. Meanwhile, we panic about death, which we cannot ever experience. Yet it is this illogical fear that motivates our lives. We gore each other and mutilate ourselves for victory and fame, as if these might swindle mortality and extend us somehow. Then, as death bears down, we agonize over how little we have achieved. My own life, for example, has been so inadequately realized. I will scarcely be recorded anywhere. Except, of course, in your eccentric newspaper. I won't question why you've chosen me — thank God someone has! It extends the lease on my illusions."

"That's much too modest."

"Nothing to do with modesty," she retorts. "Who reads my books anymore? Who has heard of me at this stage?"

"Well, me for one," he lies.

"Oh dear — listen to me," she goes on. "I say that ambition is absurd, and yet I remain in its thrall. It's like being a slave all your life, then learning one day that you never had a master, and returning to work all the same. Can you imagine a force in the universe greater than this? Not in my universe. You know, even from earliest childhood it dominated me. I longed for achievements, to be influential — that, in particular. To sway people. This has been my religion: the belief that I deserve attention, that they are wrong not to listen, that those who dispute me are fools. Yet, no matter what I achieve, the world lives on, impertinent, indifferent — I know all this, but I can't get it through my head. It is why, I suppose, I agreed to talk to you. To this day, I'll pursue any folly to make the rest of you shut up and listen to me, as you should have from the start!" She coughs and reaches for a fresh cigarette. "Here is a fact: nothing in all civilization has been as productive as ludicrous ambition. Whatever its ills, nothing has created more. Cathedrals, sonatas, encyclopedias: love of God was not behind them, nor love of life. But the love of man to be worshipped by man."

She leaves the room without explanation and her heaving coughs are audible, muted by a closed door. She returns. "Look at me," she says. "No children, never a husband. I reach this stage of my life, Mr. Gopal, with the most comical realization: that the only legacy is genetic material. I always disdained those who made children. It was the escape of the mediocre, to substitute their own botched lives with fresh ones. Yet today I rather wish I'd borne a life myself. All I have is one niece, an officious girl (I shouldn't call her a girl — she's going gray) who looks at me as if through the wrong end of a telescope. She comes in here every week with gallons of soup, soup, soup, and an entourage of doctors and nurses and husbands and children to look me over one last time. You know, there's that silly saying

'We're born alone and we die alone' — it's nonsense. We're surrounded at birth and surrounded at death. It is in between that we're alone."

Erzberger has veered so far off topic that Arthur is unsure how to lead her back without appearing rude. She herself, from the industry of her smoking, seems to sense that this is not what he came for.

"Can I use your bathroom?" He closes the door after himself, rolls his shoulders, consults his watch. It's already so much later than he'd wanted. He must get some usable quotes. Nothing she has said will work. But the task feels insurmountable. All he wants is another career, one that pays him to make Nutella sandwiches and cheat at Monopoly with Pickle.

He checks his cellphone, which is set on silent mode. It shows twenty-six missed calls. Twenty-six? That can't be right. Normally, he doesn't get twenty-six calls in a week. He checks again — but yes, twenty-six calls in the past hour. The first three are from home, the remainder are from Visantha's mobile.

He steps from the bathroom. "Sorry, I have to make a call. Excuse me." He goes out onto the porch. The air is freezing.

Erzberger smokes on the leather couch,

hearing the murmur of his conversation but not the sense of it. His talking stops, but he does not come back in. She stubs out her cigarette, lights a new one. She swings open the front door. "What's going on? You're not even on the phone anymore. What are you doing out there? Are we finishing this interview or not?"

"Where's my bag?"

"What?"

He walks past her into the living room. "Do you know where my bag is?"

"No. Why? Are you leaving? What are you doing?" she shouts after him. He doesn't even close the front door after himself.

In the following days, Arthur does not return to the paper. Soon, everyone knows why. Kathleen telephones to offer her condolences. "Come back whenever you feel ready."

After a few weeks, his colleagues begin to grumble.

"Hardly makes a difference with him or without him," they say.

"We have interns doing Puzzle-Wuzzle now."

"And doing it better."

"He used to leave early every day. I mean, I *do* feel bad for the guy. But, you know? This is kind of — kind of pushing it. Don't you think? How long's he gonna be gone?"

The news editor, Craig Menzies, turns out to be Arthur's truest ally during this period. He lobbies on Arthur's behalf, arguing that the paper should leave him alone as long as he needs. But after two months Accounts Payable informs Arthur that he must return in the New Year or lose his job.

Menzies suggests that Arthur soften his reentry by attending the Christmas party — it'll be a relatively painless way to see everyone in one go. The party involves prodigious amounts of booze, posturing, and flirtation, which means the rest of the staff should be too occupied to pay much attention to him.

Menzies greets Arthur and Visantha outside the office and leads them up, where they immediately bump into a group of colleagues.

"Arthur. Hi."

"You're back."

"Arthur, man, good to see you."

None of them appear glad; they seem abruptly sobered.

Menzies intervenes. "Where are the free drinks kept?" He shepherds Arthur and Visantha away.

Intermittently, staff members approach Arthur, repeating how good it is to see him.

The brave ones raise the topic of his absence, but he interrupts: "I can't discuss that. Sorry. And things here? Same as ever?"

In the far corner of the newsroom is a Christmas tree, its base surrounded by presents wrapped in brilliant red paper and tied with curled golden ribbons. Children rush over to collect theirs, shaking little boxes that mustn't be opened quite yet — the company has a tradition of giving gifts to employees' kids ahead of Christmas. Menzies and Arthur had forgotten that children would be at the party, but are keenly aware now. Menzies positions himself before Arthur and Visantha, standing erect and speaking loudly to block sight and sound of the young ones in the corner.

Clint Oakley circles Arthur, Visantha, and Menzies from a wide radius, throwing glances and touching his lips to an overfull glass of punch. When Visantha and Menzies step away to get a plate of hors d'oeuvres, Clint swoops. "Good to see you, buddy!" He slaps Arthur's shoulder, sloshing punch on the filthy carpeting. "Are you gracing us with your presence full-time now, or is this just a one-night stand? We miss you, man. You gotta come back. Puzzle-Wuzzle barely works without you. How long you been off now?" He continues to talk in this jackhammer fashion, never allowing Arthur to respond. "Nice of us to let you in here so you can drink our liquor. Eh? Good of us, ain't it. My kids got their free Christmas presents. Some nice shit this year — I made 'em show me. Just to see how cheap the Ott Group is. But it's some not-bad shit. Like, toy guns and Barbies and whatever. I shouldn't have peeked. Not supposed to before Daddy Claus comes down the chimney, right? But I never could hold out. You know, like when it was Christmas morning and, like, your parents were asleep and shit, and you snuck down and pulled open the wrapping paper? You know what I mean, right, my Hindu buddy? You did that when you were a kid, right? I know you did! Only, don't go stealing a Christmas present for the kiddies this year. You don't get one this year, buddy. I'm gonna get me some cake." He struts away.

When Menzies returns with the hors d'oeuvres, Arthur asks him, "Does Clint know?"

"Know what?"

"What happened."

"How do you mean? With Pickle? I'm sure he does. Why?"

"Doesn't matter. I just needed to check. Have you seen Visantha?"

On the cab ride home, he and his wife find nothing to talk about.

He digs into his pocket. "Not sure I have change. Do you?"

As arranged, he returns to the paper in the New Year. He drops by Kathleen's office to signal his arrival, but she is on the phone. She covers the receiver and mouths, "I'll come see you later."

He sits in his cubicle in the far reaches of the newsroom and turns on his computer. As it rumbles to life, he glances around, at the senior editors' offices along the walls, the horseshoe copydesk in the center of the newsroom, the spattered white carpeting that smells of stale coffee and dried microwave soup, its acrylic edges curling up but held down in places with silver gaffer's tape. Several cubicles are empty nowadays, the former occupants long retired but never replaced, their old Post-its fluttering whenever windows open. Under the abandoned desks, technicians have stashed broken dot-matrix printers and dead cathode-ray-tube monitors, while the corner of the room is a graveyard of crippled rolling chairs that flip backward when sat on. Nobody throws anything away here; nobody knows whose job that is.

Arthur returns to routine, preparing This

Day in History, Brain Teasers, Puzzle-Wuzzle, the Daily Ha-Ha, World Weather. He listens to the demands of Clint and obeys. Apart from this, he talks to no one but Menzies. And he no longer leaves early; he leaves on time.

Eventually, Kathleen stops by his desk. "We haven't even had a coffee yet. I'm sorry — nonstop meetings. My life has become one long meeting. Believe it or not, I *used* to be a journalist."

They chat in this vein until Kathleen deems that enough time has been devoted to her bereaved subordinate. She'll leave and, ideally, they won't speak again for months. "One last thing," she adds. "Could you possibly call Gerda Erzberger's niece? She's rung me about a thousand times. It's nothing important — she's just venting about you not finishing the interview. But if you could get her off my back I'd really appreciate it."

"Actually," he says, "I'd like to go back up there and finish that piece."

"I don't know if the budget can afford a Geneva trip twice for one obit. Can't you finish it here?"

"If you give me a day off, I'll pay my own travel costs."

"Is that a ploy to get a day away from

Clint? You've only been back a week. Can't say I blame you, though."

Arthur flies to Geneva this time and finds that Erzberger has been moved to a hospice in the city. She has no hair; her skin is jaundiced. She removes her oxygen mask. "I run out of breath, so take notes fast."

He places his tape recorder on her bedside table.

She turns it off. "Frankly, I don't know if I'm talking to you at all. You wasted my time."

He collects his tape recorder, his overcoat, and he stands.

"Where are you going now?" she asks.

"You agreed to this meeting. If you don't want to cooperate, I don't care. I'm not interested."

"Hang on. Wait," she says. "What happened exactly? My niece said you went away for 'personal reasons.' What does that mean?" She takes a breath from the oxygen mask.

"I don't intend to discuss that."

"You must give me some sort of answer. I don't know if I want to bare myself to you anymore. Maybe you'll just go to the toilet and not return again."

"I'm not discussing this issue."

"Sit down."

He does.

"If you won't tell me anything interesting about yourself," she says, "at least tell me something about your father. The famous R. P. Gopal. He was an interesting man, no?"

"He was."

"So?"

"What can I say? He's always remembered as very charismatic."

"I know that. But tell me something you yourself remember."

"I remember that my mother used to dress him — not choose his clothes, I mean literally dress him. I only realized in my teens that this wasn't normal or common. What else can I say? He was handsome, as you know. When I was younger, the girls I went out with were irritatingly impressed by family photos. He was always much cooler than I am. What else? His war writings, of course, from India. I remember him composing poetry: he used to do it while sitting in my old crib. He said it was comfortable in there. I don't remember much more. Except that he enjoyed his drink. Until it took him, of course."

"So all you do is obituaries? What did your father think of that?"

"I don't think he minded. He got me my

first job in the business, on Fleet Street. After that, he didn't seem bothered one way or the other. But I never really had the journo bug. I just wanted a comfortable chair. Not an ambitious man, me."

"Meaning you're a bit of a dud."

"That's very kind of you."

"Compared with R. P. Gopal, anyway."

"Yes, you're right. I don't compare to him. He didn't leave me his mind, the bastard." He looks at her. "Since you're being scathing about me, I hope you won't mind my being direct. Actually, I'm not sure that I care. You really are at odds with your writing, you know. When I read your memoirs before our first meeting, I was nervous about interviewing you. But you're much less admirable in person."

"I'm starting to like this conversation. Is all this going in the obituary?" She coughs painfully, wheezes into the oxygen mask. When she speaks again, it is a rasp. "This is a quiet room," she says. "I was lucky to get my own. My niece comes to visit every day. Every single day. Did I tell you about her?"

"Yes, you complained about her. Said she tormented you with hot soup and cold comfort."

"No, no, no," she responds, "I *never* complained about her. You're remembering wrong. I adore my niece. She's the dearest woman. Gerasim — that's my nickname for her. Her real name is Julia. She's an angel. I'm devoted to her. You can't imagine her kindness in these past months." She coughs. "I'm running out of words. I'm losing my voice. I'll shut up. Though I've said nothing. Nothing useful." She produces a pad and writes, "I'm supposed to communicate with this thing." She sits at the ready, but he asks her nothing.

The only noises are medical machinery and her wheezing.

Until he speaks: "Here's something interesting. Actually, I'll tell you something. It doesn't matter but . . . This thing that happened." He stops short.

She nods and writes on the pad: "I know. An accident. Your daughter."

"Yes. My daughter. It was an accident."

She writes, "It is over now."

"I can't talk about it." He puts his tape recorder and pens in his pocket.

She takes off her mask. "I'm sorry," she says. "I had nothing to say to you in the end."

As he waits to board his flight back to Rome, he writes out all he can recall about Erzberger. He works on the plane and, once home, looks for a space where he will be undisturbed. Only one is free, Pickle's former room. He sits on her bed and taps away at his laptop until 4 A.M., sipping whiskey to keep himself going — an old trick of his father's. The next day, he stays late at the office, compiling background on Erzberger. He stacks her books on the edge of his desk, his efforts plain to all. Kathleen passes, noticing.

Erzberger, as she depicted herself in writing, is morally bold, uncompromised by her epoch, endearing, even inspiring. In person, she showed little of this. But when Arthur writes the obituary he adheres to the Erzberger of the memoirs, the fictional Gerda, overlooking the woman he met. This is the article they want. To add an air of authority, he inserts the phrase "in a series of interviews conducted shortly before her death." He revises the piece until he can imagine no further amendments. He reads it aloud to himself in Pickle's old room. He has made an effort this time. It's almost as good as something his father would have submitted. He emails it directly to Kathleen, bypassing Clint. This is irregular, and she points it out. In her office, Arthur explains: "I thought you'd have a better feel for this edit. I don't want to step on anybody's toes. But if you have a chance to glance at it,

that'd be great. If not, or if it's inappropriate, of course no trouble."

She does read it, and is impressed. "When
Gerda dies," she says, "we'll run this as it is.
Full length, if possible. This is exactly the
sort of writing we need more of. With a real
voice. With something to say. Really terrific.
You captured her perfectly. Make sure Clint
gives you the proper space. Okay? And if
there's any trouble, say I said so."

He takes the opportunity to propose a few
more stories to Kathleen — not obits but
general features. She doesn't object, so he
pursues them in his own time. Maintaining
precedent, he files directly to her, not
ostensibly for her to edit but because, as he
puts it, "I'd really appreciate your opinion,
if you have a second." Once she has read
each and enthused, he forwards it to Clint
with a note stating, "KS edited." With that,
Clint cannot touch a word.

Gradually, Arthur converts Pickle's old
room into his study. That is, he calls it his
study. Visantha won't.

One night, he looks up from his notes.
"Hi. What's up?"

"You busy?" she asks.

"Fairly. What's going on?"

"I'll come back later. I don't want to inter-
rupt."

"What's up?"

"Nothing. I just wanted to talk."

"About?" He turns off the desk light. He sits in darkness. She is silhouetted in the doorway. He says, "I can't talk about that."

"I haven't said what."

"I'm done here for the night."

"Age-wise," she says, "it's a rush. If we want to."

"I got a fair amount done tonight, I think."

"Because of my age. I'm just saying."

"No, no," he says, rising. "Not for me. No. Couldn't bear that. I'm done in here. Done for the night." He approaches and touches her shoulders. She responds, expecting an embrace. Instead, he shifts her gently aside and passes.

The next day, a Cuban man who claimed to be 126 years old dies. Nobody believes the claim, but the paper needs to fill out page nine. So Arthur is assigned to write eight hundred words. He steals the basics from the wires and adds a few clever flourishes. He reads it over a dozen times, emails it to Clint. "You have the fake Cuban," Arthur informs him, and does a last check of his email in-box before heading to the door. He finds a message from Erzberger's niece: Gerda has died.

Arthur checks the time to see if he can

still make deadline. He calls the niece, offers his condolences, inquires about a few compulsory details: when exactly Gerda died, what the official cause was, when the funeral will be. He types these updates into the obit and walks into Clint's office. "We need to knock something off page nine."

"Not at this hour."

"An Austrian writer, Gerda Erzberger, just died. I have preparedness ready to go."

"Are you insane? We've got the fucking Cuban on nine."

"You need to kill him and put in Erzberger."

"I *need* to? Kathleen didn't say I need to do nothing."

"Kathleen wanted it in."

Each man cites Kathleen's name as if hoisting a club.

"Nuh-uh. Kathleen wanted the 126-year-old Cuban. She said so at the afternoon meeting."

"Well, *I* want Erzberger in. At full length."

"Who heard of this dumb-ass Austrian, anyway? Look, man, I think we can safely hold your masterpiece till tomorrow."

"Kathleen specifically said she wanted something in the paper as soon as Erzberger died. Obviously, we could tack a brief onto

84

the bottom of the world's oldest liar and that might satisfy her. But I don't want to do that. This is my personal request, nothing to do with Kathleen: dump the Cuban and run Erzberger. And *don't* hack my piece. I don't want to open the paper tomorrow and read it as a brief at the end of the Cuban. Is that clear?"

Clint smiles. "I'll do whatever I got to do, man."

Arthur sleeps poorly that night — he's too impatient. When the paper arrives, he flips immediately to page nine. "Yes!" he declares. "Oh, Clint, dear, dear Clint!" Just as Arthur had hoped, Clint has destroyed the Erzberger article, condensing her life into one hundred words and making it a brief at the bottom of the dead Cuban. "Perfect," Arthur says.

He composes himself and phones Kathleen from his study. "Sorry to bug you this early at home, but did you see our obits today?"

"Obits plural?" He hears her flipping pages. Her voice turns metallic. "Why did we run this as a brief?"

"I know — I don't see why we couldn't have just held it for a day."

"You didn't know it was running like this?"

"Not a clue. I'm only seeing it now. The thing that bothers me is — well, a few things, I guess. First, there's all the money the paper spent sending me up there. Second, there's the effort I took in going back. Especially after everything that happened." He kicks the door of the study closed so Visantha won't hear.

"Exactly," Kathleen says.

"But more than anything else," he goes on, "it feels like a disservice to Gerda. An important twentieth-century writer, a serious thinker, in my view. Already she's way too overlooked. And what do we do? Clint turns her into a brief. At the bottom of some Cuban liar. I don't want to get anyone in trouble, but I find it offensive. And it makes the paper look bad. It makes us look like philistines, when all Clint needed to do was hold it for one day and then run it at full length, as I told him to. As I said *you* wanted. I told him, 'Don't run anything today. Kathleen would want you to hold it until tomorrow.' Anyway. I'm sorry — I'm bitching," he says. "I don't mean to slag off Clint. It's just —"

"No, you're right to be angry. I'm pretty annoyed myself."

"Could we run my piece at full length today?" He knows the answer.

"We can't report her death twice," she says.

"What stuns me is that I specifically brought up your name when Clint and I discussed this."

"Seriously?"

"I was crystal clear."

"You know what," she says, anger mounting, "I don't want your stuff under Clint anymore. This is ridiculous."

"But politically? I mean, I have to be under Clint. I'm on page nine. Which is his."

"Nothing is *his*."

"What about my fixtures: the puzzles and all that?"

"You shouldn't have to do that crap anyway. An intern could do that."

"Clint will give you a hard time about this."

"I'm not worried."

"I don't want to get ahead of myself here," he says, picking at the Scotch tape holding one of Pickle's old magazine clippings to the wall. "But I've been meaning to talk to you about something."

When Arthur is named the new culture editor, he moves into Clint's former office. It is deemed too blatant to make Clint sit in Arthur's old cubicle, so they find him one at the edge of the sports department, facing a pillar.

At home, the atmosphere between Arthur and Visantha is strained. She is openly hunting for a job back in the United States, and there is no talk of his returning with her. Indeed, he will be relieved when she leaves — the old Visantha is long gone anyway, just as the previous Arthur has perished.

These days, he prefers to stay late at work. After-hours, he admires his new office. True, it is smaller than those of the other section chiefs. And he is farther from the cupboard of pens. Then again, the watercooler is a good deal nearer. And this is a consolation.

1954. Corso Vittorio, Rome

The paper was established on Corso Vittorio Emanuele II, a broad east–west thoroughfare lined with dirty-white travertine churches and blood-orange Renaissance palazzi. Many of the buildings in central Rome were colored as if from a crayon box: dagger red, trumpet yellow, rain-cloud blue. But the paper's dour seventeenth-century building seemed to have been colored with a lead pencil: it was scribble gray, set off by a towering oak door large enough to swallow a schooner, though human beings entered through a tiny portal hinged within.

A doorman sized up new arrivals from his glass booth, pointing down the long hallway, its brilliant burgundy runner halting just short of the elevator cage, the metal door ajar, its operator sitting on a velvet stool. "*Che piano, signore?* What floor, sir?"

For Cyrus Ott, it was the third, formerly the headquarters of a Fascist movie magazine that went bankrupt after the fall of Mussolini. Ott rid the place of its dusty furniture and had all the interior walls knocked down, creating a wide-open newsroom, rimmed with tidy offices that looked inward, like box seats directed toward the stage. He bought wooden swivel chairs, varnished desks, brass banker's lamps, a custom-built horseshoe table for the copy editors, shiny black phones for the reporters, thirty-eight Underwood typewriters imported from New York City, thick crystal ashtrays, and thick white carpeting, with a discreet cocktail bar in the east wall.

Six months later, any visitor stepping out of the elevator at the third floor landed directly in a vibrating newsroom, the secretary's desk ahead, a handful of typing reporters left and right, a half-dozen copy editors defacing proofs at the horseshoe table. In the offices along the walls, salesmen hocked ad space, a stenographer copied down classifieds, the accountant inked ledgers. In the northwest corner was Ott's office, with *PUBLISHER* etched on the frosted door; in the northeast corner were Leopold T. Marsh, editor-in-chief, and Betty Lieb, news editor. Ranged nearby were senior staffers specializing in business, sports, wire copy, photos, layout. Copyboys buzzed back and forth like pollinating bees.

Printing took place in the subbasement, but it could have been another land. Unionized Italian laborers ran the deafening press down there, yet few of them ever met anyone who wrote the paper just floors above. In the late afternoon, a truck arrived with a vast roll of newsprint, which the workers slid down the incline at the back, slamming it into the loading bay shuddering the building up to the third floor. Any journalists lazing around up there — joshing with one another, legs kicked up on desks, brimmed hats dangling on shoe tips, cigarettes smoldering in ashtrays — jerked upright in immediate panic. "Fuck, is it that time already?"

Miraculously, by the 10 P.M. deadline the paper had filled every line down every column, no matter the last-minute heart palpitations and blaspheming. Editors rose from their desks for the first time in hours, shrugging tortured shoulder muscles, attempting to exhale.

Most of the journalists were men, Americans chiefly, but with a few Britons, Canadians, and Australians, too. All had been based in Italy when hired, and all could speak the local language. But the paper's newsroom was strictly Anglophone. Someone hung a sign on the elevator door that read, LASCIATE OGNI SPERANZA, VOI CH'USCITE — OUTSIDE IS ITALY.

And when staffers went downstairs for sandwiches they'd say, "I'm headed to Italy — anyone need anything?"

The first full year of operations, 1954, was packed with news: the McCarthy hearings, the Soviets testing a nuclear weapon, the Dow Jones closing at a record high of 382 points. Initially, the paper suffered under the suspicion that it was an international mouthpiece for

Ott's business empire, but this was unfounded. The greatest influence over content was necessity — they had holes to fill on every page and jammed in any vaguely newsworthy string of words, provided it didn't include expletives, which they were apparently saving for their own use around the office.

Betty and Leo ran the editorial operations jointly. He liked to say, "I handle the big picture." But it was Betty who wrote — or rewrote — most of the copy; she had an effortless way with prose. As for Ott, he handled the money side and offered advice when solicited, which was often. Betty and Leo speedwalked across the newsroom to his office, each trying to get in the door first. Solemnly, Ott listened, staring at the carpet. Then he looked up, pale blue eyes flitting between Betty and Leo, and issued his ruling.

The three of them got along splendidly. Indeed, the only awkward moments arose when Ott stepped away, at which point Betty and Leo spoke to each other as if newly introduced and watched the door for their publisher to return.

Normally, Ott was ruthless about profit. But the paper was an anomaly: financially, it stank. Back in the United States, his business rivals observed this Italian venture with suspicion. It must be a scheme of sorts, they figured.

If so, the aim was far from clear.

He never explained his business plans to Betty and Leo, and was even more opaque on personal matters. He had a wife, Jeanne, and a young son, Boyd, but had never explained why they remained in Atlanta. Leo sought to tease out details but failed — Ott had the ability to insert full stops in conversations, when and where he wished them.

■ ■ ■ ■

"Europeans Are Lazy, Study Says"

· · ·

BUSINESS REPORTER — HARDY BENJAMIN

■ ■ ■ ■

Hardy spends her morning on the phone to London, Paris, and Frankfurt, wheedling quotes from grumpy financial analysts. "Is an interest-rate hike imminent?" she asks. "Is Brussels extending the shoe tariffs? What about the trade imbalance?"

She is unfailingly courteous even when her sources are not.

"Hardy, I'm busy. What do you need?"

"I could call back later."

"I'm busy now; I'm busier later."

"Sorry to be so annoying. Just wondering if you got my voice mail."

"Yes, I know — you're doing another China story."

"I'll be quick, I swear."

"You know my line on China: 'We should all start learning Mandarin. Blah-blah-blah.' Can I go now?"

By midafternoon she has written a thou-sand words, which is greater than the number of calories she has consumed since yesterday. Hardy is on a diet that started, roughly, at age twelve. She's thirty-six now and still dreaming of butter cookies.

She takes a break at the espresso bar downstairs, where she meets up with her friend Annika, who is unemployed and therefore usually free for coffee. Hardy empties a packet of artificial sweetener over her cappuccino. "Nothing epitomizes the futility of human striving quite like aspartame," she says and sips. "Ah, but this is good."

Meanwhile, Annika floods her caffè macchiato with an endless stream of brown sugar.

They are an unusual duo at the bar: one is pinkish, geeky, short (Hardy); the other is bosomy, stylish, tall (Annika). The pinkish one waves for the barman, but he doesn't notice; the bosomy one nods and he bolts forward.

"You're annoyingly good at hailing boys," Hardy says. "Though it's demeaning how they slobber over you."

"It doesn't demean me."

"It demeans *me.* I want counter staff to treat *me* like an object," she says. "Did I tell you, by the way, that I had another nightmare about my hair?"

Annika smiles. "You're sick, Hardy."

"In my dream, I was looking in the mirror and I saw this apparition blinking back at me, surrounded by orange frizz. Horrifying." She glimpses herself in the mirror behind the bar and turns from the sight. "Grotesque."

"For the record," Annika says, "I adore your hair." She pulls one of Hardy's curls. "Look how it boings back. And I love auburn."

"Auburn?" she says, eyebrows raised. "My hair is auburn like carrot soup is auburn." Her cellphone rings, and she drains the last sip of cappuccino. "It's gonna be Kathleen with questions on my story." Hardy assumes her professional voice and answers. But after listening a moment her tone changes to alarm. She responds in Italian, copies down an address, and hangs up. "It was the police," she tells Annika. "My apartment was burglarized. Apparently, they caught a couple of *punkabbestia* druggies coming out with all my stuff."

Back home, she finds the drawers flung open and food dumped on the floor. In place of her mini stereo and tiny flat-screen TV are wires. Thankfully, her laptop was at the office. Her apartment is on the ground floor and the kitchen window, which gives onto an alley, has been smashed. That's where they entered, the police say. Apparently, the two suspects stuffed all they could into plastic bags, then fled. But the bags — already jammed with stolen goods from another apartment in Trastevere — tore under the weight and disgorged loot all over the roadway outside. The culprits tried to stuff the swag back in, but the commotion attracted the authorities.

On a long table at the police station are strewn her CDs, mini stereo, little flat-screen TV, DVDs, perfume, and jewelry, mixed with the possessions of the other, absent victim: a nylon necktie circa 1961, a handful of spy thrillers in English, a Catholic catechism, and, strangely, a pile of ratty boxer shorts.

She states for the record that her belongings are among those recovered, but is not allowed to retrieve anything — the other victim must be present to avoid disputes over ownership, and the police cannot find him.

That night, Hardy phones Annika to coax her over. "It's creepy with the window smashed," Hardy says. "You don't want to come and protect me? I'll cook."

"I wish I could, but I'm still waiting for my fella to get home," Annika says, meaning Craig Menzies, the paper's news editor.

"You could always come hang out with us."

"I don't want to go overboard. It's fine."

Hardy checks the deadbolt and settles on the couch, blanket laid over her legs, feet snuggled beneath, a carving knife within reach. She gets up and checks the lock again. As she passes the mirror, she raises a hand to block the sight of herself.

She inspects the window in the kitchen — air rushes under the cardboard that patches over the shattered pane. She prods the card. It holds, but is hardly safe. She nestles under the blanket and opens her book. After eighty pages — she's a fast reader — she gets up to investigate what's available in the kitchen for dinner. She settles on rice crackers and a can of chicken broth on the top shelf, which she is too short to reach. Using a ladle, she taps the can to the edge. It wobbles, falls, and she catches it with her free hand. "I'm a genius," she says.

Days pass and the police cannot find the other victim, which means that Hardy is still forbidden to reclaim her possessions.

"At the start," she complains to Annika, "I imagined this guy as some kind of sweet, innocent English monk, with the spy thrillers and the catechism and all that. But I'm starting to hate him. I have this image now of some pervert priest, you know, with the

101

cilice and the drooling problem, hiding out at some pontifical institute to avoid criminal charges in the States. Regrettably, I've seen the man's boxers."

Almost two weeks later, the police locate him. By the time she arrives at the station, he's already sorting through their stuff. She turns angrily to a policeman. "I can't believe you didn't wait for me," she says in Italian. "The whole point was for me and him to divide up the stuff together."

The officer melts away and the other victim turns cheerfully toward her. He's not a priest, after all, but a scruffy twentysomething with blond dreadlocks. *"Buongiorno!"* he says, conveying in one word his utter inability with the language.

"Weren't you supposed to wait for me?" she replies in English.

"Ah, you're American!" he says, speaking with an Irish accent. "I love America!"

"Well, thank you, but I'm not actually the ambassador. Look, how do we want to do this? Shall we start going through the CDs?"

"You go ahead. A person needs lots of patience for that kind of thing. And Rory is alien to lots of patience."

"You're Rory?"

"Yes."

"You refer to yourself in the third person?"

102

"The what person?"

"Forget it. Okay, I'll get my stuff." She loads up her duffel bag, then scans the remaining items. "Wait — something of mine isn't here." All that's left on the table are his tie, books, CDs, and boxer shorts.

"What are you missing?"

"Just something private. Damn it," she says. "It's not worth anything — just sentimental value. A Rubik's Cube, if you must know. It was a present. Anyway . . ." She sighs. "Are you making a report for the insurance?"

"I hadn't planned to, to be honest." He leans his head out the door and glances down the hall. He returns and, in a whisper, tells her, "I'm not exactly living in my flat legally. It's a commercial space, in the strictest-speaking sense. I can work there, but I'm not supposed to be living there."

"And what's your work?"

"Teaching work."

"What sort?"

"Bit of a nightmare with these coppers, what with me not living there officially in the formal sense. I thought about not picking up my things at all. But I needed these." He touches the pile of boxers, grinning.

"Okay, but my insurance has nothing to do with you living in a commercial space."

"They might start sniffing around, don't
you think?"

"Sorry — what did you say you teach,
Rory?"

"Improv," he says. "And juggling."

"Not at the same time, I hope."

"Sorry?"

"Doesn't matter. Where are you from in
Ireland? County Cork, by any chance?
Everyone I meet from Ireland seems to be
from County Cork. I think it must be empty
by now."

"No, no — lots of people there," he
responds guilelessly. "Is that what you're
hearing? That it's emptied out?"

"I'm joking. Anyway, back to business. My
insurance company isn't going to be interested in you, so I will have to file a report.
The burglars smashed my window, and in
Rome that's going to cost me a fortune."

"A window? Is that all? Jesus, I can sort
that out."

"You're going to replace my window?"

"Sure."

"How?"

"Put in some glass."

"You yourself will?"

"Absolutely."

"Okay, but when?"

"Right now, if you like."

104

"I can't — I have to get back to work. Plus, don't you need materials?"

"Like what?"

"Glass, for example."

"Ah," he says, nodding. "You have a point."

"I don't want to be difficult here, but it took the police practically two weeks to track you down. I can't spend my life corralling you into fixing my window."

"You don't trust me?"

"It's not that I *dis*trust you. I just don't know you."

"Here, take my business card." He hands her one, then removes his watch. "You can keep this, too, as a deposit till I fix your window."

"Your digital watch?"

"If you don't want that, take your pick — anything you like from the table." His junk is laid out there: CDs, dog-eared spy thrillers, the Catholic catechism, the boxer shorts.

A smile crosses her face. She glances at him. She sweeps the boxers into her duffel bag. "Now *that's* a deposit."

"You can't take those!" he exclaims. "What am I gonna wear?"

"What have you been wearing this past week?"

At the espresso bar, she tells Annika about the Irishman. "And I stole his boxers."

"Why would you take some old guy's underwear?"

"He's a kid, actually. From Ireland. Has blond dreadlocks."

"Dreadlocks on a white guy? That is sad."

"I know, but he's tall, which makes it slightly less horrific. Doesn't it? I'm a total idiot, though — I ran out without leaving him my contact details."

"Look, you've got the guy's underwear — he'll turn up."

But he doesn't. She phones the number on his business card and leaves a message. He doesn't call back. She leaves another. Again, no response. Finally, she visits his address, which looks like a boarded-up garage. He answers the door, blinking at the daylight. "Well, hello there!" He stoops to her low altitude and kisses her cheek. She pulls away in surprise. He says, "I clean forgot. You know that — I clean bloody forgot about your window. Aren't I terrible! I am sorry. I'll sort that out for you right now."

"Actually, I'm going to have to file that insurance claim."

He toys with a dreadlock. "I should get rid of these stupid things. Don't you think?"

"I don't know."

"Bit of a tradition about them. One of my odysseys."

"Odysseys?"

"Like, trademarks."

"You mean 'oddities'?"

"Daft, though, aren't they. Come on — you chop them for me. All right?" He beckons her in.

"What are you talking about?"

"I give you scissors. You cut them off."

His place was clearly not intended as a living space. It is windowless and illuminated solely by a halogen lamp in the corner. A yellowing mattress is pushed against the wall, with a battered backpack beside it, a heap of clothing, juggling balls and clubs, a toolbox, and his spy thrillers and catechism. A basin and a toilet are affixed to the wall, without a divider for privacy. The room smells of old pizza. He rummages in the toolbox and emerges with a pair of industrial scissors.

"Are you serious?" she says. "Those things are the size of my torso."

"What do you mean by 'torso'?"

"I'm just saying they're big scissors."

"It'll be fine! Don't you worry, Hardy."

He sits on the closed toilet seat. He's now almost the same height as she is standing.

She rises on the balls of her feet and snips, handing him the first amputated strand. "This is actually kind of fun," she says, and cuts another. The discarded locks pile up like kindling. His ears, bared now, are bent slightly, like a rabbit's. He raises a mirror. Both are reflected: Rory studying his shorn head; she studying him. He grins at her and she laughs, then catches sight of her own face and recoils, shaking hair from her shoes. "That look okay to you?"

"Looks brilliant. Thanks very much. My head feels so light." He shakes it, like a wet dog. "You know, I'm starting to think getting robbed wasn't so bad after all. I got my stuff back *and* I got a free haircut out of it."

"Fine for you, maybe. I didn't get all *my* things back."

The next morning, Hardy awakens thinking of Rory. At noon, she sends him a text message. Thereafter, whenever a mobile beeps she checks hers. But it's never him. She rues having sent that pathetic message ("I still have your underwear!") and hopes that somehow he never received it. After a few hours, she can't bear waiting any longer, so she phones him. He picks up and promises to "pop by" later.

By midnight, he still hasn't showed. She phones again, but no answer. It's almost 1

A.M. when he appears, grinning, on her doorstep. She makes a point of looking at her watch. "I'll get the stuff now," she says. "It's kind of freezing if you leave the door open like that."

"Should I come in, then?"

"I guess." She fetches the plastic bag containing his underwear. "I hope those weren't your only pairs."

"Course not." He takes them. "I wondered before why a thief would want my underpants. But now I see they're a pretty popular item."

"So, okay, I guess that's all. Or, uhm, did you want a drink or something?"

"Yeah, nice one, yeah. Lovely."

"I have stuff to eat. If you want."

"Super, super." He follows her into the kitchen.

She opens a bottle of Valpolicella and heats up a casserole of lasagna that she had planned to bring to the office. (She cooks abundantly and expertly but eats none of it; she has seen the bricks of butter, shovels of sugar, gallons of double cream that disappeared into the mix, ready to reappear on her hips. So her creations — the Leaning Tower of Potato, the Seattle Swirl Cookies, the Sesame-Crusted Salmon Cakes with Lemon Tarragon Sauce — end up at the paper, spread out for the staff, nibbled by distracted editors, spilled on the carpeting, as she observes from her desk, feeding only on their praise.)

Rory devours the lasagna, downs most of the wine, and chatters, all at once. "Lovely. Super." He tells her about his father, who owns a plumbing company outside Dublin, and his mother, a secretary at a medical-supplies company. He briefly attended university in Ireland but quit short of a degree and traveled to Australia, Thailand, Nepal. Next, he was in New York, working at pubs. He took a class there in improv comedy and performed at an open mike in the East Village. After that, he trekked through Europe, took a ship from Marseille to Naples, passed a few months in the south of Italy, then made his way up to Rome.

She fills his glass. "I'd never have the courage to teach a class in anything. Not that I'm qualified to. Let alone in a foreign city. It's pretty brave."

"Or plain stupid."

"Brave," she insists.

He asks about her work. "Hate to admit it," he says, "but I've hardly read a newspaper in my life. So bloody small, isn't it."

"Small?"

"The writing. You need to make the writ-

110

ing bigger."

"Mm," she says. "Maybe."

"What do you write about then, Hardy?"

"Business." She sips her wine. "Sorry, I'm not keeping up with you here."

"You won't keep up with me," he replies good-naturedly.

"Can I pour you some more?" She does so. "Well, I was hired to write about personal finance and luxury goods. But I seem to have become a one-woman business section. We had this ancient guy in Paris called Lloyd Burko who used to do the occasional European business story. But now, essentially, it's just me."

"Nice one, Hardy." He notices something in her expression. "What's funny?"

"Nothing — I just like how you call me Hardy."

"That's your name, is it not?"

"Yes. But I mean how you say it."

"How's that?"

"Say it again."

"Hardy."

She smiles, then resumes: "Basically, financial reporting is this sinkhole at the center of journalism. You start by swimming around it until finally, reluctantly, you can't fight the pull anymore and you get sucked down the drain into the biz pages."

"That bad, is it?"

"Not really. I tend to dramatize. The sad truth is that I'm secretly into this stuff — I'm the kind of person who reads Morningstar stock reports on vacation. My feeling is that, at heart, every story is a business story."

"Ah, right," he says.

"But I'm weird that way."

He carries his dirty plate to the sink. She jumps to her feet. "No, no — you don't need to do that." She stumbles. "Oh — I think I'm a bit drunk." In the restricted space of her kitchen, they are close. She looks up. "You're irritatingly tall. It's like an indictment of everything I stand for."

"You're not so short."

"Who said I was short? I'm a minimalist."

He leans down and kisses her. "Your nose is freezing, Hardy."

She touches it. She's no longer trying to sound clever. "Can you do that again?"

"What?"

"That thing you did before."

"Calling you Hardy?"

"No, the thing you did after that. The thing you just did."

"What thing?"

She kisses him. "*That* thing. Keep doing it, please."

Activities shift into the bedroom.

Afterward, they lie in the dark, side by side on her bed. "Can I get you anything?"

"No, no, Hardy. I'm lovely."

"I quite agree. A last bit of wine, maybe?"

"A wee dram wouldn't hurt."

She pours him a glassful and speeds back to the bedroom in bare feet. Before entering, she says, "I wasn't cold before, I was just nervous." She hands him the glass. "My nose, I mean."

He sips. "Delicious."

"You sound a bit drunk. Nice drunk, though. Charming drunk." She leans into him. "What's that tattoo, by the way?"

"It's a wolf. I got it done in Sydney. You like it?"

"A wolf? I thought it was a seal. A seal howling at the moon. Anyway, it's very nice." She kisses his shoulder. "It's so nice to have someone here."

The next day at the espresso bar, Annika asks for details. "Did your Irishman fix the window?"

"We got slightly drunk, actually."

"Oh really? Continue."

"No, nothing."

"No, something."

"Okay, something."

"And the window?"

Hardy hires a glazier — she doesn't want Rory to feel pressured about it each time he drops by. But a week later he hasn't dropped by again, hasn't called, hasn't answered her messages. She visits his place, ready for a sad scene. But when he opens the door he kisses her on the mouth and asks where on earth she's been. She ends up taking him home, feeding him, watering him, giving him lodgings, as before.

"I like coming here," he says, propped up in her bed as she dresses for work the next morning. "You have a proper bathtub."

"Is that the extent of my appeal? You're overlooking my shower."

"I prefer baths myself."

"You're not going to vanish again, are you?"

"What do you mean?"

"Vanish. As in absence of Rory. Deficit of Rory. Apartment devoid of Rory."

"Don't be batty. I'll give you a ring."

"When?"

"How's about tomorrow?"

"When you say tomorrow, do you mean two weeks from tomorrow?"

"I mean tomorrow. Actual tomorrow."

"As in two days after yesterday?"

He doesn't call. She wants to scream. But this is how he is: easygoing, which means

114

tough-going for everyone else. She can hardly be surprised at this stage. She collects him from his hovel down the road in Trastevere as if he were a puppy, rescued from the pound for the umpteenth time, wagging at the sight of her yet certain to scamper away the minute she absents herself. His time without her, as far as she can tell, is occupied by reading books on the CIA and drinking plonk with his Italian hippie friends. His improv classes turn out to be more hypothetical than real. But everyone needs something they do, she decides, especially if they're not doing it.

What money he has comes from his father in infusions that arrive irregularly, so he is flush one week and broke the next. He spends it strangely: on a lime-green alarm clock, for example, although he has no reason to get up in the morning and no food in his apartment. When he's broke, she hides money in his jacket pocket. Now and then, she encourages him to start those improv classes, or seek employment of another kind — teaching English, perhaps. But his dream is to make it as a comedian and he's convinced that fame is around the corner, though how he might achieve this in Italy is beyond her. What's more, while he is a cheery fellow, he's not a markedly funny

115

one. Hardy refuses to hear his stand-up routine. She's polite about this but firm.

One afternoon, Annika asks her, "What if I found Rory a one-off gig?"

"How would you do that?"

"You don't sound too enthusiastic."

"No, I am. Tell me."

Annika saw a flyer advertising a fund-raiser at a local pub for the Vatican Radio soccer team. The organizers already have a band arranged but are looking for other acts. "It wouldn't pay, but it'd be practice for him," Annika says. "And no pressure — just a bunch of friendly drunks."

"You're more intent on getting his career going than he is," Hardy says.

"I noticed."

Hardy and Rory meet up with Annika and Menzies at the pub. The crowd is large and boisterous, and a drum kit is set up on the stage at the back, with a microphone stand before it. They find a free table.

"This is marvelous, this is," Rory says and disappears to count the crowd.

Hardy grips Annika's leg under the table. "I'm so nervous."

"You're nervous?" Annika says. "You're not the one doing it."

"I know, but . . ."

Rory returns, beaming.

"You're excited, then?" Menzies asks him.

"Absolutely. Not a lot of opportunities in Italy to do stand-up in English."

"Almost none, I'd think."

"You're probably right."

"What sort of comedy do you do?"

"What do you mean?"

"Well, how would you describe your act?"

"You're gonna love it."

Hardy leans toward Rory and whispers, "Might be time to buy a round." She slips him a fifty-euro note under the table.

He taps Menzies on the shoulder. "I'm getting this one, folks. Same again, ladies?"

The emcee — an Englishman who normally delivers somber bulletins on Vatican Radio but is this evening dressed as a Harlequin — jogs across the stage. "Ready, everybody?"

"I think it's me now," Rory tells the table. He nods at Hardy and heads for the stage. The patrons part before him and strangers slap his back.

Annika tells Hardy, "Nothing to worry about — it'll be fun."

The crowd murmurs as he climbs onto the stage. He tugs the microphone baffle down tight, shades his eyes from the spotlight. "All right," he says.

"Who is this guy?" a drunk bellows.

Rory identifies himself.

Derisory hellos spray back at him.

Hardy squeezes Annika's leg again. "I can't bear this."

"What are you worried about?"

Rory begins his routine. "The Internet is amazing, isn't it." He clears his throat. "Did you realize the U.S. military invented it? It's true. I read that. They wanted to be sure that if there was a nuclear war everyone would still be able to get pornography." He pauses for laughter.

No one laughs.

"And," he persists, "come to think of it, if the world was at the brink of destruction, with Armageddon and all that, perhaps a bit of a wank would be in order."

A few dubious snorts.

Hardy closes her eyes and lets go of Annika's leg.

"Since this is a Vatican crowd," he continues gamely, "I thought I'd talk about religion. I'm a Catholic myself. In the Bible there's that section on God killing everyone in Sodom and Gomorrah. But I don't get it. I mean, we know why everyone in Sodom got punished. But what did the Gomorrans ever do to anybody?"

Once more, the room is silent.

"This," Menzies whispers, "is what's

known in comedy circles as 'dying.' "

"That's not helpful," Annika responds.

"I feel like I'm going to be sick," Hardy says. "I have to get out of here. Is it going to be obvious? I don't want to hurt his feelings."

"Maybe it'll get better."

Rory changes topics. "Let me tell you about my girlfriend. This girl — have you heard of the biological clock? Hers is at about half-past midnight. She is so desperate, you have no idea."

"Maybe," Annika suggests hurriedly, "you should take this opportunity to go to the toilets."

Hardy hustles away.

As she passes the bathroom mirror, she raises her hand to block the reflection and enters a stall, sits, her chin on her hands. The echo of Rory's voice drifts in. She plugs her ears. After ten minutes, Annika taps on her stall. "It's safe to come back now."

"I drank too much — that's the story if he noticed."

"Gotcha."

"You seem kind of weird," Hardy says.

"Did you not hear his act?"

"No. Why?"

"It was totally inappropriate. All sorts of private stuff about you. I'm extremely pissed off right now."

"I don't want to know."

"I'm tempted to punch him."

"What should I do?" Hardy asks.

"I can't tell you." Her expression, however, does.

Rory is at the bar, seeking the bartender.

"So?" Hardy says, trying to sound enthused. "How'd you think it went? Did you enjoy it?"

"Brilliant. Absolutely brilliant." He clearly didn't notice her absence.

"Let's snag that table in the corner," she says.

"We're not going back with the others?"

"They're in the middle of a talk. Let's give them a few minutes."

A U2 cover band plays its first set. During the intermission, Annika and Menzies, their coats on, stop at Hardy and Rory's table. "We're off now, I'm afraid."

Hardy stands and gives Annika a hug.

"You all right?" Annika asks.

Hardy doesn't respond.

For the rest of the week, she finds ways out of their afternoon coffee break.

"Kathleen has me slaving away on a massive takeout," she tells Annika by phone.

"What's the subject?"

"It's supposed to be called 'Europeans Are Lazy.' "

"I don't believe you."

"I'm serious. What kind of deranged person lies about differential rates of labor productivity?"

"You, probably. I want coffee. You must come. I command you."

"I can't. I'm sorry." Hardy adds, "I know you don't like him, by the way."

"What does that have to do with anything? And I don't dislike him. I just . . . He's sucking all the funny out of you."

"I'm still funny. I'm just not funny ha-ha. More funny weird."

"Nothing new there."

"I don't want to get into my situation with Rory. It's fine. I'm happy about it."

"You don't seem any more happy than you were before."

"Well, you're wrong."

"Why are you getting angry?" Annika says.

"I'm not."

"I just think you have to have standards."

"Thanks."

"I don't mean it like that."

"What am I supposed to do?" Hardy says. "Be furious? Outrage hasn't gotten me anywhere, ever."

"Are you in love with this guy?"

"Look, I stopped waiting for that particular sentiment sometime around 1998. At this stage, I'm satisfied if he can reach the top shelf without using my ladle."

"But *this* guy?"

"You have to understand, Annika, that I have pretty much resigned myself to spinsterhood since, I don't know, since approximately my entire life. But just because I act chirpy about it doesn't mean that I'm chirpy about it. You have Menzies. Me? I dread weekends. How depressing is that? I wish I didn't have vacation time — I have no idea what to do with it. It's like a four-week reminder of what a loser I am. I don't have anyone to go anywhere with. Look at me — I'm practically forty and I still resemble Pippi Longstocking."

"Quit it."

"Are you saying I should dump him? Wait for true love? And if that doesn't happen? I can't count on my friends. You guys all have other things to do — husbands, families. Anyway, it's not as if your man is about to set the world ablaze."

"Menzies is Menzies. At least he's smart."

"Brains don't keep me warm at night."

"This guy is taking advantage of you."

"No one takes advantage of me. Not without my say-so."

After this, their tradition of afternoon coffee breaks ends.

But Hardy barely notices — she's too occupied. Rory is set to move in.

When the day arrives, his Italian hippie friends turn up to help move boxes. She has promised to cook a hearty meal in exchange for their labors, and the loading and unloading is a jolly affair, sploshed with cheap red wine. Fortunately, Rory owns nothing of value and his few possessions survive the increasingly inebriated moving team.

"Is that it?" she asks.

"I think so." He pats her on the top of her head.

"What was that for?" She pulls him down by the shoulders to her height and kisses him, pressing as hard as she can, then draws back, her hands against his face. She lets go. "I'm going over to your place to give it a final clean."

"No need for that," he says.

"I know, but it's polite."

The evening air is crisp, and dusky Trastevere is unusually tranquil. She breathes out contentedly and unlocks his old apartment. It's a terrible mess. She shakes her head indulgently.

She wipes down the stubble-clogged sink, gathers a discarded razor and a strand of dental floss. Old pizza boxes are folded up everywhere. She sweeps and airs out the walk-in closet, which tinkles with metal hangers.

She notices something: dumped in the corner is her old Rubik's Cube, the one that the burglars stole.

She is still for nearly a minute.

Beneath the toy are a few of her CDs that were never recovered, and rings that went missing, too; Rory must have helped himself before she arrived at the police station. On the panels of the Rubik's Cube are letters in her father's handwriting. It was a present on her fourteenth birthday and he wrote a wish in marker on the squares, then scrambled the puzzle so that she had to solve it in order to read the message. But the cube is scrambled again now, spelling nonsense: RYH and HEE and AYR. Mechanically, she twists it back into its correct position, reviving the message, which is composed horizontally across four sides:

AVE	RYH	APP	Y14
FOR	DEA	RHA	RDY
ALL	MYL	OVE	DAD

To this day, her father in Boston is the only person who Hardy *knows* esteems her. With the rest, she must be clever, must cook sublimely. Her father's affection alone is unconditional. Yet it has been years since she has returned home; she can't be in his company anymore. Each time they meet, his expression states so fixedly: how is it possible that you are still alone?

When she goes back to her apartment, Rory and his friends are debating which spy agency is the best — MI6, the CIA, or the Mossad. She proceeds past them, her over-coat pocket heavy with the stolen toy. She lays the coat across a kitchen chair and finishes preparing the meal.

The men drink heartily and gorge themselves on everything she brings out, forking in more even as their mouths steam with hot helpings. She herself doesn't eat, instead clattering about the kitchen with dirty pots, opening cupboard doors just for somewhere to stare. Must she mention what she found?

"Rory," she calls out, "I'm so dumb — I left something over at your place."

In the dark of his apartment, she digs her nails under the stickers on the Rubik's Cube. She peels off the squares one by one. The Rubik's Cube is smooth now, plain black. She reaches for the farthest point in his closet and drops the toy. It lands with a clatter on the CDs and the rings that he stole.

Back home, she finds the men boozily debating Guantánamo Bay, flopping forward to make their points and flopping back to listen. She asks if they have everything they need, then excuses herself to the kitchen. She washes her hands, rips off a paper towel, dries herself. She ought to go in there and confront him.

"Hardy!" he calls merrily. "Hardy, where are you?"

"Coming."

She catches sight of herself in the silver kettle and studies the reflection, not recoiling this time. She tucks her carrot hair behind her ear and grabs a fresh bottle of Valpolicella.

On the arm of his chair she sits, watching him struggle with the cork.

"Pop," he says finally, pouring the first dash into his own glass.

"Pop," she says and presses a kiss into his shoulder. No reason to mention anything at all.

1957. *Corso Vittorio, Rome*

The paper increased to twelve pages a day, adding a culture section, Puzzle-Wuzzle, and the obituaries. Circulation broke fifteen thousand, with most of the copies sold in Europe, plus a sprinkling in the Maghreb and the Far East. Despite all predictions, Ott was still there, running the show.

His life, beyond the paper, was lived alone on the Aventine Hill in a sixteenth-century mansion that he had bought from an impoverished Italian noble family. The place was four stories of stone, painted orange and brown, with long yellow shutters, giving the impression of habitable marzipan. A spiked fence surrounded the property, and maids and cooks and odd-job men made their way in and out through the squeaky front gate. Inside, the ceilings were covered with frescoes of a highly sentimental nature — cheeky cherubim and plump lovers frolicking by waterfalls. Ott disliked these and was tempted to have them painted over.

However, he rarely looked upward, focusing instead on the walls, which he covered with paintings. His proclaimed interest was financial — Europe was full of bargains after the war, he said. But it was Betty who adored art. During her years in Rome, she had become passionate about paintings, haunting Renaissance churches to study dimly lit master-pieces, or using her press pass to sneak into newly opened art exhibits. So Ott made her his counselor: whatever she admired, he bought.

They frequented a private gallery near Quattro Fontane run by a flamboyant Armenian émigré named Petros, whose chief preoccupation was the provenance of works rather than their artistic merit. He listed illustrious past owners and recounted barely credible tales of how the pieces had ended up in his hands: train wrecks in Chungking, cutlass duels in the Crimea, pouches of counterfeit rubies. He rarely deigned to identify the artists, so Betty conveyed this detail to Ott: "That's Léger, I think. Not sure about this one. But that's Modigliani, for certain. And this is a Turner."

Betty even decided where in Ott's mansion each work should hang. She nudged the frame a little to the right, a little to the left. "Straight now?"

He stood a distance back, studying the shipwreck by Turner, all swirling doom and sinking sailors. "Tell me what's good about this one," he said.

She took a step back and, hand on hip, strove to explain. Her confused answer — he half smiled as he listened — grew all the more

128

fervid as clarity failed her.

"If you don't get it," she concluded, "well, then, you just don't get it."

"Who says I don't?" he responded, winking. "Maybe I just like watching you tell me."

Downstairs for lunch, Betty placed a vast *mozzarella di bufala* upon a plate and fetched the carving knife and fork. Poised above the cheese, she paused, not looking up. "What," she asked, "are you doing out here?"

"The paper," he replied.

"I know, but . . ." She inserted the fork: a milky pool expanded across the plate.

He took the cutlery from her hands, speared a piece, and fed it to her off the knife.

■ ■ ■ ■

"GLOBAL WARMING GOOD FOR ICE CREAMS"

• • •

CORRECTIONS EDITOR — HERMAN COHEN

■ ■ ■ ■

Herman stands before the copydesk, torch-eyes passing over the three editors on duty. They halt in mid-keystroke. "And I haven't even accused anyone yet," he says darkly, opening that morning's paper as if it contained a murder weapon. What it does contain is worse: a mistake. He touches the error with contempt, pokes at the despicable word, as if to shove it off the page and into a different publication altogether. "GWOT," he says. He slaps the page, shakes it at them. "GWOT!"

"G what?"

"GWOT!" he repeats. "GWOT is not in the Bible. And yet it is here!" He jabs the article, driving a sausage finger through page three.

They deny responsibility. But Herman has infinitely less time for pardon than for blame. "If none of you nitwits know what GWOT means," he says, "then why is

GWOT in the paper?"

An arctic silence settles upon the copy-desk.

"Have you *read* the Bible?" he demands. "Any of you?" He glances at the sorry trio of copy editors before him: Dave Belling, a simpleton far too cheerful to compose a decent headline; Ed Rance, who wears a white ponytail — what more need one say?; and Ruby Zaga, who is sure that the entire staff is plotting against her, and is correct. What is the value in remonstrating with such a feckless triumvirate?

"Sooner or later . . ." Herman says, and allows the partial threat to hang there. He turns from them, prodding the air. "Cred-ibility!" he declares. "Credibility!"

He elbows into his office, and the momen-tum of his belly topples a stack of books — he must tread with caution in here, for this is an overstuffed room and he an overstuffed man. Reference works clutter the room — classics like *Webster's New World College Dictionary, Bartlett's Familiar Quotations, National Geographic Atlas, The World Alma-nac and Book of Facts,* along with idiosyn-cratic tomes like *The Food Snob's Dictionary, The Oxford Dictionary of Popes, Technical Manual and Dictionary of Classical Ballet, The Visual Dictionary of the Horse, The Complete*

Book of Soups and Stews, Cassell's Latin Dictionary, Albanian-English/English-Albanian Standard Dictionary, and *A Concise Dictionary of Old Icelandic.*

He notices a gap on the shelf and searches the book skyscrapers rising from the floor for the missing volume. He locates it (*A Dictionary of Birds, Part IV: Sheathbill — Zygodactyli*), slides it back into place, hikes up his belt, lines himself up with his desk chair, and inserts his bottom — one more bulky reference work returned to its rightful home. He drags the keyboard to his bunchy gut and, condescending to the screen, types a new entry for the Bible:

• **GWOT:** No one knows what this means, above all those who use the term. Nominally, it stands for Global War on Terror. But since conflict against an abstraction is, to be polite, tough to execute, the term should be understood as marketing gibberish. Our reporters adore this sort of humbug; it is the copy editor's job to exclude it. ***See also:*** **OBL; Acronyms;** *and* **Nitwits.**

He hits save. It is entry No. 18,238. "The Bible" — his name for the paper's style guide — was once printed and bound, with a copy planted on every desk across the newsroom. Now it exists solely within the paper's computer network, not least because the text has grown to approximately the size of metropolitan Liechtenstein. The purpose of his Bible is to set down laws: to impart whether a "ceasefire" is, properly speaking, a "cease-fire" or indeed a "cease fire"; to adjudge when editors must use "that" and when "which"; to resolve quarrels over prepositions, false possessives, dangling modifiers — on the copydesk, fisticuffs have broken out over less.

Kathleen raps on his door. "Such were the joys," she says wearily.

"Which joys are these?"

"The joys of trying to put out a non-embarrassing daily with roughly five percent of the resources I need."

"Ah, yes," he replies. "The joys of the paper."

"And you? Whose self-esteem are you dismantling today?"

He massages his fingers and dips them into his trouser pocket, which is swollen as if with pebbles. He retrieves a mound of sucking sweets that have melted together. "You'll be thrilled to hear," he informs her, popping the candies into his mouth, "that I have a new copy of *Why?* ready." By this, he means the monthly internal newsletter in which he decants his favorite blunders from the paper. It is fair to say the staffers do not greet each edition of *Why?* with elation.

Kathleen sighs.

"Duty does call, I'm afraid," he says. "Now, what can I do for you, my dear?"

She often stops by for advice. Her deputy may be Craig Menzies, but Herman is her true counselor. He has worked at the paper for more than thirty years, has held most editorial jobs here (though never reporter), and served as the acting editor-in-chief during interregnums in 1994, 2000, and 2004. Staffers still shiver to recall his stewardship. Yet for all his bluster Herman is not disliked. His news judgment is envied, his memory is an unfailing resource, and his kindness emerges for all those who hang around long enough.

"What are your thoughts about my culture shake-up?" she asks.

"You managed to dislodge Clint Oakley finally."

"Very proud of myself over that," she says. "And you were right: Arthur Gopal isn't a write-off. Things remain ugly on the stringer front, though. Still no one in Cairo. And Paris remains unmanned."

"How can Accounts Payable refuse to

replace Lloyd?"

"It's insane."

"Outrageous."

"You here tomorrow?"

"Day off, my dear. Wait, wait — before you wander away, I wanted to warn you that I have a delightful new correction upcoming."

She groans; he grins.

Corrections have proliferated of late. A handful even earned a place on Herman's corkboard: Tony Blair included on a list of "recently deceased Japanese dignitaries"; Germany described as suffering from "a genital malaise in the economy"; and almost daily appearances from "the Untied States." He types out his latest publishable correction: "In an article by Hardy Benjamin in the Tuesday business section, the former dictator of Iraq was erroneously referred to as Sadism Hussein. The correct spelling is Saddam. We doubt that our typographical error impinged on the man's credibility, however, we regret —" He checks his watch. Miriam leaves tonight, and Jimmy arrives tomorrow. Herman still has much to do. He slips on his coat, jabs a finger in the air. "Credibility!" he says.

The front door to his apartment in Monteverde won't budge, so he shoulders it halfway open and, with a grunt, squeezes inside. His wife's luggage is blocking the passage. She is scheduled on an overnight flight from Rome back to Philadelphia to visit their daughter and grandchildren. The *click-clack* of her heels sounds down the hallway. "Sweetie pie," he calls, and edges past the luggage. "Sweetie pie, I'm afraid I banged one of your suitcases. The red one."

"Burgundy," she corrects him.

"That's not red?"

At work, Herman makes the corrections. Not here.

"I hope I didn't break anything. Were there presents in there? Should we open and check? What do you think?" Awaiting her judgment, he contorts as if before a teetering vase.

"It was packed perfectly," she says.

"I'm so sorry."

"I took ages doing that."

"I know. I'm terrible. Can I help?"

She kneels to unbuckle the luggage straps, and he raises a finger — not to prod the air this time but to beg permission. "Darling, might I possibly make you a drink? Might that be nice?"

"Can I check my bag first?"

"Yes, yes, of course."

He takes refuge in the kitchen, dicing car-

139

rots and celery. At the sound of her clicking heels, he swivels around. "A nice, hearty soup to fill you up for the long trip."

"You make me sound like a thermos."

He resumes chopping. "These vegetables are delicious — could I slice you a few?"

"Such a pity you can't come. But I guess you prefer Jimmy."

"Don't say that."

"Sorry," she says. "I'm being awful." She steals a carrot.

"Are you worried about the flight?"

She blinks in affirmation, then studies his soup mix. "Needs salt."

"How can you say?" he protests, then tastes it. She is right. He salts the soup, stirs it, kisses her cheek.

After dinner, he sees Miriam off at the airport and speeds home in their dented blue Mazda, a tiny model that, with him inside, looks like a bumper car. He tucks fresh sheets on the spare bed for Jimmy and tidies up. But there is not as much preparation as he'd expected. He runs a finger around the pot of cold soup (*acquacotta di Talamone:* chopped carrots and celery, chopped pancetta, pumpkin, zucchini, kidney beans, lima beans, artichoke hearts, grated pecorino, ground pepper, eight boiled eggs, fourteen pieces of toast). He and Jimmy met in Baltimore in the late 1950s, the only Jewish kids at a Presbyterian private school. Herman had been sent there by his father, a foul-tempered Zionist and a dead ringer for Karl Marx who believed the best school in the district should be forced to swallow a fat little Jew, namely, his son. The fat little Jew himself saw few benefits in being someone else's battering ram. But, thankfully, he had been preceded at the school by another Jewish kid, Jimmy Pepp, who enjoyed legendary status there for having climbed atop the church library and smoked a pipe on the roof. They said he had descended via the drainpipes and kept the tobacco smoldering all the way down. And it had been windy. The tale was dubious, but there was no denying that as a youth Jimmy had kept a pipe, a curved marvel with a meerschaum bowl and mahogany body that he puffed on the hill behind school, often leaning over a book of poetry — E. E. Cummings, say, or Baudelaire. He was also notable as the only pupil not to wear the school blazer, which he evaded with a falsified doctor's note claiming "seborrhoeic dermatitis." None of the teachers dared ask what this affliction consisted of — a fortunate turn, since Jimmy himself could only have guessed. The reason for his subterfuge was simply that he preferred to wear a donnish tweed jacket with elbow patches, in whose left pocket he kept a copy of *Ulysses* —the Modern Library edition, missing the dust jacket — and in whose right pocket he stored his calabash pipe and a tin of Mac Baren Club Blend tobacco. The balance between left and right pockets was grossly uneven, *Ulysses* being a notably heavy volume, so he evened it out with fountain pens, which often exploded, bleeding a constellation of indigo blotches into his right pocket. For a reason Herman never understood, Jimmy protected him at school from the day they met.

He is among the last to emerge off the afternoon flight from Frankfurt.

"Welcome," Herman says, beaming and reaching for Jimmy's bag, then changing his mind and throwing a thick arm around his narrow friend. "You got here."

He leads Jimmy to the car and they set off for the apartment. "Since I didn't know where your body clock would be," Herman explains while driving, "I have four possible dinner options. Scrambled eggs with truffle oil — very nice, I recommend it. Alternatively, homemade pizza. Or fresh *bresaola*, salad, and cheese — I have a great Taleggio. Also, there's leftover *acquacotta di Talam-*

one, which is a soup. Or we could just eat out. Is that four options?"

Jimmy smiles.

"What?" Herman asks, grinning back. "It's my job to fatten you up, no? Sorry, I have to concentrate here — I'm gonna crash us." He drives on in silence for a minute. "Good to see you," he says.

Jimmy journeyed from Los Angeles via Frankfurt, and the trip totaled almost twenty-four hours. He stays awake as long as he can, then falls asleep in the spare room. The next morning around dawn, he is padding around the living room in boxers with a design of lipstick kisses. His chest hair is white. Herman emerges in pajamas, kneading a knot in his back. "You want coffee?" he asks, and gives Jimmy the morning paper. Over breakfast, they talk politics — who's ruling America, who's ruling Italy. Soon, it's time for Herman to go to work. "You only just arrived, and I'm already abandoning you — some host," he says. "You got everything you need? You want to use the computer? It's outdated, but we have the Internet. And I got the technicians at work to install word processing so you can work on your book while you're here. Here, let me log you on."

With his rumpled copy of the paper under

his arm, Herman strides into the newsroom, shooting accusatory glances. Reporters murmur "Morning," and editors compress their lips and nod at the floor. He elbows into his office, pops a sucking sweet, and spreads out the day's paper, his yellow highlighter poised to lasso any sins. A stack of unopened letters to the editor sits on the edge of his desk. Sometimes it seems the readers do nothing but complain. They're usually on the old side — he can tell from the palsied scrawl and the diction ("Dear Sir, I expect you receive a great many letters, yet I must express my dismay over . . ."). Admittedly, the paper's readership is only about ten thousand people nowadays, but at least they are passionate. And the postmarks come from all around the world, which is heartening. For many, especially those in remote locales, the paper is their only link to the greater world, to the big cities they left, or the big cities they have never seen, only built in their minds. The readers constitute a sort of fellowship that never meets, united by loved and loathed bylines, by screwed-up photo captions, by the glorious corrections box. Speaking of which.

He spots Hardy Benjamin gossiping at the other end of the newsroom — he still hasn't finished the Sadism Hussein correction. From the doorway of his office, he bellows, "Miss Benjamin, I'll need you later."

"Something wrong?"

"Yes, but I'm too busy to talk now."

"Is it serious?"

"What I'm occupied with *now* is serious. You'll have to wait, Nancy Drew." He closes his door, irritated with himself. Imagine if Jimmy saw me bossing them like this, he thinks, and yanks a book at random from the shelf, the *International Dictionary of Gastronomy.* He flips its pages, landing at the entry for "churros." The first time he and Jimmy shared a home was on Riverside Drive at 103rd Street, on the Upper West Side of Manhattan. Herman was in his first year at Columbia University, while Jimmy had just returned from three months in Mexico, where he'd been romancing an older woman, an artist who sculpted Aztec monsters and whose husband in Houston had hired a kid to thump Jimmy on the head with a brick, though the kid just threw it and missed. Jimmy claimed that this was the reason he'd returned to America. But Herman suspected, guiltily, that there was another reason: that Jimmy had intuited from Herman's letters how disheartened he was alone at college in New York. There was only a single bed in his studio apartment, so Jimmy slept on the floor without sheets or pillows, which he claimed to prefer. Within a week, he had an entourage of peculiar friends and Herman's home had been transformed from monastic cell to bustling salon, crammed with all the weird of the metropolis: Dyer, the baby-faced waiter from New Orleans, who couldn't have been sweeter until he robbed everyone and bit a policeman's horse; beanpole Lorraine, who smoked marijuana cigarettes and opened her purse to show erotic drawings of herself with spiders; and Nedra, dark eyes disconnected from reason, who said she'd been born in Siam or Brooklyn, who smelled of underarm sweat, whom any street drunk could have and whom most had, though Jimmy let her sleep on the floor beside him and never touched her. Herman asked what had happened after that kid in Mexico threw the brick and missed. Jimmy said that he and the would-be assassin had started laughing. Then, Jimmy said, he'd bought the kid churros.

Herman closes the *International Dictionary of Gastronomy* and feeds it back into its slot on the shelf. He opens the paper to the culture pages, which have improved considerably under Arthur Gopal. Nevertheless,

146

Herman spots an offender: the word "literally." He snarls, wakes up his computer, and types:

• **literally:** This word should be deleted. All too often, actions described as "literally" did not happen at all. As in, "He literally jumped out of his skin." No, he did not. Though if he literally had, I'd suggest raising the element and proposing the piece for page one. Inserting "literally" willy-nilly reinforces the notion that breathless nitwits lurk within this newsroom. Eliminate on sight — the usage, not the nitwits. The nitwits are to be captured and placed in the cages I have set up in the subbasement. *See also:* **Excessive Dashes; Exclamation Points;** *and* **Nitwits.**

On his way home, Herman drives to Enoteca Costantini in Piazza Cavour to pick up a bottle of Frascati Superiore. Tonight he is preparing a traditional Roman meal for Jimmy: deep-fried *fiori di zucca* and *carciofi alla giudia,* a straightforward *bucatini all'amatriciana,* homemade *pizza bianca* to mop up the sauce, and *pangiallo* for dessert (this last item, alas, is store-bought).

At the apartment, he finds Jimmy flopped

on the spare bed, back turned. He rolls over.

"How you feeling?" Herman asks. "Jet-lagged?" He readies dinner as Jimmy recounts his day. He went for a walk and got lost, and someone followed him for a while — a thief, he thinks — but the guy gave up.

"Sounds more successful than my day," Herman comments. "My style guide is out of control. It's ridiculous. Those poor putzes I work with!"

At dinner, Jimmy eats little and drinks only water. As for tobacco, he has quit completely — it's curious to see him without the customary cloud of smoke. Herman asks about life in L.A., and Jimmy says he's busy — time just races by, consumed by all the minor activities: buying groceries, watching his TV programs, going to the laundromat. And crime is a worry.

Herman pats his gut, sauntering with intent toward the liquor cabinet. "Care for a *digestivo?*" he asks. "One thing I don't have, I'm afraid, is your favorite: Barbancourt rum, right?" The old Modern Library copy of *Ulysses* remained in Jimmy's pocket throughout the 1960s. Leopold Bloom was his hero, not least because they shared a taste for animal innards — fried pork kidneys in particular. However, the overpowering sizzle and stench of Jimmy's food in their shared New York apartment diminished over that decade as he spent more time in Mexico, pursuing his drama with the married sculptress. He claimed she resembled Molly Bloom, which amused Herman — what on earth does Molly Bloom look like? Herman graduated from Columbia with a degree in political science and took a job as a copyboy at a city newspaper. In his conception, this was all backward — Jimmy, not he, was supposed to go into journalism, starting out as a sportswriter, say, or covering cops, then writing a Runyonesque column about booze and betting and all the affable lunatics who gravitated toward him like bugs to a bulb. The next step for Jimmy would be to cover a war overseas and perhaps take part, like Hemingway or Orwell, then publish a book about it. His first novel would follow. After that, Jimmy's career would take off. Years later, Herman could write a biography — the definitive account, composed by Jimmy Pepp's best friend, who had known the great writer from school days in Baltimore to the mad nights in New York to the sculptress in Mexico to the first crackle of publishing success and the iconic fame that followed. But at the time of this reverie Herman was alone again in New York, a gopher at a local newspaper, fetching quarts of bourbon for ulcerated editors, making smoke runs, picking up corned beef on rye on Ninth Avenue, with the inevitable "No, hang on, kid, make mine pastrami on brown with extra mustard, and don't forget the napkins." Other copyboys busied themselves by stuffing live mice into the pneumatic tubes that connected the various departments, rocketing the creatures through the network until they popped out squeaking in the secretaries' pool. With this sort of competition, it was easy for Herman to shine.

The editors gave him a tryout as a proofreader, and he had a knack for it — finally, arcane knowledge and pedantry came in handy. The day of this promotion, he happened to meet Miriam at a friend's party and, inflated by professional success, found the courage to ask her on a date. In the coming months, he fell in love with her. But he worried about introducing her to his best friend, afraid that he, Herman, would wilt by comparison. Yet when Jimmy next passed through the city, Herman bravely arranged for them to meet for dinner. He was nervous all that day. Surprisingly, Jimmy seemed somewhat witless during the meal: his romantic exploits in Mexico sounded childish, his writing came off as half-baked. He spent most of the meal praising Herman, boasting of his friend's brilliance at Baltimore Presbyterian (untrue), of his sparkling college career (a gross exaggeration), and of the triumphant future that inevitably lay ahead for Mr. Herman Cohen (hardly credible). After dinner, they split up. Herman felt odd parting from Jimmy and going home with Miriam — he and his oldest friend still had all the real catching up to do.

Miriam said she liked Jimmy all right but couldn't see what Herman had been going on about. And that, Herman knew, had been the point of Jimmy's performance. He saw Jimmy off at the train station and smiled at the sight of *Ulysses* jutting from his luggage. "Is that the same copy from school?" Herman asked. Jimmy opened it. The pages had been cut out, and planted inside was a leather flask. "It wasn't always like that, was it?" Herman asked. Jimmy offered a sip and said how beautiful it was to see him with this girl, to see him happy. Herman blushed. "What is this poison?" he asked. Jimmy took a swig as if to double-check, then identified it as his favorite drink, Barbancourt rum.

Herman peruses the Bible on his computer screen at work, grinding a hard candy between his teeth. Ever since Jimmy arrived, Herman has turned against the Bible. It's nothing but a list of complaints — whining, organized alphabetically. No time to brood, though. He has work to do. He turns to the Sadism Hussein correction. He calls Hardy into his office.

"I thought I might have escaped," she says.

"Take a seat."

"That mistake was slipped in on the copydesk." This is every reporter's excuse.

"Who on the copydesk?"

"I'm not going to say."

"Yes, you are."

"Are you going to waterboard me if I don't?"

"Probably. Was it Ruby Zaga, by any chance? No matter. Whoever was responsible, it makes us look like nitwits. Now listen, your reporting is solid. And you write well, which is the highest praise from me. You are one of the strongest members of this staff. I hope that's been made clear to you." He taps the Sadism Hussein correction on his monitor. "But I have to think about credibility."

"I realize that. The thing is —"

"Hang on, hang on. If credibility is our goal — and at this point credibility is pretty much all we have left — then we should

152

strive to maintain the reputation of strong staffers. So I wonder if we shouldn't let Sadism Hussein die."

"Seriously?" she says. "Thank you, thank you, thank you. I'll never use spell-check again."

"So it *was* you."

"And I'll memorize the dictionary, I promise."

"Dictionary, schmictionary."

"The Bible," she corrects herself. "I'll memorize the Bible."

"That's better." He dismisses her and sneaks out for lunch with Jimmy at Casa Bleve, an eatery tucked inside a sixteenth-century palazzo near Largo Argentina. "I took you here on a previous visit, remember?" Herman says. "When you came with Deb."

Jimmy frowns, but can't remember. He says he can't retain anything anymore.

"I'm the same," Herman says. "I used to have perfect recall, but my memory's shot now. I have this new technique: I write everything down. Lists. That's the answer." He's lying. His memory remains impeccable. "Long lists for everything. Consider it. It works. Any idea I have — not that what I do amounts to ideas — but any gripe I have with the paper, I jot down. Thank God

I'm not attempting anything as complex as what you do. I admire that. I could never write a book." He flaps the napkin out on his lap. "Do you mind if I ask about the book? I'm wondering — and I don't want to intrude here — but I'm curious to know if you brought the manuscript. My bigger question, I guess, is when do I get to read it? And you should feel free to work on it out here, if you want. You don't have to feel obliged to meet up with me for lunch. I can leave you in the study, bring you bowls of soup, whatever. I spent years in New York bringing food and drink to writers — I know what I'm doing in this field! Seriously, though, I'd be delighted if you made some progress while you're here. And if I could be of use in looking over the thing, I'd be honored. Again, not that there's any obligation. Sorry, I'll shut up."

When Herman was offered a position at the paper in the 1970s, he hesitated: going off to Europe before Jimmy had established himself was all wrong. Then again, Jimmy wasn't even in New York anymore. His affair in Mexico had ended badly and, rather than returning to Manhattan, he had accepted a job taking publicity photographs for the equestrian circuit, traveling the United States in trucks with event technicians. He wrote infrequent memos to Herman about his wanderings. The letters were captivating, the events bizarre. Herman kept the correspondence in a cherrywood box — they'd be useful one day in the biography. He imagined Jimmy's existence: moving on a whim, walking out when jobs annoyed him, staying up all night and waking with unknown women. Herman resented it slightly, as if he were somehow footing the bill for Jimmy's freedom. Miriam encouraged Herman to take the job in Italy, especially while their daughter was young enough to make the transition. It was tempting: the paper held a cosmopolitan allure for Herman. To his mind, it was the publication that a weathered novelist or a spy might fold under his arm. And the 1970s were thrilling times at the paper, with an inventive new editor, Milton Berber, a vibrant young staff, and buoyant spirits all around. So he took the position and urged Jimmy to take advantage of the free lodgings in Rome — he could come and write his book there, full-time and for as long as he liked. (Within limits set by Miriam, naturally.)

Instead, Jimmy settled in Arizona with Deb, who weaved artisanal rugs and had an infant daughter. He married Deb, adopted the girl, and, to bring in money, qualified as a paralegal. Herman was disappointed when he finally met Deb — he'd expected a marvel, and she wasn't that. It rankled that Jimmy should be detained by mediocrity in Arizona when he could have been sparkling in Rome. Herman could easily have got Jimmy hired at the paper, and he'd repeatedly offered to do so.

When the bill comes for their lunch at Casa Bleve, Jimmy pulls out his credit card.

"No, no," Herman says. "This is mine. I'm the one with the job."

But Jimmy insists.

"Okay, how about this then," Herman says. "I'll let you pay on one condition: that you write something for me — an article, any kind you like — and I get to print it in the paper. What do you say? Obviously, we'll pay you, though I'm afraid we have a lousy freelance rate these days after all the budget cuts. But you can write about anything. An opinion piece, something funny — anything. It'd be a real feather in my cap to publish you. How's that sound?"

That night, Jimmy sits before the computer, leaning his gaunt face into the screen, slender fingers hovering above the keyboard. Herman leaves him there, closes the door, and shakes his fist triumphantly. As the hours pass, Herman paces back and forth in the kitchen, nervously eating slices of homemade lemon-pistachio polenta and browsing cookbooks. He approaches the computer room, places his ear to the door, hears the slow tapping of fingers on the keyboard. It is almost 2 A.M. when Jimmy emerges. The article is there on the screen, but he can't figure out how to work the printer. He's tired, says good night, goes to bed.

By the end of the 1980s, Deb had divorced Jimmy. A few years later, they remarried. But soon she left him a second painful time, and he moved to Los Angeles to get away from the situation. He freelanced as a paralegal, which kept him afloat. But he had no health coverage, so when a molar went rotten he yanked it himself with needle-nose pliers. He was drunk at the time and bungled it, splintering the tooth and leaving chunks in the bloody gum. Herman happened to call a few days later and heard about the tooth and the fever that had followed. He demanded that Jimmy go to the hospital. At the emergency room, they told him the wound had gone septic. While waiting for the on-call dentist, he suffered a heart attack. Jimmy was fifty-six, but by the time he was discharged he had become an

157

old man. In the following months, he aged further, grew forgetful and anxious, suspected that people were walking up behind him. He checked endlessly that his doors and windows were locked, that the gas was off. He often called in sick at the law firm where he freelanced, then eventually retired — it was foisted on him, really. At the time, Herman welcomed the news: finally, Jimmy could focus on his writing. He'd always said he'd finish his book once he retired.

And now he's here, in the spare room, asleep. Still no sign of the full manuscript, but at least here is a taste of Jimmy's writing. Herman prints a copy of the article and two pages emerge. He snatches them from the printer tray, rushes to the sofa, plops down to read.

It takes a moment before he can focus on the text, so excited is he. How many years has he waited for this! Sure, it's just a few hundred words, but it's a start. Might Jimmy have a full manuscript in that bag over there in the corner? Herman would never snoop, but how he longs to.

He focuses on the pages before him.

He reads through them.

Herman has worked as an editor for forty years. It doesn't take him long to realize. This article is no good.

It's a sort of editorial, but without any clear argument, touching on life in L.A., on the proliferation of guns in America, on declining civility. The article is full of grammar mistakes and platitudes. It's amateurish. Is this the right document? Maybe this is a rough draft? He goes to check the computer. By the mouse pad, he finds a scrap of scrunched paper and pulls it apart. It bears Jimmy's handwriting and contains a long list of notes, written, rewritten, crossed out, full of scribbles and question marks and lines and dashes and variations. Hours of effort have gone into this, a worthless piece of writing.

Herman can't sleep that night. He keeps sitting up in bed, turning on the lamp, stuffing himself with hard candies, then brushing his teeth all over again. At 6 A.M., he rises for good — he intends to escape the apartment before Jimmy wakes up. That way, Herman can study the article at the office and work out what to do.

But Jimmy appears from the spare room, saying he wanted to catch Herman before he left: there's a spelling mistake in the article.

"Don't worry. I'll fix it," Herman says.

Jimmy insists on doing it himself. He disappears into the computer room, makes his correction, and hands Herman a memory stick containing the article.

At the office, Herman shoots off an email to Kathleen, saying he may have a late addition to the editorial page. He isn't bound by this, but it leaves him the option. Does he have to run the piece? He could tell Jimmy it was good but that it needed more focus. Then again, honestly, can anything be salvaged from it? And the paper isn't his to fill as he pleases. It's not disloyal if he spikes the piece, is it? What about credibility? "Credibility," he mutters, and it is a sodden, fraudulent word on this day.

He resolves to publish the article. He has the power to. And he will. It'll appear in a single edition, down two half-columns, with a bloated headline and a pull quote to fill out the space, deep in the inside pages. He'll show the clipping to Jimmy tomorrow morning, he'll thank him, he'll throw a thick arm around his narrow friend and say, "After all these years, we got to work together."

He plugs the memory stick into his computer and opens Jimmy's document. But the text of the night before is gone. All that appears is a note: "Don't worry, kid. I deleted the thing. Did you know tonight is my last night in town? I'm taking you for dinner, and I pay. No arguments. Jimmy."

Kathleen asks about the editorial, and Herman tells her it was a false alarm. She points out a headline on page seven — "Global Warming Good for Ice Creams" — and proposes it for his next edition of *Why?* She adds, "I find it idiotic on so many levels."

"No, yes, you're right," he says, though he's not listening.

Jimmy chooses a touristy restaurant near the Vatican for their last dinner. Herman wishes he himself had picked — he can see from the curled menu outside that this place isn't serious. Food is not the point, of course, but he's on edge: his friend leaves tomorrow and nothing has been achieved. During dinner, Jimmy drinks three glasses of wine, which is the most he's had since the heart attack. As alcohol seeps into him, he rambles charmingly, like in the old days, when he was legendary for tipsy philosophizing, reciting Yeats or Yevtushenko from memory, blathering on about Joyce, and proclaiming the funniest word in the English language to be "rump." Herman associates Jimmy's drunken chatter with their happiest times.

They don't mention his article at first. But the evening is going so well that Herman says, "This whole thing could be an impetus, don't you think? A little reminder, you know. To really write something now."

Jimmy sits up straighter, clears his throat. "Herman," he says calmly, "I'm not writing anything. I haven't yet, and I'm not going to now. I never was going to. I knew that from, maybe, age twenty. You're the one who kept going on about it."

"I didn't go on about it," Herman says, taken aback. "It's just that I thought — I think — that you are capable of something great. Something outstanding. You always had such talent."

Jimmy taps his friend's earlobe affectionately. "There's no such thing as talent, kid."

Herman pulls away. "I'm serious."

"So am I. I should have made it clear forty years ago that you had the wrong idea about me. But I'm vain. I guess I was trying to make a good impression. Only I'm too old to keep trying. So please stop talking about what I'll do. It only emphasizes what I didn't. I've had a good enough life, an average life. And that's fine."

"It's hardly been average."

"No? If not, then what proof is there to the contrary? I have the proof of sixty-five years."

Herman begins to dispute this, but Jimmy

162

talks over him.

"You know what I liked about that article you had me do?" he says. "I liked working with you, Herman — that I enjoyed. Hearing how you'd get it into print. You really know the world of journalism, boy. See — *you* do useful work. Hard work. Not the hooey I've done. Standards. That's what you have. And I liked getting a sense of how you do it. That's a real pleasure for me. To see how far you've come."

"Don't be crazy. You're the one who wrote that article. Think how quickly you rolled it out. Professional writers sometimes take *days* over a piece, weeks even, months. Imagine if you really put some time into it? Doesn't that inspire you? To go back and work on something a bit more permanent?"

"I haven't got it in me," Jimmy says. "And I don't like leaning on you anymore. I take advantage of you too much. Always have. Your generosity. Me sleeping on the floor at Riverside Drive? I never paid a dime of rent in how many years?"

"You weren't my tenant. You were my friend. You didn't owe me anything."

Jimmy smiles. "You got a nutso perspective on certain things, Mr. Herman Cohen."

When they leave, Herman takes a handful of business cards from the restaurant and rests his hand on Jimmy's shoulder. As they emerge onto the street, Herman makes a show of looking around for a taxi to hide the fact that he's choked up.

At Fiumicino Airport the next day, Jimmy mentions that he may move back to Arizona. His adopted daughter, now in her thirties, has a place in Tempe. She works in real estate and lives alone. She'd enjoy the company.

As Herman listens, he envisions this life for his fading friend. He and Jimmy are not, as Herman has always believed, gradations of the same man — he the middling version and Jimmy the superlative one. They are utterly different: Herman would never move in with his daughter, would never let himself fall insolvent at age sixty-five, and never need a place to stay. Even now, the notion of retirement is preposterous to him — his fingers still jab far too well, poking that paper to credibility.

They part at airport security and Herman walks toward the exit, but he pauses at the sliding doors. Perhaps Jimmy still needs him for something. What if there's a problem?

He turns back and spots his old friend in the security line. Jimmy hauls his carry-on luggage, jacket slung over his forearm. He yawns — he never did get over the jet lag.

He is jostled from behind and scratches his forehead testily, muttering. He has little hair left, a dusting of snow above each ear. His eyelids hang heavy, his ears are long. How Herman has adored provoking laughter from that face over the years! And how thin it has become. A spindly neck knocking around inside a collar, an abdomen retreating into a spine. The security line inches forward until it is Jimmy's turn. With difficulty, he heaves his bag onto the conveyor belt and Herman's shoulders strain involuntarily as if to help the bag up there. Jimmy raises his arms to be scanned, collects his bag, walks out of sight.

Herman drives the blue Mazda slowly home to Monteverde. He finds himself considering it all: Miriam (he smiles), their daughter (what a fine young woman), their grandchildren (each has such a different personality), these extraordinary years in Rome (Miriam was right about us moving here), his satisfaction at the paper (I've been useful). All this has been the most extraordinary surprise; he had expected an unhappy life, yet ended up with the opposite. It's barely credible.

When Miriam arrives home, she raves about the trip to Philadelphia and shows off all the photos on her digital camera. They are so wrapped up in talking about the grandkids that they hardly discuss Jimmy's stay. She turns to Herman on the sofa — they are sitting side by side.

"What?" he asks suspiciously. "What is it?"

"I was just thinking how handsome you are."

"How fat, you mean."

"No," she says. "Handsome." She kisses his cheek, then his lips. "You are. And I'm not the only one who thinks so, either."

"So I've got admirers now?"

"I'm not about to tell you, am I. You might run off."

"I made soup, by the way."

"Yes," she says, amused. "I know."

A couple of months later, Herman receives an email from Jimmy. It is long and rambling, full of philosophizing and poetic citations. Which is another way of saying he's in splendid spirits with his daughter in Tempe, Arizona.

The email, for no reason Herman can articulate, upsets him. He sees no reason to write back, and perhaps that is why.

1960. Aventine Hill, Rome

Ott opened his copy of the paper across the dining-room table and touched a finger to his tongue, which was dry from all the medication the doctors had him on. He flipped the pages: Eichmann caught in Argentina, African colonies declaring independence, Kennedy running for president.

He was proud of what the paper had become but sorry to read it here in his mansion and not in the office, among his staff. He had not visited Corso Vittorio in weeks. He'd told Betty and Leo that he was traveling in the United States; he'd told his family in Atlanta that he was on the road in Italy. The only travel he did, however, was to clinics in London and Geneva.

His symptoms had been worsening for months: blood, pain, exhaustion. He came to despise his bathroom in the mansion, all the intimate revulsions awaiting him there. He had the cooks prepare steak, eggs, liver pâté, but still he grew thinner.

A surgeon in London cut out half of Ott's cancerous insides, but the procedure did no good. On his return to the mansion, he ordered the servants away. A delivery boy dropped each day's paper outside the gate; a maid left him food. Otherwise, he was on his own.

He washed in the bathtub, soap bar bruising his skin, bumping bones beneath. He climbed out, arms straining on the rim of the tub. In the fogged mirror, he caught sight of himself, thick white towel around jagged hips. He was dying.

He walked across the mansion, bathwater dripping off him, over the floorboards, up the stairs to the second floor. Cautiously, he lowered himself into the chair at his desk — no buttock flesh to cushion him anymore — and opened his letter pad.

The first note he addressed to his wife and son, whom he had left in Atlanta years earlier. "Dear Jeanne and Boyd," he wrote. "The important thing to realize, and I need to make this clear."

His pen hung above the line.

He glanced at the wall, at one of the paintings Betty had chosen, the Turner. He approached it and reached behind himself, as if to take her wrist, to lead her closer. "Tell me about this one. I don't understand it. Explain it to me."

He returned to his desk and started a new letter. It was time, he decided, to explain matters.

As days passed, copies of the paper piled up outside the mansion. The maid who left Ott's meals noticed that they were not being consumed. She unlocked the mansion. "Mister Ott?" she called out. "Mister Ott?"

His family in Atlanta, against all evidence, had always expected him to return. Now they could not even retrieve his body. Legally, there was no way: his will specified burial in the Protestant Cemetery in Rome. They refused to believe this had been his wish and boycotted the funeral in Italy, holding an alternative service in Atlanta.

The paper came out with a black border around page one, accompanied by a front-page editor's note in tribute to the founding publisher. Leo sent Ott's brother, Charles, a letter of condolence (he did not respond), then followed up with a polite entreaty that the paper be allowed to survive. Again, Charles — now chairman of the Ott board — did not respond. Nor did he halt funding.

Six anxious months passed before Charles announced that he was coming for a visit. On arrival, he shook hands coldly with Leo and ignored Betty altogether. He made one demand — that at the top of the masthead, in bold print and in perpetuity, it state: "Founded by Cyrus Ott (1899–1960)." Betty and Leo heartily endorsed the idea.

"This is an enterprise that mattered a great deal to my younger brother," Charles said. "Letting it end now would be, I believe, a smear on his memory."

"I thoroughly agree," Leo said.

"How many copies do you people sell?"

"Around fifteen thousand on a good day."

"Well, I want more. I want my brother's name in front of as many eyes as possible. It may not mean much in the grand scheme, but it does mean something to me and to my family."

"We were extremely fond of him," Betty said.

This irked Charles for some reason. He concluded the conversation and went into the newsroom to address the staff.

"Putting out the paper each day is your business," he told them. "But that the paper gets put out — this is my business. I consider the enterprise to be a standing memorial to my brother, and it'll keep standing as far as I'm concerned."

The staff, seeing that he had finished, broke into applause.

■ ■ ■ ■

"U.S. General Optimistic on War"

. . .

EDITOR-IN-CHIEF — KATHLEEN SOLSON

■ ■ ■ ■

When she realizes that Nigel is having an affair, her first sentiment is satisfaction that she figured it out. Her second is that, despite all the palaver about betrayal, it doesn't feel so terrible. This is pleasing — it demonstrates a certain sophistication. She wonders if his fling might even serve her. In principle, she could leave him without compunction now, though she doesn't wish to. It also frees her from guilt about any infidelities she might wish to engage in. All in all, his affair might prove useful.

She toys with this while onstage during a media conference at the Cavalieri Hilton in Rome. The subject of the panel discussion is "How the International Press Views Italy," an enduring preoccupation in the country. She resents having to attend — it's clearly a task for their young publisher, Oliver Ott. But he has gone missing again and ignores her phone calls. So the conference is left to

173

Kathleen and the paper must manage in her absence. It is not managing well, if the constant stream of text messages on her BlackBerry is any indication.

"Will the newspaper industry survive?" the mediator asks her.

"Absolutely," she tells the audience. "We'll keep going, I assure you of that. Obviously, we're living in an era when technology is moving at an unheralded pace. I can't tell you if in fifty years we'll be publishing in the same format. Actually, I can probably tell you we *won't* be publishing in the same way, that we'll be innovating then, just as we are now. But I assure you of this: news will survive, and quality coverage will always earn a premium. Whatever you want to call it — news, text, content — someone has to report it, someone has to write it, someone has to edit it. And I intend for us to do it better, no matter the medium. We are *the* quality source among international newspapers, and I encourage anyone who doubts this bold claim to buy the paper for a month. Better yet" — lilt in voice; complicit smile to audience; pause — "better yet, buy a two-year subscription. Then you'll really see why our circulation is rising." The audience laughs politely. "My work is putting together *the* outstanding publication in its class. If we can do that, readers will turn up. Those of you who have followed the paper's progress since I became editor in 2004 will know the radical changes under way. There are more to come. It's thrilling to be a part of, to tell the truth."

What truth? The paper is hardly at the cutting edge of technology — it doesn't even have a website. And circulation isn't increasing. The balance sheet is a catastrophe, losses mount annually, the readership is aging and dying off. But she has acquitted herself well onstage. The audience applauds and hurries out for the free lunch, while she excuses herself to the organizers. "I wish I could stay," she tells them, "but that's life at a daily newspaper."

On her way to the cloakroom, she is approached by a Chinese American student from the audience. He introduces himself as Winston Cheung, dabs sweat from his face, wipes his glasses, and proceeds to rattle off his academic credentials. Since he won't get to the point, she gets there for him. "Okay," she interrupts. "And the punch line is, Do I have a job for you? You said you're studying primatology, right, so I'm guessing you'd be interested in a science section, which we don't have. If you wanted to report general news, lots of publications are hunting for people with language skills. Do you speak any Asian languages?"

"My parents only spoke to me in English."

"Pity. Languages are key. You don't, by any lucky chance, speak flawless Arabic?"

"Not flawless Arabic, no."

"Meaning you speak *flawed* Arabic?" she says. But this guy is a nonstarter — no experience, no languages, and look how jittery he is. She needs to get rid of Winston Cheung. "Look, if you want to send us something — purely on spec — we'd look at it." She rattles off Menzies' email address and ducks into the cloakroom.

As she heads for the exit, someone touches her shoulder. She turns irritably, expecting Winston Cheung again. But it's not him.

She steps back with surprise. "My God," she says. "Dario."

Dario de Monterecchi is the Italian man she lived with in Rome during her twenties. When she left the city in 1994 to take a reporting job in Washington, she left him, too. Now here he is, temples graying, eyes bagged, slightly handsome but slightly jowly, wearing the sleepy surrender of the family man. "Sorry to sneak up like that," he says. "Did I scare you?"

"You have to try harder than that. I am

176

somewhat caught off guard, though. My God, it's so strange seeing you. How are you?"

"I'm well," he says. "And you were excellent today. I'm most impressed. But are you leaving?"

"Sadly, yes. I have to. They need me at the office," she answers. "I'm sorry, by the way, that I haven't been in touch since I got back to Rome. It's been crazy. You knew I was back, right?"

"Of course."

"Who from?"

"Just heard — you know how small Rome is."

"Weird having my private life pop up when I'm in professional mode. Puts me off balance," she says. "You might not believe this, but I really wish I didn't have to go."

"Not even time for lunch?"

"I don't get lunch, alas. We close the first edition in a couple of hours. If I'm not there, the world ends. What are you doing at this event anyway?"

He hands her his business card.

"Oh, no," she exclaims, reading the card. "I'd heard a rumor about this. But Berlusconi? Ouch."

"I do press for his party, not for him personally."

She raises her eyebrows skeptically.

Dario says, "I *was* always on the right, remember."

"Yes, yes, I know. I remember you."

"Well, anyway," he says, "I should let you go." He kisses her cheek. She rubs his back. "You don't need to keep comforting me," he says, smiling. "I'm not still upset."

She grabs a taxi outside. As the cab speeds toward the city center, she consults her BlackBerry, which is pulsating with messages from Menzies: "General Abizaid testifying to Senate about Iraq. How should we cover?? Call please!" Meanwhile, Dario — who slept beside her and woke beside her for six years of her life — has vanished from mind. She can't help it: she's of the newspapering temperament, and he's no longer front page. When, she wonders, do people have time to contemplate anything? But she has no time to answer that.

She passes through the paper's various departments to consult on tomorrow's edition. Her arrival halts conversations, prompts sheepish expressions and flurries of phone calls that should have been made earlier. The afternoon meeting is a farce. The usual suspects trickle in and settle around the oval table. Kathleen listens. Then she speaks. She isn't shrill — she never is. She is deliberate and pulverizing. She commands actions, concludes with "All right?" and walks out of the room.

Her chief ally — the only person she holds to be her intellectual equal at the office — is Herman Cohen. He is waiting in her office when she returns. At the door, she covers her face playfully to block him from view, then enters, crossing her index fingers as if before a vampire. "Please don't."

"You know you want it," he says, handing her the latest copy of his in-house newsletter, *Why?*, with which he chronicles mistakes in the paper. "Everything well, my dear?" he asks.

"I go out for one morning and this office turns into the monkey enclosure."

"You're starting to sound like me."

"And I'm getting bombarded with emails from Accounts Payable," she says, meaning the chief financial officer, Abbey Pinnola. "Supposedly I have to offer human sacrifices."

"She wants layoffs now?"

"So it seems. Not clear how many."

"Technical staff or editorial?"

"We'll see. Who would you pick from editorial?"

At the top of his list is Ruby Zaga, a copy editor who's notorious for inserting errors into stories.

"Is she really the worst?" Kathleen asks.

"I forgot, Ruby's a friend of yours."

"Hardly a friend. But can't we fire Clint Oakley?"

"Someone has to put together Puzzle-Wuzzle, my dear."

"I'm telling Accounts Payable that I'll *consider* layoffs if I get money for a stringer in Cairo, plus someone to replace Lloyd in Paris."

"Good for you. Stick to your guns."

"It's beyond me," she says, "how Abbey can say that covering Cairo and Paris is a luxury. How is that a luxury? It's a necessity. Luxury these days is actually having a conversation about what goes in this paper. All I do is cover over cracks. It's depressing."

"Learn to delegate."

"Who to?"

"I beg your pardon?"

"To *whom*," she corrects herself. "I thought I'd delegated to you. Aren't you supposed to be helping me?" She means this but must convey it as jest — he is an institution here, and she can't risk alienating him.

"I was delegated to be in charge of these." He shakes a packet of hard candies at her.

As she closes her glass office door after

him, a few staffers in the newsroom glance over, then look away. It's strange to be the boss, knowing they discuss you, doubt you, resent you, and — since they are journalists — complain, bitch, and moan about you.

Her BlackBerry rings. "Menzies," she answers with a sigh, "why are you phoning me? I'm right here across the room." She raises her hand.

"Sorry, sorry — didn't see you. Can you come over? We need you."

She obliges.

That night for dinner, Nigel makes osso buco.

"Smells wonderful," she says, arriving home later than promised, as always.

Their apartment off Via Nazionale is spacious enough for an extended family but houses only the two of them. It is thinly furnished, as was her intent, with chrome chairs in the living room, granite in the bathroom, a gas range and matching overhead fan in the kitchen. In each room, the only decoration is a giant black-and-white photograph framed in the center of the wall. Each is obliquely themed to its room, so the kitchen contains a huge photo of cooks stuffing dumplings at the Luk Yu Tea House in Hong Kong; the dining room has a gargantuan picture of empty tables at El

Bulli on the Costa Brava; the salon shows the interior of Skogaholm Manor in Stockholm; and in the bathroom is a vast photograph of the crashing sea off Antarctica.

"Glass?" He pours her one.

"What is it tonight?"

He displays the bottle, then reads the label: "Montefalco. Caprai. 2001." He thrusts his nose into the wineglass.

She takes an unceremonious gulp. "Not bad, not great," she says. "You must be starved. Sorry I kept you. Can I get us some water?"

"Allow me, pasha."

Nigel, an attorney-at-rest since they left D.C. more than two years earlier, thrives on this life: reading nonsense on the Internet, buying high-end groceries, decrying the Bush administration at dinner, wearing his role of househusband as a badge of progressive politics. By this hour, he's normally fulminating: that the CIA invented crack cocaine; that Cheney is a war criminal; that the September 11 attacks were conceived by agents of Big Oil. (He talks a lot of shit about politics. She has to smack him down intellectually once a week or he becomes unbearable.) This evening, however, Nigel is restrained. "Good day?" he asks.

"Mmm, yeah, not bad." She's amused —

he's so transparent. He has clearly done something and is writing about it. That English girl — Nigel and she had been meeting weekly to discuss the failure of the left. Then, abruptly, he stopped mentioning her. To Kathleen's knowledge, the left hasn't stopped failing. Presumably, an act occurred.

And yet, savoring her osso buco, tickled by his mendacious face hiding in a fishbowl wineglass, she cannot bring herself to care terribly. If it *is* a full-blown affair, she will be angry — such a development would jeopardize their situation. But this doesn't have that feel. He is more a skulking fornicator, not a marriage-busting cheater. If Kathleen ignores the matter, what happens? It will seep away.

At work the next day, her desk phone rings.

"Hi there — it's me again."

"Sorry, who is this?"

"Kath, it's me."

"God — Dario, I didn't recognize you."

"I wanted to invite you to lunch. Forza Italia will foot the bill."

"In that case, definitely not," she says. "No, I'm kidding — I'd love to. But I'm insanely busy. I told you, I don't get lunches, tragically." Then again, she thinks, a contact with Berlusconi's people could be useful. The Prodi government is bound to fall, meaning early elections, at which point having ties to Dario could prove handy. "But it would be nice to meet up. What about an early *aperitivo?*"

They meet at the Hotel de Russie garden bar, a courtyard of shaded café tables upon *sampietrini* cobblestones, as if this were a private Roman piazza for the use of paying guests only.

"If you misbehave," Kathleen says, studying the drinks menu, "I'll order you the Punjab health cocktail: yogurt, ice, pink Himalayan salt, cinnamon, and soda water."

"Or how about the Cohibatini?" he responds. "Vodka, Virginia tobacco leaves, eight-year-old Bacardi rum, lime juice, and corbezzolo honey."

"Tobacco leaves? In a drink? And what is corbezzolo honey?"

"Boringly," he says, "I'm taking the Sauvignon."

"Boringly, me too."

They close their menus and order.

"Odd weather," he remarks. "Almost tropical."

"Sitting out in November — not bad. I think I'm in favor of global warming." She resolves to stop making this fatuous remark, which parachutes off her tongue anytime someone mentions the climate. "Anyway, nothing more boring than talking about the weather. Tell me, how are you?"

Thin — that's how he is on second sight. He wears a mauve tie and a spread-collared shirt that hangs on his shoulders as if upon a hanger. His countenance — naïve and affectionate — is the same, and this makes him younger somehow.

"You're not the same," she says.

"No? Well, that's good. Imagine if I was unchanged after all these years."

Unchanged: this is how she thinks of herself. Fresh as ever at forty-three, legs long and strong under the business slacks, tight midriff under tight waistcoat, lustrous chestnut hair with only a couple of strands of gray. She takes unearned pride in her looks. "So funny to see you again," she says. "Kind of like meeting up with an old version of myself." She asks about their old friends and his family. His mother, Ornella, sounds as cold as ever. "Is she still reading the paper?"

"Hasn't missed a copy in years."

"That's what I like to hear. And Filippo?" she asks, referring to Dario's younger brother.

"He has three kids now."

"Three? How un-Italian," she says. "And you?"

"Only one."

"That's more like it."

"A boy, Massimiliano. Just turned six."

"So, married, obviously."

"Massi? We're waiting till he turns seven." She smiles. "I mean *you* must be married."

"Yes, of course. And you?"

She caricatures her domestic situation, rendering Nigel as a comic subaltern, as is her habit. "He feeds me grapes most evenings," she says. "It's part of his duties."

"That must suit you."

"Depends on the quality of the grapes. But hang on," she says. "I still don't have a sense of what's going on with you."

"I'm well, very well at the moment. I did have a rough patch last year. But that's over. The family weakness." By this, he means depression, which afflicted his father, ultimately ending the man's career in diplomacy. The ambassador's breakdown in 1994 came the week that Kathleen left Dario. "They were good about it at work," he goes on. "Say what you will about Mr. Berlusconi."

"And how is your father, incidentally?"

"Well, sadly, he died about a year ago now. On November 17, 2005."

"I'm so sorry to hear that," she says. "I really liked Cosimo."

"I know. We all did."

"But your problem wasn't as serious as his used to be, right?"

"No, no. Not nearly. And they have much better medicine these days."

They taste their wine and glance around the garden bar — its potted lemon trees, a discreetly burbling fountain, the leafy escarpment climbing to Villa Borghese Park.

"I asked to meet up for a particular reason," he says.

"Ah, the ulterior motive — are you going to fob off some Berlusconi puffery on me now?"

"No, no, nothing to do with work."

"But I *do* want to hear about *Il Cavaliere*," she says. "I'm dying to hear what it's like working for such a fine man."

"He is a good man. You shouldn't write him off."

"And this is your pure, unadulterated opinion? You do what again? Public relations, is it?"

"Can't blame me for trying, Kath. But no, I wanted to ask you something else — I need your advice."

"Shoot."

"Are you still close with Ruby Zaga?"

187

It had slipped Kathleen's mind that Dario and Ruby knew each other, but all three were briefly interns at the paper in 1987. Indeed, Ruby introduced Dario and Kathleen. "Copydesk Ruby?" Kathleen says. "I was never close with her. Why do you ask?"

"Just that I've been having a bit of a problem with her," he says. "I hadn't seen her for ages, then a few months back, not long after my father died, I ran into her on the street. We agreed to meet up for a drink, I gave her my number, and forgot about it. She did phone, though, and we went out. It was a normal night. Nothing special. But since then she keeps calling my cell and hanging up."

"That's weird."

"It's been going on for weeks. She must have called fifty times. My wife thinks I'm having an affair."

"And you're not."

He dips into the bowl of olives. "No."

"Hmm," she says. "Suspicious."

He looks up, smiling. "I'm not. Honestly. Anyway, maybe let's shift topics. Berlusconi — you wanted to talk about Berlusconi, right?"

"Well, you're off the hook for now."

"What do you want to know about him?"

"First off, how can you work for that guy?

188

The face-lifts, the hair transplants — he's such a buffoon."

"Not to my mind."

"Oh, come on."

"Don't forget, Kath, I'm on the right."

"So you keep telling me. How did I ever bear you?"

"Were you on the left?"

"Of course," she says. "But couldn't you have done better than Berlusconi?"

"Couldn't you have done better than the paper?"

"What does that mean?"

"Nothing. But please, if you don't mind, try not to belittle me. You're too good at it."

"I don't belittle you." She pauses. "What do you mean I'm good at it? Is that how you remember me?"

"Not for the most part."

"Well, if I used to I'm sorry."

"We do get great gift baskets at Christmas," he says, changing topics. "Berlusconi is unmatched in that area: *torrone*, champagne, foie gras."

Yes, this is what she's here for: the inside line on life under Berlusconi, Europe's court jester. At the least, Dario can give her an amusing tale to recount at parties. He might even feed her a story. No one can resist a Berlusconi-is-ludicrous piece. But

189

hang on, hang on — she isn't quite finished talking. "I hope I wasn't awful to you."

"Don't be crazy."

"I feel as if maybe I was."

"You know how deeply I loved you."

She takes an olive, just holds it. "That's fairly blunt."

He says, "You were goodness." It sounds like a language mistake, but his English is usually flawless.

"Now I really feel like a shit." She eats the olive.

"I didn't say you *weren't* a shit."

She laughs. "Beware — I'm probably more of one now than I used to be."

"I imagine you are. But that's normal, isn't it? One becomes more of a shit as one gets older. I, for example — and you'll find this shocking — had a minor indiscretion involving another woman."

"Oh, really?"

"And I always hated infidelity."

"I know. I remember."

"But I never felt guilty about it. Never told my wife. Just felt irritated — irritated with Ruby. She was the person, the woman."

"You had an affair with Ruby Zaga?" Kathleen says, grimacing. "Our copydesk nun?"

"I never slept with her. I kissed her."

"Does that count as an affair?"

"I don't know. Anyway, it was ridiculous. It was that time we went for a drink. A boring night, in all honesty. We disagreed about something minor — can't remember what. She got all touchy. I paid, went outside, waited for her. She came out, crying. I tried to calm her down and — I don't know why — I found myself kissing her. We did that for a while in this alley in Trastevere, near her place. I remember it stank of garbage." He shifts with embarrassment. "Anyway, nothing happened after that. We had no further contact. Until a few weeks later, when she started calling me. As I told you, she never talks, never says anything. But it's starting to cause problems. She doesn't get the hint."

"Well, well, well," Kathleen says.

"Mm," he says.

"I wouldn't have guessed that one." She utters a dry laugh. "Ruby Zaga!"

"I'm mortified to confess this. But you're the only person I know who knows her."

"What can I suggest? Just change your cellphone number."

"I can't. I gave her my work cell, which is what every journalist has. If I change that, I'm suddenly out of contact. My whole job is being in contact."

"I've barely spoken ten words to Ruby since I moved back to Rome. I could try to broach it with her, but it'd be deeply weird," she says. "I'm asking myself now whether you did this sort of thing when we were together."

"Of course not. We didn't lie to each other back then."

"I lied to you — I never told you I'd applied for the job in Washington. You didn't know I was going to leave."

"True, true."

"Sorry," she says.

"Forget it. Far too much time gone by."

They sit eating olives.

She gets a funny look. "Listen," she says, "would you be willing to do something unusual?"

"I don't know. What?"

"Well," she says, "would you be willing to tell the *entire* truth about me, about what you thought of me? From the old days — what you thought of me then. I'll do the same for you."

"What for?"

"To hear all the bits that you can't say to a person when you're still with them. Aren't you curious?"

"I'd be afraid to hear."

"I'd like to. I'm curious," she says. "I'd

like to understand myself better. Even improve myself, heaven forbid. And I trust you. Your opinion. You're smart."

"You and intelligence!"

"What about me and intelligence?"

"You're very preoccupied with it, with ranking brains. Yours, in terms of everyone else's."

"That's not true."

"We can't do an honesty exchange if you get defensive."

"If I promise not to, will you?"

"It's silly, don't you think? Dissecting ourselves like that? Are we good in bed, are we bad — that sort of underbelly stuff. Sleazy, no?"

"This is why you got out of journalism while I never did: I can't tell the difference between interesting and sleazy. Oh, come on! It'll be fun. Be heartless. Say anything."

He shifts in his seat, then nods. "All right. If you want."

She smacks her thighs with delight. "I've always wanted an opportunity like this. Let me get another drink as I steel myself for your ruthless critique." As she awaits a second glass of Sauvignon, she telephones Menzies to say that she'll be out of contact for fifteen minutes. She switches off her BlackBerry.

"A quarter of an hour?" Dario says. "That's all the time we need to rip each other apart?"

"This isn't ripping apart. Just honest commentary. That's what I want. And be heartless: I have a hideous ass or I'm a bad lay or whatever. Really."

"You want something sexual, then?"

"Why, *is* there something sexual?"

"Not necessarily."

"There is."

"Let me think of something." He pauses. "It's not a big deal, really. Just I guess you were kind of aggressive."

"How? Sexually?"

"Yes. I was slightly intimidated by you."

"For six years you were intimidated by me?"

"Pathetic, I know. It's hard to explain. It was sort of like, sort of like being screwed rather than doing the —"

"Rather than doing the screwing," she says uncomfortably. "Go on."

"Although, at the same time, you never seemed to have much of a sex drive. Making love with you felt like something else. Like, I don't know, an act of a different sort."

"It didn't seem to revolt you so much back then."

"See, you're getting defensive."

"I'm not."

"Do we continue this, Kath? It's turning kind of unpleasant."

"No, no. I'm interested."

"I'm just someone who —"

"Who wanted a more submissive woman."

"Maybe less aggressive. Is that bad?"

"You should have gone for Ruby from the start."

"I know you're kidding, but that's probably what attracted me to her."

"You're attracted to women who sob when you buy them a drink?"

He doesn't respond.

She says, "Sorry. It's funny, though — you hated that I made you submissive. And I hated that you were so passive, that I was always the one initiating it. You know? But God, you make it sound like I was forcing myself on you, slobbering all over."

"There was a *little* slobbering," he jokes.

She laughs.

"There," she says, exhaling. "That wasn't so hard. Any other thoughts about me?"

"Not really," he says, hesitating. "Well, one tiny thing — not sexual. Just that I always thought you were kind of an instrumentalist with people. Can I say that in English? I mean, you were always looking to

195

gain something. I remember watching you meet people — I could see the cogs turning in your mind. Doing calculations."

"You make me sound horrendous. I'm the person who you —" She balks at saying loved. "Who you claim to have liked so much."

"I don't mean this as criticism."

"No, no, it sounds like a huge compliment," she says sarcastically. "But is it possible that your view is colored by how I left?"

"I don't care about that now. I'm happy you went. If you'd stayed, I wouldn't have met my wife, I wouldn't have had Massi. I did love you. But the thing about you back then was that you were completely conditional."

"As opposed to what? To stupid? I hope I was conditional. Everything intelligent is conditional."

"That's a strange thought."

"So, to summarize: I'm emasculating, calculating, and unloving. What a nice portrait. If I was any of that stuff, it was inexperience. I was in my twenties. But," she continues, "I have to wonder if you're not being slightly naïve here. I mean, are you saying you want *nothing* from people? You have no motives? Everybody has motives. Name the person, the circumstances,

196

I'll name the motive. Even saints have motives — to feel like saints, probably."

"That's pretty cynical."

"It's realistic."

"Which is what cynics always say. But honestly, Kath, do you calculate everything? Even in your private life?"

"Maybe not. Not like I used to. I was a bit bad that way with you, I admit. But still, the point of any relationship is obtaining something from another person."

"I can't see it that way."

"So why do you kiss someone?" she asks. "To give pleasure or to take it?"

At dinner that evening, Nigel irritates her. The paper, he complains, has already published a look-ahead to the World Economic Forum in Davos, though it's weeks away, while there hasn't been a word on the World Social Forum in Nairobi. The mainstream media care only about rich white guys, he says. She notes that the paper has no reporters in Africa and so couldn't cover the World Social Forum. He opens his mouth to contest the point, then closes it.

"You *are* allowed to disagree," she says.

"I know."

"That's all you're going to say? How about: 'The fact that you don't bother to hire anyone in Africa only proves what I'm

197

saying'? Or, 'A setup story doesn't need to be written with a Kenya dateline'? Both of which would be pretty good arguments. You could even roll out your thing about the paper's European-to-African ratio. What is it? 'One dead white man equals twenty dead Africans'? None of that tonight? Just because you're feeling guilty doesn't mean you have to be a pushover, Nigel."

"Feeling guilty?"

"I'm guessing it's over your girlfriend."

"What are you talking about?"

"The English girl. Right?"

He goes into the bathroom. After a few minutes of silence, the faucet runs. Once it stops, he remains there, in hiding. She takes this as confirmation. When he emerges, a conversation will ensue. He must be sitting on the edge of the bathtub, hunting for a way out of this mess. What will result from the coming confrontation? What if he's seriously entangled with this English girl? Kathleen is annoyed with herself — she's still raw from Dario's critique and has misplayed this exchange.

Nigel emerges and makes coffee. She watches his rigid movements around the kitchen. He acts as if he's not within his own home but trespassing in hers. He's lazy, Kathleen thinks. He dreads employment more than he dreads humiliation. He'll cling to this marriage.

"I know," he says. "I know."

"You know what?"

He won't look at her.

Before marrying, they set a policy on adultery that sought to be as grown-up as they considered themselves to be. Statistically, at least one of them was bound to cheat. So, they decided, when it happens the guilty party is categorically forbidden to let on.

"This is exactly what was *not* supposed to happen," Kathleen says. "I actually feel more hurt by this than I expected. Idiotic."

"It's not. You're not idiotic."

Dario's description of her sexuality crosses her mind. She won't degrade herself by demanding details from Nigel. "I want to ask you details," she says.

"Don't."

"I won't. But I keep wanting to."

"Don't. It's stupid. Of me, I mean. Not you."

"We agreed this wasn't supposed to happen, but never worked out what to do if it did. Unless, of course," she says, "you intend to make this important. Ending-marriage important."

"Don't be insane." He opens and closes

the fridge for no apparent reason. "I don't know. I'm sorry. I'm an asshole. It was such a total nothing. If you'd let me tell you the details, would you feel better? To see how dumb it was?"

"I'd feel worse."

"So what do we do?"

She shrugs.

He tries to lighten the atmosphere. "Now you have a fling and we'll be even."

She isn't amused. "Me, have sex with someone else?"

"I'm kidding."

"Why kid about it? Maybe it's a good idea."

"I didn't mean it."

"Look, I don't want to have an affair. For God's sake. I'm just more hurt than I expected."

"Than you expected? You expected this?"

"I knew this was happening. You're easy to read," she says. "And who knows — maybe I'll take you up on your idea of a free affair, maybe I won't. You can wonder sometimes."

"Are you kidding?"

"No."

"What can I say — if you want to be that way, fine. I can't stop you, but I really regret it."

"*You* regret it?" she says, raising her voice. "*I* fucking regret it. *I* didn't precipitate this. *I* fucking regret it."

In the coming days, she is rude to the interns — always a litmus test of her mood — and seeks confrontations with reporters, then batters them. She phones the publisher, Oliver Ott, and leaves another message on his answering machine, demanding an increase in the budget, implying that her resignation is not unthinkable. She sends an email to the Ott Group board in Atlanta with a similar warning.

The way she left matters with Nigel disgusts her. A free affair — what kind of people are we?

Later that week, she turns up at Dario's office in Berlusconi's party headquarters on Via dell'Umiltà. He meets her downstairs. He is more lordly than he used to be, has more confidence; his colleagues clearly respect him. He ushers her into his crimson-carpeted office, a muted flat-screen TV on the wall playing an all-news network, a Napoleonic cavalry battle frescoed on the ceiling. "Maybe you're right about Berlusconi if he hands out office space like this," she says, leaning out the open shutters over a courtyard four floors below.

"Can I order you a coffee?"

She sits. "Don't have time, I'm afraid."

"This is just a quick hello, then?"

"Just a quickie," she says. "Funny, isn't it — our offices are so close, but we never bumped into each other around here."

"I knew you were back at Corso Vittorio, so I steered clear."

"You shouldn't have."

"I know — it was stupid."

"Anyway." She stands.

"That *was* quick." He rises, rounds the desk.

She touches a hand to his neck. She moves to kiss him.

"That's actually not a good idea." He pats her hand but does not remove it from his neck.

"One kiss? To remind myself what it's like?" She's kidding — she releases him. "Sorry. I couldn't resist you."

"Nice to be irresistible."

"No, then?"

"Not a good idea."

"If we closed the shutters?" She raps suggestively on his leather-topped desk.

He laughs. "You're crazy."

"What time do you finish here?"

"We have a dinner strategy session after work."

"What time does that finish?" She cuts

the distance between them and rests her hands on his shoulders. He places his palms on hers. While they kiss, she looks at him. His eyes are closed. They step apart, their hands sliding down until they find each other's hips.

"That was."

"Strange."

"Very strange."

"You. Again."

"Yes. You, again."

She buttons her coat. "I'll return after the paper closes tonight. A little after ten, say?"

"It'll be in the middle of this dinner thing."

"So come back here for some reason. I'll be downstairs."

She arrives as planned, and he escapes from his dinner. He leads her up to his office.

"I have one demand," she says.

He is uncertain whether to sit behind his desk or remain standing.

"I don't want to be like I was before," she continues. "I sounded awful the way you described me."

"I'm not like I used to be, either," he says, sitting. "Which is maybe why this doesn't make sense."

"We'll just talk, then. But can we at least

talk on the same side of the desk? Or are you afraid you're going to launch yourself at me?" She comes around, leans down, and kisses him. She sits on his lap.

She studies him, his vulnerable face. Look at him: he wants to have sex with her. Reading this, she is suddenly quenched. She flips a forelock from her brow and exhales. "What time is it?" she asks. "I guess I should leave."

She checks her BlackBerry on the way home. She has an email from Accounts Payable saying the Ott board is considering her request for fresh investment. The only condition is that the paper cut labor costs. If a few layoffs win her money for new reporters overseas, it's well worth it.

She tips the cabbie generously and takes the elevator up to her apartment, imagining all that the paper will now be able to afford. A proper correspondent in Paris, finally. A full-time stringer in Cairo — God, that would make such a difference. She walks in with the standard apologies to Nigel, who hands her a glass of Vermentino. She pats him affectionately and sips. "Mmm, delicious. Really nice."

"Nothing that special," he replies modestly, but is clearly buoyed by her approval.

"Hits the spot. Truly does. Good choice. I

felt like something like this. By the way, I have very cool news." Triumphantly, she recounts her victory over the tightfisted Ott board. He grows enthused along with her and, filling each other's wineglasses, they plot what the paper might do with the money.

She allows him to go first. He works himself up, eyes glowing, as if this modest tranche could transform the publication. She indulges him, touched by his excitement. Then he looks up and says, "I don't know, maybe that's dumb." He's a funny man, she thinks — he strikes these bombastic poses, then shrinks when our eyes meet, as if his every intellectual foray were like being caught singing in the shower.

At the office, she leaks news of the possible investment, shrewdly omitting specifics, so that each department becomes charged up and hopeful. Rumors spread about merit raises. She tamps down the most exuberant fantasies but allows a bit of pleasant dreaming to percolate through the newsroom.

She receives an email that afternoon from Dario but doesn't immediately open it. Must she answer right now? Maybe she shouldn't answer at all. How would a dalliance look? Highly unethical. The paper reports regularly on his employer. And Berlusconi is such a joke. If people knew she was mixed up with a Berlusconi flack, it would not look good. It's a double standard, she thinks. Everyone is so censorious when professional women have affairs — they can't pay attention at work, their judgment is affected, they're under the sway of their lovers. Yet when a male editor seduces some P.R. babe, it's he who has the upper hand, he who's taking her for a ride. It's bull. However, she has heard women demolished over less. She'll go back to the States someday, back as something bigger. She needs her reputation intact. This job, whatever its flaws, should upgrade her; she intends to leave here as executive material. Don't risk stains.

Meaning? Well, meaning Dario. A pleasant man, but weak. He had a breakdown, poor guy. Not a total surprise. Perhaps he ended up in P.R. because that's what he is: P.R. material. A sweet person, but not an exceptional one. Maybe he's found his level.

She reads his email. It's merely a remembrance of a trip they took on the Adriatic in 1988, when they rented a yacht that neither could navigate. She smiles at the mention of *ajvar,* the Yugoslav vegetable spread they ate throughout the vacation to economize.

She pinches her hand, disgusted with herself — that assessment of Dario was such a betrayal. She rereads his email and responds: "Hey, shall we get a drink after work?"

They meet at the cocktail bar in 'Gusto. The hostess crams them into a low table by the window. A jazz band is playing at the back, and they must sit close in order to hear each other.

"Have you tried a *caipiroska?*" Dario asks. "They make it with strawberries here. Let me order you one."

"What is it?"

"It's like a caipirinha, only with vodka instead of *cachaça.*"

She laughs. "I have no idea what you're talking about."

"You don't drink cocktails?"

"Pretty much wine for me. I see you've gotten into cocktails since I left."

He winks. "Drowning my sorrows."

"Don't people drown their sorrows in things like scotch? Not strawberry whatever-it's-called."

"*Caipiroska.* I'm ordering you one. Come on."

This isn't innocent, she thinks. This is flirting. She triggered something in him when they were in his office. She visits the toilets and, on her return, finds their drinks on the table: a strawberry *caipiroska* for her and a glass of pinot grigio for him.

"After all that," she exclaims, sitting, "I'm stuck with the girl drink and you got wine! Unfair!" She tastes hers. "Mmm. It's got bits of real strawberries."

"I told you."

She takes another sip. It's one of those fruity mixes in which the liquor goes straight to the knees. "I could drink this all day." She wants to touch him across the table. She won't. It's irresponsible. She has to make clear that this is going nowhere. She needs to put down the strawberry whatever-it's-called and concentrate. "Hey," she says, taking his wrist.

He places her hand in his palm and grips her fingers.

She says, "So nice to be with you again." What is she doing? This is cruel. He's clearly still in love with her.

"It was really difficult after you left Rome," he says.

"I know. I'm so sorry."

"And it's difficult seeing you again."

She considers kissing him.

He places her hand gently on the table. "I have to say something."

"I know, I know." Her mind races for a

way to stop him — he's about to announce himself. She's going to have to jilt him yet again. She must cut him off.

He goes on, "I have to make clear, Kath, before this goes any further, that we can only be friends."

She sits back. She leans forward, then sits back again. "Well." She takes another sip of her cocktail.

"Not drift back into anything like before, I mean. Is that . . . ? What do you think?"

"This thing is cloying, has a cloying taste. It's too sweet." She puts down the straw. "Yes, I completely agree. I was about to say that myself." She looks around the room. The jazz band is too loud. She takes another sip. "Hmm."

"What's the hmming for?"

"No, nothing." She pauses. "How come, though? I mean, I agree — I'm not trying to change your mind. But I'm kind of confused. A few days ago, if I'm not mistaken, you wanted to have sex with me in your office."

"No, I didn't."

She gapes at him. "Did that not happen? Was I hallucinating?"

"Nothing more was going to happen."

"It almost did happen, Dario."

"It didn't. It wouldn't have."

"Oh, come on."

"It wouldn't have happened," he insists. "I'm not attracted to you anymore."

"How do you mean?" It's perfectly clear what he means, but she is prevaricating until she can compose herself.

"I'm not sexually attracted to you anymore," he says. "I don't mean to be harsh."

She flips her hair aside. "Evidently I need to start dyeing out the gray."

"It's not age."

"Yes, right — Ruby's older than me and age never stopped you with her."

"I told you, with you it's like you're the aggressor. And I don't understand you sometimes. Even in my office, you seemed eager but then, when I responded, you just went away."

"You're fixated on how things *used* to be between us. But we agreed that we wouldn't revert to our old habits, no? And I'm not like that anymore, if I ever was."

He drinks the last of his wine; her cocktail is gone, too. But neither is ready to leave. This encounter has been so sour.

"Another drink?"

"I'd have another."

He catches her smiling. "What? What's funny?"

"Us. We had my dumb honesty session

before — it was supposed to get rid of all my bad habits! But instead." She shakes her head. "You really are smart, you know. I haven't given you enough credit." She runs her forefinger down the bridge of his nose.

"I know you haven't."

She holds her head in her hands, peeking theatrically through her knitted fingers. "I sound so awful when you describe me. And I can't even disagree. Well, I can. But not honestly."

He shifts his stool closer and, as her face emerges, he strokes her hair. He touches her forehead. "You," he says. "You again. You're still dear to me. You are goodness." He smiles. "I told you that before."

She shifts away. "What," she says hurriedly. "What are you talking about?"

"You — you're so driven. Like a mole burrowing in the earth, just pushing ahead. But I remember you." He smiles. "I remember you waking up. You sleeping. You getting the hiccups at the movie theater."

She can't talk.

"But it makes me sad," he concludes. "You make me sad a bit. I still love you, but we're not going to start anything."

Her eyes well up. Quietly, she says, "Thank you." She wipes her nose. "When I'm old and bent and sitting in a chair, you come

211

and hold my hand. All right? That's your job. Okay?"

He takes her hand and kisses it. "No," he says. "When you're old and bent, I'll be gone. I'll hold it now. Later, you'll have to remember."

1962. Corso Vittorio, Rome

Newsroom noises drifted into Betty's office: guffaws and murmured gossip, the clack and bing of typewriters, copyboys emptying crystal ashtrays into the garbage can. She sat at her desk, unable to work, spirits sunk beyond all reason.

Ridiculous — that's how she felt. Absolutely laughable. She had no right to be mourning still. To have cultivated the notion that she and Ott had a particular bond. Looking at paintings together. But what about the old days in New York?

Everyone felt this way about Ott, she supposed — this amplified sense of their importance in his life. He had that effect. His attention had been a spotlight; all else dimmed.

However, she had exerted no such force on him. He had left her in New York, had gone back to Atlanta, pursued his life of profit and expansion. He had married, produced a son.

213

Betty should have forgotten about him; his absence shouldn't have mattered as much as it had and for as long. Eventually, she moved away from New York, traveling to Europe to report on Hitler's war. In London, she met a fellow American reporter, Leo, and they married. After the war, they settled in Rome, she consuming more Campari than she'd imagined the first time she tasted the stuff, writing less than she'd planned, too.

Then Ott had turned up, his presence at once magnifying all the small compromises she had made over the years, while offering an escape from them. She wanted to write again and believed she could. He installed her as the voice of the paper. Leo had the title of editor-in-chief, but everyone knew she was the brains of the operation. She came back to life with Ott across the newsroom. But outside the paper?

Ott had never sought to resume anything with her. Their outings to buy paintings, their lunches at his mansion — meaningless. Look, she reminded herself, he never even told me he was sick. He never asked for help. He never contacted me when he was dying. I didn't have that role in his life. I have no right to this grief.

One night, when Leo was out boozing with the staff, Betty took a taxi up to the Aventine

Hill and stood before the spiked fence surrounding Ott's old mansion. Nothing remained in there. Only the paintings they had collected together: the swan-necked Gypsy by Modigliani; Léger's wine bottles and bowler hats; the acrobatic blue chickens and emerald fiddlers by Chagall; Pissarro's cozy English parsonage, smoke twisting out the chimney; the sloshing shipwreck of Turner — all of them, hanging in the pointless dark. She held down the buzzer, ringing the empty house, knowing it to be futile yet pressing till her fingertip went bloodless white. She let go; the house fell silent.

Without Ott around, Betty and Leo diverged more and more on how to run the paper. They hid their discord at the office, but barely. So it was with trepidation that they greeted news of a visitor from headquarters in Atlanta: Ott's son, Boyd, who was to pass the summer of 1962 in Rome before starting his junior year at Yale.

Leo, eager to curry favor, lined up a series of glitzy events to impress the young man and dispatched cleaners to dust off the old mansion on the Aventine Hill.

As a teenager, Boyd had flown to Rome each summer to spend a few weeks with his father. The pinnacle of those visits came when he and his father spoke alone. Even Ott's most cursory remarks entered Boyd as purest fact, as certain as the planets. When each vacation drew to an end, Boyd yearned to stay, to quit school in Atlanta, to live in Rome with his father. But Ott never invited him. On the flight home, the teenager mocked himself mercilessly, recalling his errant remarks, stinging at the memory, deeming himself an idiot, a disgrace.

Now, two years after his father's death, Boyd had returned to the city, a young man. To everyone's surprise, he spurned Ott's old mansion in favor of a hotel. And he showed no interest in carousing with Leo and the staff. Boyd disdained alcohol, disliked food, and betrayed no sense of humor. His goal in Rome, he said, was to learn the business of newspapering. But he seemed more interested in learning the business of Ott. "What did my father think about this?" he asked. "And what did he say about that? What was his plan for the paper?"

"The kid strikes me as sort of angry," Betty remarked. "Do you get that at all?"

"Well, I happen to like him," Leo responded, almost scolding.

"That wasn't what I was saying."

Not until Boyd returned to Atlanta did Betty and Leo separate. She liked to say, "I got the record player, he got the paper."

Betty moved back to New York and found a desk job, editing features at a women's magazine that specialized in recipes utilizing cans of condensed mushroom soup. She rented a one-bedroom apartment in Brooklyn that overlooked a primary-school playground and, every weekday morning, awoke to children's squeals. She pulled her dressing gown from the nail on the door and sat at the window, watching them: boys wrestling, examining bleeding kneecaps, resuming battle; new girls casting about for friends, digging their hands into pinafore pockets.

Betty never did return to Rome.

■ ■ ■ ■ ■

"THE SEX LIVES OF ISLAMIC EXTREMISTS"

• • •

CAIRO STRINGER — WINSTON CHEUNG

■ ■ ■ ■

He lies under the ceiling fan, wondering how to start. Every day in Cairo, news events take place. But where? At what time? He connects his laptop and reads the local press online but remains bewildered. These news conferences — how does one get in? And where does one obtain official statements? He wanders around his neighborhood, Zamalek, vaguely hoping a bomb might explode — not too close, of course, but within safe note-taking distance. He'd make front page of the paper, get his first byline.

No bombs go off that day, however. Nor in the following days. He checks his email constantly, anticipating a flaming missive from Menzies demanding to know what in hell he's doing. Instead, Winston finds an email from another person trying out for the Cairo stringer position, Rich Snyder, who announces his imminent arrival, end-

221

ing with the line "Can't wait to see you!"

That's friendly, Winston thinks. But are we supposed to meet up? He composes a cordial response: "I hope you have a safe flight. Regards, Winston."

This prompts an immediate answer: "Hope you can pick me up! See you there!" He includes his flight number and arrival time.

Is Winston expected to fetch the man from the airport? Aren't they rivals? Perhaps it's professional courtesy. Nobody from the paper mentioned this. Then again, he hasn't a clue how journalism works. Since he has nothing else to do, he takes a taxi to Cairo International.

"You came all the way out here — that is so awesome," Snyder says. He grips the younger man's shoulder and lets a bag slide from his own. Snyder is nearing fifty and wears an army surplus jacket and a white T-shirt, souvenir dog tags clinking around his neck. A corona of thick curly hair encircles his head and pinprick eyes dart about under a thick brow. It's hard for Winston to ignore: Snyder resembles a baboon.

"Wicked to be back in the Mideast," Snyder says. "I am so exhausted, you have no idea. Just got back from the AIDS conf."

"The AIDS what?"

222

"The AIDS conference in Bucharest. It's so dumb — I hate getting awards. And journalism is not a competition. It's not about that, you know. But whatever."

"You won an award?"

"No big deal. Just for the series I did for the paper on Gypsy AIDS babies. You saw that, right?"

"Uhm, I think maybe. Possibly."

"Bro, where have you been? It got suggested for a Pulitzer."

"You've been nominated for a Pulitzer Prize?"

"Suggested," Snyder specifies. "Suggested for one. What pisses me off is that the international community refuses to act. It's like nobody cares about Gypsy AIDS babies. In terms of the Pulitzer." He points to his carry-on bag. "You mind lugging that to the car? I've got serious vertebrae issues. Cheers." He snaps open his cellphone to check the screen. "I'm totally paranoid — keep thinking I'm gonna call someone by mistake while I'm talking about them. This thing is off, right?" He snaps it shut. "I love Kathleen," he continues. "Don't you love her? She is so great. When she was at her old job, Kath was always trying to hire me as, like, Washington's main national-desk writer. But I was deep in Afghanistan at the

223

time, so I was, like, 'Appreciate that, but your timing sucks.' She's still kicking herself. Missed ops. Whatever. You dig her?"

"Kathleen? I don't know her that well — I only met her once, actually, at a conference in Rome."

Snyder continues snapping his mobile open and shut. "Entre nous," he confides, "she's a bitch. Those aren't my words. That's what people say, entre nous. I myself hate the word 'bitch.' But I'm a feminist." He checks his phone. "Keep that entre nous, 'kay?"

"That you're a feminist?"

"No, no — tell people that. I'm saying, entre nous, Kathleen is out of her league, according to some people. Some say 'affirmative action,' though personally I find that term offensive." He walks out to the airport parking lot. "Feel that heat, bro! Which ride is us?"

"I thought we could share a taxi."

Blinking in the sun, Snyder turns to Winston. "How old are you, anyway? Seventeen?"

Winston gets this a lot — puberty left little trace on him; he still can't grow stubble. He attempts to age himself by wearing a suit, but in this muggy climate the most salient effect is sweat; he walks around wiping his face and fogged glasses, generally looking like a panicky congressional page. "I'm twenty-four."

"Little baby," Snyder says. "When I was your age, where was I? In Cambodia reporting on the Killing Fields? Or with the rebels in Zaire? I forget. Whatever. Get the cab door? My back is a mess. Appreciate that." Snyder stretches across the backseat of the taxi. "Dude," he declares, "let's commit some journalism."

Winston compresses himself into the smidgen of backseat not occupied by his rival. The cabbie swivels around, restlessly awaiting instruction, but Snyder continues chattering.

Tentatively, Winston interjects, "Sorry, which hotel are you in?"

"No worries, bro — we can drop you at your place first."

Winston recites his address to the driver.

"Ah," Snyder remarks, an eyebrow raised. "You speak Arabic."

"Not perfectly." He only started studying the language a few weeks earlier, having learned about this stringer position via an email exchange with Menzies. Previously, Winston had been studying primatology at grad school in Minnesota. But, suffering grave doubts about a future within the

225

confines of academia, he made a radical shift, quitting the program to remake himself into a foreign correspondent.

"I'm sure you're awesome at Arabic," Snyder insists. "I remember when I was in the Philippines during People Power back in the 1980s, and everyone's all, like, 'Oh, man, Tagalog is so hard.' And I'm, like, 'Bull.' And within days I'm, like, picking up chicks in Tagalog and stuff. That was after two days. Languages are totally overrated."

"So your Arabic must be excellent."

"Actually, I never speak foreign languages anymore," he explains. "I used to get so keyed into cultures that it was unhealthy. So I only talk in English now. Helps me maintain my objectivity." He squeezes Winston's shoulder. "I'm dying to work out, bro. Where's your gym? You got a gym out here, right? I'm into extreme sports myself: ultramarathons, kitesurfing, tennis. I still got buddies on the tennis circuit. Back in the day, they kept bugging me to turn pro and I was, like, 'I got nothing to prove.' " He gazes out the window, flexing a pectoral muscle. "Where did you come from anyhow?"

"Near Minneapolis."

"Dude," Snyder interrupts, "I mean, where were you *working* before this?"

"Ah, right, right. Uhm, I freelanced

226

mainly. A bunch of local Minnesota publications." This is a lie: his last piece of writing was a college essay on teaching monkeys sign language (a bad idea, it turns out).

But, thankfully, Snyder isn't interested in fact-checking. "How many places have I reported from now?" he says. "Can't remember. Like, sixty-three? I'm including countries that don't exist anymore. Is that allowed? Whatever. It's just a number, right? How many you up to?"

"Not that many."

"Like, fifty?"

"Ten, maybe." Winston hasn't even visited ten countries.

"Ten versus sixty-three. I doubt they'll take that into consideration when filling this job." He smirks.

"This is a full job, then? Menzies said in his email that it was just a stringer position."

"Is that what they told you?" He snorts. "Sonsabitches."

They arrive at Winston's apartment in Zamalek. Snyder gets out, too, rolls his neck, and jogs on the spot. "Stops blood clots," he explains. "Could you get my bag? Hey, thanks."

"But are you staying nearby?"

"Was just gonna grab a quick shower *chez*

227

toi, if that's cool."

"What about your hotel?"

"Look, bro, it's just water — if you don't want me to use your precious shower, say so. I did just get off a massive flight. But whatever."

The cabdriver thrusts out his hand.

"Only got Romanian currency, dude," Snyder tells him.

So Winston pays.

An hour later, Snyder emerges from the bathroom, one of Winston's towels wrapped around his midriff. He climbs into a pair of camouflage cargo pants and lets the towel fall to the carpet, briefly baring his bushy loins. Winston turns away but is not quick enough, condemning himself to the sight of Snyder tucking his penis down the left trouser leg. "Commando style," he says, buttoning his pants. "Always go commando style."

"I'll keep that in mind."

"So," Snyder goes on, "how long you been in this place?"

"A couple of weeks. This woman called Zeina, who went to my college, works here as a wire-service reporter. I found her through the alumni list. She's renting me the place short-term."

"And you got Internet access?"

"Yes, why?"

"Need to check something." He settles in at Winston's laptop. As he reads, he exclaims constantly: "Can you believe that!" or "That is wild!"

"How long do you think you'll be here?"

"Do you not want me here or something?" Snyder says, spinning around.

"Just that I might need the Internet later."

"Awesome." Snyder turns back to the laptop.

By early evening, he is still at the computer, rising only to gorge himself on Winston's food and spread his possessions across the floor. Various items of Snyder's — a hairbrush, Kevlar messenger bag, sports socks, deodorant spray — appear on the carpet around him in a widening radius. The baboon is marking his territory.

"Sorry," Winston says finally, "but I really need to get going. I have to log you off."

"What's the big rush, man?"

"I need to eat."

"I'm totally finished here. Gimme a sec. Let's go to Paprika together. I love that place." A half hour goes by. "I'm done now. Totally done." Another half hour passes.

"Just join me when you're finished," Winston says, clenching and unclenching his fists.

"Relax, bro!"

At 11 P.M., Snyder logs off. Finally, they step outside. "Where's my key?"

"How do you mean?"

"If you're still at the restaurant when I get back, I'll be locked out," Snyder says. "All my stuff is inside."

"You're not coming to dinner?"

"Did you think I was? Ohmigod! I hope you weren't waiting for me. No way. That is hilarious. But I'll totally be back before you. The keys?" He plucks them from Winston's hand. "Awesome, man — you're totally awesome." He jogs down the street, waving for a cab.

"Hang on," Winston cries. "Wait."

"Dude," Snyder calls back. "I'll be gone, like, ten minutes. I'll be back before you've even ordered." He jumps into a cab and is gone.

By this hour, all the local restaurants have closed. There is a twenty-four-hour deli, Maison Thomas, but it's shut for renovation. Winston resorts to a grubby convenience store. He buys potato chips, a candy bar, a can of Mecca-Cola, and consumes the lot outside the apartment complex, studying his watch and feeling horribly reduced by the whole Rich Snyder experience.

At 3 A.M., Snyder ambles back. "Ohmigod, what are you doing outside?"

"You have the keys," Winston replies.

"Where's yours?"

"You have them."

"Well, that was dumb." Snyder unlocks the door. "I'm taking the bed because of my back." He flops diagonally across the mattress. "You're cool with the armchair, right?"

"Not especially."

But Snyder is already snoring. Winston would dearly love to throw this guy out. However, he desperately needs instruction from someone who understands journalism. Winston studies Snyder with distaste, splayed out there across the bed. Perhaps this is how journalists are supposed to act. Winston settles down in the armchair.

At nine, Snyder shakes him awake. "What've you got for breakfast, guy?" He pulls open the fridge door. "Somebody needs to go shopping. Dude, we got, like, thirty minutes."

"Till what?"

"We'll start with man-on-the-street. I know it's bull, but that's the job."

"Sorry, I don't understand."

"Translations — I'm letting you interpret for me. I told you, I never compromise my objectivity by speaking foreign languages."

"But I have my own articles I'm working on."

"Like?"

"I was thinking of writing something on the U.S. peace initiative — Abbas and Olmert might start holding regular meetings, I heard."

Snyder smiles. "Don't write about diplomacy. Write about human beings. The tapestry of human experience is my press office."

"Is that a joke?"

"How do you mean?"

"Or something on Iran and nuclear weapons, maybe."

"Writing about Tehran from Cairo? Ouch. Listen, dude, let me tell you a story. Back when I was reporting from Bosnia, I heard that shit was going down in Srebrenica. I didn't say a word to anyone, got in my Lada, drove there. Along the way, I bump into some aid groupie. She's, like, 'Where you going, Snyder?' I'm, like, 'Vacation.' "

"I don't get it."

"If I'd said one word to her, Srebrenica would have been swarming with even more aid groupies and reporters and shit. And where would I have been? I was, like, a day ahead of everyone on the massacre. Ever since, *The New York Times* has been aching

to hire me. Till this big-shot editor there
says I don't fit their culture or something. I
was, like, I wouldn't work for you guys
anyway."

"It must have been pretty upsetting."

"Not getting the *Times* job?"

"Covering a massacre."

"Oh, totally."

"But," Winston says uncertainly, "I
vaguely remember some *other* reporter
breaking the Srebrenica massacre."

Snyder opens and shuts his cellphone to
ensure that it's off. "I never trash talk. But,
entre nous, that guy is an unethical, schem-
ing louse. Whatever — you have to live your
life. My motto is 'End hate.' "

Winston isn't sure how all this pertains to
his story idea on Iran's nuclear activities,
but deems it wise to shift topics. "Still," he
says, "I do need to get an article in the
paper. I mean, I am applying for this position."

"Applying? You are *getting* this job. I have
total faith in you."

"I appreciate that. But I haven't done a
single story yet, and I've been here two
weeks."

"Don't be so stressed. You gotta have fun
with it. And, listen, I am totally ready to
throw you a contributor's tag. What do I

233

care about bylines — I mean, how many do I have by now? Ten thousand?" He scans Winston's face for signs of awe. "Come on — I'll toss you the contributor's tag, 'kay?"

"My name and yours on the story?"

"If that rocks your world, bro."

Hurriedly, Winston showers and slips into a suit and tie. He finds Snyder at the door, in his faux-military garb, laptop under his arm.

"Is that my computer?" Winston asks.

"It's the one that was on the table," Snyder replies. "Let's roll, bro!"

"Why are you bringing my laptop?"

"You'll see." He walks outside, leading Winston down the Twenty-sixth of July Street, and points at an approaching businessman. "Get that dude over there."

"What do you mean, Get him?"

"Get quotes. Man-on-the-street. I'm grabbing a coffee."

"What am I supposed to ask him?"

But Snyder is already inside Simonds café.

Gingerly, Winston shifts into the path of the businessman. The man quickens his pace and sweeps past. Winston scouts other victims. But, as each nears, Winston loses his nerve. He slinks into the café. Snyder sits there on a high stool with Winston's laptop open, interviewing locals in English and consuming a platter of miniature buns. He types with two sticky forefingers.

"So?" he asks, swallowing. "The businessman give good quote?"

"You mind if I grab a coffee?"

"No time." He snaps the laptop shut. "I'm going to Khan el-Khalili, and I strongly advise you to follow."

"I've hardly eaten since yesterday — couldn't I get a quick bite before we leave?"

"Have this." He flicks over the final morsel of baby croissant, bearing soggy teeth prints.

As they climb into a taxi, a tall thin man steps from the café, observing them. He enters a black sedan, which pulls out behind them. Winston watches through the taxi's rear window: the black sedan is following them. They arrive at the street market, but the sedan is nowhere to be seen.

Snyder points at the bustling crowd. "Get that chick."

"What chick?"

"The one in that coat thing."

"The burka, you mean?"

"Get her, big guy. We need man-on-the-street quotes."

"But a woman in a burka? Couldn't I do man-on-the-street with a man on the street?"

"That is so racist." Snyder wanders away

to investigate a spice stall.

Under his breath, Winston repeats his most practiced Arabic phrase: "Excuse me, do you speak English?" His armpits prickle with sweat. He gathers his courage and approaches the cloaked woman. But his voice emerges in such a tiny peep that she doesn't hear. He taps her shoulder and she turns with surprise, addressing him in Arabic. A few shoppers shift, watching. He repeats, "Excuse me, do you speak English?"

She responds again in Arabic.

"You don't, then?"

More Arabic.

"This is a problem."

Further Arabic.

A frowning young man intervenes. "What is matter? Why you bother her?"

"You speak English — great. No, it's nothing. I was just hoping to ask her a couple of questions."

"Why for?"

"It's okay — I'm a journalist."

"You touch her?"

"What? No, no. I didn't touch her."

"You touch her!" the man shouts, stepping forward.

"I didn't, I swear. I just want to ask her a question. For a news story."

"What question?"

"It's hard to summarize."

"But what is question?"

That itself is a good question. Snyder hasn't told Winston what to ask or indeed what their topic is. He's constantly talking about terrorism — perhaps Winston should inquire about that. "Could you ask her if there's much terrorism in this area? And if so, where, if she knows. And if you could write that down, too — in English ideally, or even with a map, if possible."

The crowd stirs. The frowning young man crinkles his face even further. A few people gesticulate indignantly. The woman herself throws up her arms and turns away. Winston wipes off his fogged glasses, apologizes to the crowd, and rushes over to Snyder, who is still smelling spices at a nearby stall.

"What'd you get?" he asks.

"She's against it," Winston blurts. "In favor, basically. But sort of against it."

"Okay, but what did she say, exactly?"

"Uhm, yes, I think so."

"What?"

"Uh-huh."

"Take a deep breath, dude. What did you ask her about?"

"About terrorism."

"Sweet."

"And about the clash of civilizations and

237

that. The *hijab* and so forth."

"Isn't that a burka?"

"Yes, exactly," Winston says. "But she prefers the *hijab*. Only, her husband won't let her wear one. Because of the Taliban."

"The Taliban? There's no Taliban in Egypt."

"Metaphorically. The metaphorical Taliban. At least that's how I took it."

"We need to air this out. Go get her again."

"I think she's gone."

"She's right there by the fruit stand, dude." Snyder shoves Winston forward. "You want the job, right?"

Agonized, he sidles up to her once more. The crowd watches his second pass, a few people smirking, others shaking their heads. "Excuse me?" he says. "Hi, sorry — excuse me?"

She turns sharply and harangues him in Arabic.

"What's she saying, dude?" Snyder asks.

"She mentioned her husband again."

"The Taliban guy? Push for more on that."

Winston — recalling the Just Listen 'n Learn Arabic course he did on the flight over — dredges up the word for "husband." He utters it as if it were a question.

This riles the crowd further.

Snyder whispers, "Ask her if she plays around. Is that common in Islamist circles?"

"I can't ask that," Winston says, meaning this in every sense.

The crowd is growing in size and hostility.

"Maybe she's had a lesbian experience," Snyder remarks.

"But she's wearing a burka."

"Women in burkas can't express their sexual orientation? That is so racist."

"I can't ask her stuff like that."

"Islamist swingers would be an awesome story, bro. Serious awards material."

At this, the tall thin man who followed them from the café steps forth from the crowd. "What do you want to obtain here?" he demands in crisp English.

"It's okay," Winston sputters. "We're journalists."

"Who do you work for?" The man addresses Winston but looks at Snyder.

"For the paper," Winston answers. "Are you a journalist, too?"

"I'm with the interior ministry."

At this, Snyder steps forward. "Rich Snyder, foreign correspondent. Good to meet you. You speak awesome English, man. I totally envy you having a second language. We Americans are a disgrace. What's your name again?"

"I'm with the interior ministry," the man repeats, then barks a command to the onlookers, dispersing them at once. He returns his attention to Snyder. "I don't appreciate these topics of yours. You wish to write about sexual perversions in Egypt. There are no sexual perversions in Egypt. Sexual perversions are a Western phenomenon."

"I wish, bro."

The ministry man smiles thinly. "Find another topic. Something pleasing. Something cheerful about my country. Not all this" — he winces — "mixing up of people."

"What topic should I write about, then?"

"That is *your* job, is it not? I suggest you study *The Egyptian Gazette.* They publish some excellent articles."

"About Mrs. Mubarak being a good housewife? Look, if you don't want me to write about Egyptian sex practices, give me something better."

"What are you looking for?"

"I want what everybody wants. I want the Mideast money shot: terrorism."

The ministry man turns sharply to Winston. "Put your notebook away! This is not on the record!"

"I want Gamaa al-Islamiya," Snyder goes on. "Bang-bang in Upper Egypt. I want to know about security cooperation with the United States. I want interviews with special forces."

"Step into my car."

Seemingly, this request does not apply to Winston, who is left by the fruit stand as the black sedan pulls away.

He remembers too late that Snyder has the house keys. He calls Snyder's mobile, but there is no answer. Around nightfall, Snyder finally picks up. "Hey, man, why didn't you come?"

"I didn't know I was invited."

"Can't hear you. I'm at the military airport."

"When are you getting back? I'm stuck outside again."

"I'm totally coming back."

"But when?"

"Weekend at the latest."

"I need the house keys!"

"Ohmigod, relax. You worry way too much. Just have fun with it. Listen, I'm getting on a C-130 in, like, two hours. I need you to do some research." He reels off names and organizations.

"What about my keys?"

"Call me in five minutes."

"And you still have my laptop."

Snyder hangs up.

Winston calls back every few minutes for three hours, but Snyder's mobile is turned off. Winston must ask Zeina, the wire-service reporter who rents him the apartment, for a spare key. By way of apology, he insists on buying her a drink at a nearby pub.

She orders for them in fluent Arabic, picks a table, and carries over their pints of Sakara beer. She sits, sweeping aside gelled strands of her black hair, revealing a rakish grin. "So," she asks, "you enjoying Cairo?"

"Oh, yeah. It's really interesting," he says. "I have a couple of gripes, but they're pretty minor."

"Like?"

"Nothing serious."

"Tell me one."

"Well, the air is kind of hard to breathe, with all this pollution. Sort of like inhaling from an exhaust pipe. The heat makes me faint sometimes. And the food isn't all that edible. Or maybe I've just been unlucky. Also, it's a police state, which I don't love. And I get the impression the locals want to shoot me. Only when I talk to them, though. Which is my fault — my Arabic is useless. But basically, yeah," he summarizes, "it's really interesting."

"What about Snyder? What do you make

of him?"

"You know Snyder?"

"Oh, sure."

"And what do I think of him?" Winston hesitates. "Well, I suppose that, on the surface, I have to admit, he did come off as slightly, uhm, sort of ambitious. But now that I know him better I'm actually starting to think that he's —"

"Even more ambitious."

With unintended candor, he responds, "Sort of a jerk, I was going to say." He wipes his glasses. "Sorry. I'm not offending you, am I?"

"Don't be crazy. He's not a friend of mine," she says. "What are you guys working on, anyway?"

"I'm not even sure. To be fair, before he arrived I wasn't writing a thing. But I was making progress. Or I thought I was. I was getting to know the city, studying my Arabic. I was going to produce something eventually. Then he colonized. He stole my laptop. He has this strange power to trample me and make me feel obligated at the same time. He *is* encouraging — he's constantly saying I'm a shoo-in for the stringer job, that he has no chance, that I'm the obvious choice, and so forth. Yet the more time I pass with him, the more ridiculous I feel.

And I don't understand why a guy with that sort of experience is even trying out for this position."

"Iraq," she explains. "He's trying to get into Iraq. Snyder has been looking for a way in ever since the war started. Did he tell you what he was doing before he came to Cairo?"

"Something about an award?"

"He wrote a blog about Iraq. Or, rather, about trying to get into Iraq. About him getting turned back at the frontier with Iran, with Turkey, with Syria, with Jordan, with Saudi Arabia, with Kuwait. Thank God Iraq has so many borders — it gave him lots of material. I grant him this: he's determined. The guy is more than just a pretty face."

"You consider him pretty?"

"Well, he has that whole gritty war-correspondent thing going. Some women find that sexy," she says. "As far as Iraq goes, his problem is that nobody can figure him out. The Americans don't trust him, the Iranians think he's CIA, the Iraqis are just spooked by the guy. Nobody understands what he's doing there when no publication is sponsoring him."

"And why won't anyone sponsor him?"

"The guy is a handful. He's worked for everybody, then gets into pissing matches, and gets fired," she says. "But forget about Snyder for a moment. Do *you* have any stories you're doing while he's away?"

"I have some ideas."

"But you haven't filed anything, right?"

"Not yet."

"Good. Look, you don't have a laptop, so come work out of my office," she says. "I want to keep an eye on you."

On Winston's arrival the next morning, Zeina glances up from her computer, fingers still typing. "Gotta take care of this bulletin. Sit. I'll be done in two minutes." She completes it and shakes out her fingers. "Let's go — I'm taking you to your first presser."

But not so fast: Winston has no accreditation to get into a press conference and is stopped at the door of the Arab League. Zeina does her utmost but cannot pull him in with her. Eventually, she sneaks a Palestinian undersecretary out to him. The undersecretary, who speaks English, patiently explains the goings-on inside. Winston scrambles his pen across the page but has never taken down quotes before and finds speech unexpectedly rapid; within three words, the sentence is off and running while his pen straggles behind. Eventually, the undersecretary excuses himself.

"What did you get?" Zeina asks.

Winston studies his notes, which consist of opening phrases — "We believe that . . ." or "The real problem is . . ." or "What you must know is . . ." — followed by unintelligible scrawl.

"A couple of good bits," he replies.

She sets him up at a spare computer in her office and leaves him to write. He is still at it when she goes home for the night. "Call me if you're going to file anything to the paper," she says. "I want to check it first."

But by the next morning he still hasn't finished. In the late afternoon, he finally shows her a draft.

"Well," she says, after a quick read, "it's a start. Definitely a start. I do have a couple of comments."

"Please, go ahead."

"First off, a standard rule for a news article — and I don't mean to mow down your creativity here — is to identify the location and the day at some point. Also, you should cite the names of anyone you talk to. And you might want to avoid using the word 'thing' so much."

"Otherwise it looks okay?"

"Well, this is a test story — let's consider it like that."

"Do you think the paper will want it?"

"It *is* slightly old by now."

"It happened yesterday morning."

"Which is old in news terms. I'm sorry — I tend to be fairly negative, so don't take my comments too much to heart. But I have to say, you spend way too many words getting to the nut of this story. Also, I felt the undersecretary's goatee received too much attention. Frankly, I wouldn't even mention it."

"I thought it was germane."

"Not in the lead. Don't get me wrong — I like your attempts to insert color. But I felt you were trying too hard at times. Like this bit: 'As he spoke, the yellow Egyptian sun shone very brightly, as if that golden sphere were blazing with the very hope for peace in the Middle East that burned also within the heart of the Palestinian undersecretary for sports, fishing, and wildlife.' "

"I considered deleting that line."

"I'm not even sure it's grammatical. And, for the record, the origins of the Israeli-Palestinian conflict do not 'hark back to an ancient spelling mistake.' Not that I've ever heard."

"I thought that might draw the reader in."

"But it's not true."

"I don't know, Zeina — the undersecretary spoke so fast. And somebody went by selling ice cream. The noise. It distracted me."

"I know — you mention the ice-cream vendor in your article."

"A bit of local color, I thought. So I shouldn't offer it to the paper?"

"Offer it, by all means."

"Or maybe not."

"Look, come back tomorrow. We'll find you another story."

Admittedly, his first attempt flopped. But, as he heads back to the apartment, Winston is electrified — he has conducted a real interview. This was actual journalism. His mobile rings, triggering instant panic: maybe it's Menzies from the paper, demanding stories. No such luck.

"Wassup, bro?"

"Snyder, hi."

"In the Nile Valley. Military commandos. Islamists."

"I'm sorry? I'm hearing only bits of what you're saying. You're coming in telegraphically. Can you repeat that?"

"Aid groupie satphone. Charges by minute. Talk fast. How's research?"

"The stuff you asked me to do? To be completely honest, I haven't had tons of time to work on it. I've sort of been trying to do my own stories. Anyway, it sounds like you're in a rush, so I won't get into the details. Point is I've had difficulty doing the research. In part because you have my laptop."

"Did Kathleen call?"

"No," Winston responds. "Why? Was she supposed to?"

"Halt your story. Do my research."

"She said that?"

"Massive project. Award candidate. In or out?"

"Are you serious?"

"In? Or out?"

Winston settles into a carrel at the American University library. At first, he is irked at having to do Snyder's bidding, but is soon drawn into the material. He cannot deny a certain relief in being able to sift through academic tomes, fulfilling his journalistic duty without having to barge past security guards at the Arab League or grab man-on-the-street from women at the market. This library work is easily his favorite part of reporting so far. Indeed, he grows so engrossed that he's still at it three days later, when Snyder returns to town.

They arrange to meet for lunch at L'Aubergine.

Snyder arrives twenty minutes late, chattering into his cellphone. He sits and continues talking. After ten more minutes, he clicks off his phone. "Wicked to see you, bro."

"No problem," Winston says, though Snyder hasn't apologized for anything. "I've got that research you wanted."

Snyder digs a finger into Winston's hummus. "Awesome time down there. I ditched my military watchers on, like, day one. Met up with the Bedouins. Infiltrated the muj. Riding donkeys. Sugarcane fields. Choppers. Bunker-busting. Madrassas. Extremist training camps. You should have come."

"I got the sense you wanted to go alone."

"Ohmigod — are you kidding? All I want is for the news to come out."

"Did you meet any terrorists?"

"The real deal, bro." He pauses. "Not full-on Qaeda. But they're way up the waiting list."

"There's an application process?"

"Totally. OBL is whacked that way."

"Who's OBL?"

"Osama," he replies. "I don't know him *that* good. We only met, like, twice. Back in Tora Bora. Good times."

"What's he like?"

"Tall. That's what hits home most. If he hadn't taken a wrong turn, maybe a career in professional sports. That's the tragedy of this conflict — so much talent wasted. Whatever. The thing that pisses me off about GWOT is the ignorance. Don't get me wrong — I reject extremism in all forms. I only hope that, in a small way, people might read my work and hear the voice that cries out in every article."

"And what is that voice saying?"

"I'm gonna finish the hummus, 'kay?"

Winston piles three binders on the table. "Almost everything you asked for. There's a table of contents and an index."

Snyder eats without looking up.

Winston makes another attempt. "Do you want me to leave it here?"

"Keep it, guy. My present to you."

"Don't you want the research?"

"Don't you read the paper, dude? The story already came out."

Winston absorbs this. "I got a contributor's tag for a story I didn't even read?"

"But you said *not* to put your name on my story. Didn't you say that in an email or something?"

"Never."

"Yeah, you did. Since obviously it was, like, my story and stuff." He dive-bombs his hand into Winston's eggplant dip. "So, you gonna try freelancing now?"

"Well, I'm still going for this stringer job."

"Stringer for who?"

"For the paper."

"They didn't tell you? I feel so bad," Snyder says. "I'm pretty much the paper's guy in Cairo now." He opens and shuts his cellphone, ensuring that it's off. "Entre nous, this gig is just a time-killer for me. I'll be out of here in a year max. *The New York Times* will definitely want me in Baghdad. We're not in touch yet, but they'll call within the year, I guarantee. In a way, the wait is cool for me — by the time I get there, Iraq might be a failed state, which would be wicked on my résumé." Their bill arrives. "Who's grabbing this one?" Snyder asks, making no move to do so.

Sluggishly, Winston takes out his credit card.

"That is so nice of you, guy. I would totally expense this, but since you're going to."

"Actually, I can't expense anything. I don't have a job."

"Ohmigod, then that is even more cool of you to pay."

Snyder leads the way back to Winston's apartment, unlocks the door, and belly-flops onto the bed.

"Snyder?"

"Yeah?"

"What happened to my laptop?"

"What laptop?"

"The one you took."

"Where'd you have it last?"

"*You* had it last."

"Don't think so, dude."

Winston sits up most of the night, conspiring to murder this usurping baboon. But the risk of jail time in Cairo is a powerful disincentive, so he shifts to planning all the cutting remarks he'll make the next morning.

Yet at dawn, when Snyder is up and leaping about, Winston only watches, half-asleep, silently loathing. Snyder says an aid groupie is getting him on a restricted flight to Darfur. "I'm in a failed-state of mind," he declares. He gathers his belongings and leaves without even offering thanks.

Winston stretches out on the still warm bed and shuts his eyes. He runs over his interactions with Snyder, condemning himself for cowardice. He flips about for a fitful hour, then rises, determined to leave this city.

The decision is deflating, then heartening — he has longed to escape Cairo ever since he arrived. Should he inform the paper of his departure? Do they even know he's here?

He hasn't heard a peep from Menzies or Kathleen or anyone else since he arrived.

All that remains is to change his return ticket, pack, and get the keys to Zeina. He invites her for his last dinner as thanks, pledging to himself not to mention Snyder. Nonetheless, the baboon keeps popping into their conversation.

"One thing I have to say about him," Winston comments, "is that he does get amazing quotes. In my minuscule experience at it, nobody said anything particularly interesting."

"Snyder's quotes? Some people claim they are, on occasion, approximate."

"How do you mean?"

"Well, do Taliban fighters really say things like 'That bombing was sweet, now let's kick ass on the Northern Alliance'?"

"I'm not sure. I've never met the Taliban."

"To be fair, he reports the hell out of stories, goes to the front lines — he is fearless in his own weird way."

"I know. I saw him talking to an interior ministry guy once at Khan el-Khalili. Snyder just kept badgering the guy — pretty rudely, I thought. But he ended up getting a story out of it."

"Good reporting and good behavior are mutually exclusive," she explains. "I'm exaggerating, slightly."

She is a decade older than Winston, and he admires her — she's so collected and competent. He wonders if, after dinner, there might be an opportunity to kiss her. He has not seen couples kissing on the street in Cairo. Where would he make his approach?

Then again, if he were to launch himself at Zeina, what next? Already, with her clothes on, she scares him. Whatever narrow hope he has nurtured evaporates when she says, "You know that me and Snyder had a thing, right?"

"Really?" Winston responds nonchalantly. "What kind of thing?"

"A fling thing. Whatever."

That's a Snyder line, Winston realizes with a chill. "I wondered how you knew so much about him."

"Majorly bad move. But he's tempting."

"Snyder is tempting?"

"I told you," she says, "the man is sexy. But now tell me, young Mr. Cheung, looking back, has this journalism experience been a nightmare for you?"

"Not entirely."

"Did you enjoy any of it?"

"I liked going to the library," he says. "I think I prefer books to people — primary

255

sources scare me."

"Unless they're simian."

"Even then," he says. "Like one time, my thesis adviser was giving a tour of our lab to a bunch of undergrads. He was trying to demonstrate hierarchical dominance among macaques. On his cue, this male called Bingo started chewing on my thigh and corralled me into the corner of the enclosure. Before the entire class, Bingo showed that he, an unremarkable adolescent monkey, significantly outranked me."

She smiles. "Is that why you quit grad school?"

"The matters are not unrelated. The downside of studying primates, I realized, is that you grow overly conscious of rank, submissive behavior, alliance-forming. In academia, I was always going to be a low-status primate. But journalism seemed like an alpha-male profession."

"Journalism is a bunch of dorks pretending to be alpha males," she says. "Speaking of which, did I mention that Snyder called me from Darfur?"

"What for?"

"He wanted me to interpret something from Arabic. Had some pretty interesting material, too."

"Did you help him?"

"Why would I? Actually, I've been in touch with Kathleen at the paper."

For a chilling moment, he thinks Zeina has interceded to get him the stringer position after all, and that he might be compelled to stay.

This isn't what she meant. "I'm tired of wire-service hackery," she explains. "It'd be nice to actually detach my ear from the telephone and go out and report once in a while. Even if it's just as a stringer for the paper."

"I didn't know you wanted this job."

"Well, I did."

"I guess it was even more generous of you to have helped me, then," he says, wondering suddenly how much she really had helped. "Why didn't you mention this before?"

"We were opponents."

"I didn't realize."

"So you're going back to your studies in Minnesota, then?"

"I have a plan," he responds archly, but goes no further. He isn't going to reveal himself to her. And, anyway, he doesn't have a plan. "You know," he remarks, "it occurs to me that I've been wrong about something: I always assumed that age and experience weather you, make you more resilient.

But that's not true. It's the opposite." He turns to her. "Don't you think?"

But she's checking her cellphone for missed calls from Snyder and doesn't respond.

1963. Corso Vittorio, Rome

With Betty out of the picture, Leo assumed full control of the paper and declared that his first goal was to raise status. Whether he meant the paper's status or his own was a matter of debate.

His obsession was "marquee pieces," which he defined as articles to make you fall over at the newsstand. However, he distrusted his own staff to produce anything that good, so he purchased the stories from outside writers, which endeared him to no one at the office. The atmosphere grew increasingly toxic; the old collegial days were over.

Circulation declined marginally, but Leo claimed that the readership had merely grown more refined. When corresponding with the board in Atlanta, he pledged to cut costs, but privately he was cocky. After all, Charles had tipped his hand: he'd said the paper was untouchable.

In 1969, Charles stepped down as chairman of the board and Ott's son, Boyd, age twenty-seven, took over. Leo sent Boyd a letter of congratulations, with a hint that more cash would be timely — the paper could do with a few new hands. Instead, Boyd got rid of an old one: Leo himself.

The justification was that Leo had betrayed the paper and its late founder. Ott had left his family, had toiled day and night, to build a publication that served the world, Boyd said. But Leo had turned the paper into little more than a personal fiefdom. Boyd even alleged that Leo had altered the masthead to shrink "Founded by Cyrus Ott (1899–1960)" and enlarge "Editor-in-Chief: Leopold T. Marsh." A measuring stick seemed to prove the point.

Leo lingered around the capitals of Europe for a while, nosing about for a route back into the international press. In the end, he returned to the United States, taking home a before-breakfast Cognac habit and scant cash. He accepted a job in Pittsburgh running a trade publication on the coal industry and was lucky to get it.

Boyd pledged to lead the search for a replacement editor-in-chief but proved too absorbed by the rest of the Ott empire. He had grand ambitions and began by selling off many long-standing holdings, even the sugar refinery that had started it all, in favor of speculative investments overseas. It was audacious — just the sort of thing his father would have done.

Or so Boyd believed.

For he had barely known Ott, who left for Europe when Boyd was eleven. He had not even been born during his father's fabled early days, when Ott had built an empire from nothing. Most of what Boyd knew about those times came from sundry courtiers nibbling at the edges of the family fortune.

Still, these myths spurred him on. He was bold because his father had been, and proud because this, too, had been Ott's fashion. Yet Boyd's boldness lacked pleasure, and his pride lacked dignity. He styled himself a man of the people, as his father had been. But the people mistrusted Boyd, and he in turn despised them.

■ ■ ■ ■

"KOOKS WITH NUKES"

• • •

COPY EDITOR — RUBY ZAGA

■ ■ ■ ■

The jerks took her chair again, the chair she fought for six months to get. It's amazing. Just amazing, these people. She hunts around the newsroom, curses bubbling inside her, bursting out now and then. "Pricks," she mutters. She should just quit. Hand in her resignation. Never set foot in this place again. Leave these idiots in the dirt.

But wait, stop! Yes, there it is: the chair — over there, behind the watercooler. She hurries over and grabs it. "Get their own damn chair." She rolls it to its rightful place at the copydesk, unlocks her drawer, and lays out her tools: a cushion for her lower back, an ergonomic keyboard and mouse, RSI wrist braces, antibacterial wipes. She decontaminates the keyboard and the mouse. "Impossible to feel clean in this place."

She adjusts the height of her chair, pats the pillow into position, and sits. "Disgusting." The seat is warm. Someone has been sitting in it. "Should just walk out." Seriously. Wouldn't that be rich. Never have to see these losers again.

The paper is the only place Ruby Zaga has ever worked. She started here after quitting a doctorate in theology. She was twenty-seven at the time and self-conscious about taking an unpaid summer internship. At forty-six, she's still at the paper, working on the copydesk, her temper shorter and her body stouter, though she dresses just as she did on her arrival in 1987: bangles, silver hoop earrings, sweaterdress cinched with an oversize belt, black leggings, white Keds. It's not simply the same styles but the same items in many cases, dotted with fuzzballs, colors faded.

She always arrives early for her shift because the newsroom is empty then, except for Menzies, who seems never to leave. Regrettably, her colleagues on the copydesk eventually turn up. The first to do so today is the slot editor, Ed Rance, who barges out of the elevator, nose running, aerating a damp armpit with waves of his hand. He bicycles to work and sweats profusely, stains mottling his khakis. She won't allow him the chance to not say hello — she'll not say hello first. She rushes off to the toilets and hides in a stall, giving the finger to the door.

She returns, late for the start of her shift.

"Try to be here on time," Ed Rance says.

She slams her ass into the chair.

Ed Rance and the other copy editor on duty, Dave Belling, are proofreading the early edition. Ed Rance hands Ruby the last few pages — the dullest — to check over, then whispers something to Dave Belling. They laugh.

"What?" she asks.

"Not talking about you, Rube. World doesn't revolve around you, Rube."

"Yeah, well. I seriously don't need this."

In fact, they aren't talking about her but about Saddam Hussein. It's December 30, 2006, and Saddam was hanged at dawn. For amusement, they're hunting for footage of the execution on the Internet.

Meantime, all the senior editors cluster around the layout desk to discuss page one. "We got art?"

"Of what? Dictator on a rope?"

"What are the wires offering?"

"Him on the slab. His head is, like, all at an angle. Like, all twisted around to the side."

"That's gotta hurt."

"Can we do a frame grab off Al Jazeera?"

Someone jokes: "Why don't we do a frame

grab of the whole *New York Times* front page and just publish that? Then we can go home right now."

This wins a ringing endorsement and a fast-dying chuckle — they don't like to laugh at each other's jokes.

Dave Belling finds footage of the hanging online and calls over his friends, Ed Rance and Clint Oakley. The three men watch as Saddam refuses the hood. Executioners place the noose around his neck. They tighten the knot. The video stops.

"That's it? No drop?"

"Poor sweet Saddam."

"Poor adorable Saddam."

"Somewhere an angel just got his wings."

"Somewhere an angel is shooting a rifle in heaven."

Ruby wasn't invited to watch. "Jerks."

They pretend not to hear her and hunt for fresh video, something smutty this time.

She happens to like their infantile humor — it's her taste, too. But they never include her. And when *she* tells a joke they're repulsed. Why do they treat her like a freak? "Like I'm malignant."

This coven of losers, ogling babes on YouTube — and they consider *her* a menopausal troll. But she's the same as them: middle-aged, pervy, bored. Why do they have to make her feel like some piece of crap. "They're infants is why."

Copy for the late edition drizzles in. The room grows quieter. One can tell time by the noise level. Early, the newsroom is abuzz with humorless jokes. Later, now, a hush settles but for tapping keyboards and nervous coughs. At deadline, the outbursts come.

Ruby stares at the blinking cursor. They've given her nothing, not one story to edit. And then they're gonna dump Saddam on her at deadline. "Assholes."

But when the Saddam story does land Ed Rance assigns it to Dave Belling.

"Jerks." Instead of anything important, Ruby is assigned a series of mind-numbing briefs: a Nigerian pipeline blast; skirmishes in Mogadishu; the Russian gas standoff. Then Ed Rance gives her a news analysis on nuclear arms in Iran and North Korea, with ludicrous headline dimensions. The story is huge, two thousand words, but the head is tiny: one column wide and three lines deep. How do you summarize all this crap in three words? They treat her like she's a goddamn slave or something. "Pricks."

As is his habit, Herman Cohen pauses at the copydesk on his way home, standing behind each editor in turn, reading their screens. Dave Belling has a bag of sunflower seeds open and Herman digs in without asking, as he does whenever he spots open food containers. He orders tweaks to the Saddam headline, then thuds away.

The senior editors call Kathleen on her mobile to discuss page one. They put her on speakerphone so everyone can go on record endorsing her, then hang up and mock her, as if to cleanse the air of their sycophancy.

Minutes to deadline, Ruby has finished everything but a brief. She's struggling to fit "Mogadishu" into a one-column headline. Clint Oakley appears. "Who did the head on the Nigeria pipeline explosion?" he says. "Are you guys kidding me? 'Blast Kills People Again.'" He cackles with laughter. "What retard wrote that?" Ever since Clint was demoted from culture editor to obituaries, he has hung around the copydesk looking for easy targets — Ruby, above all. He knows full well it was she who handled the Nigeria pipeline story. "Who did that?" he persists. "Whoever it was should be fired. You're changing it, right? Ed Rance?"

"Already changed, Clint Oakley." The guys refer to each other by full names, as if this were boarding school.

"Cool, Ed Rance. Wanted to make sure."

He walks away, sneering. " 'Blast Kills People Again'! I fuckin' love it!"

Ruby is trembling with rage. That headline was a one-column-four and Ed Rance was screaming at her to finish it. What's she supposed to do? Now it's minutes from deadline and the word "Mogadishu" stares insolently at her. "Can't concentrate."

"I need that Somalia head," Ed Rance says.

"I know!"

"Now, Ruby."

"It's not ready!"

"We're at deadline. Put it down."

"Gimme a minute!"

"If you can't do it, put it down and I'll give it to someone who can."

"Jesus Christ!" She closes the file.

"Unprofessional," Ed Rance mutters.

Soon, the inside pages are finished. Page one is double-checked and put to bed. It's 10 P.M., the shift is over, the staff are sprung.

Tomorrow is New Year's Eve, so everyone has the day off. A few journalists and technicians linger to discuss party plans, but most slip out one by one; they stagger their departures to avoid having to share the elevator down. Soon the newsroom is empty except for Menzies, who is still at his computer, and Ruby, who packs up her tools: cushion, disinfectant wipes, RSI wrist braces, ergonomic keyboard and mouse. She locks her drawer and rakes a shivering hand through her hair, as if to dislodge spiders. "Such pricks." It'll feel good when she fucking quits. "Cannot wait."

It's dark as she heads for the bus stop. To her surprise, the paper's young publisher, Oliver Ott, is walking his dog in her direction — why is he coming to the office at this hour? He is a tall man, blemished and ungainly, and stares down at his basset hound, which sniffs the sidewalk. Oliver and the dog pass right by — her own publisher seems not to have the faintest idea who she is.

"Hello?" she says indignantly as he walks past her. She turns: "Am I invisible? Do you not see me?" He looks back. "Fuckin' asshole!" she shouts and storms away. "Good for you," she tells herself, continuing down Corso Vittorio, past her bus stop. "Good for you! Screw him!" Those weasels will use this to fire her now. "Fucking pricks. Hope they do fire me." Kathleen would love it — love to see Ruby gone. Almost worth staying just to spite her. "*Almost* worth it." Kathleen. "Bitch."

Ruby and Kathleen joined the paper in

272

the same crop of interns in 1987. Ruby arrived a week earlier, so was able to show the younger girl the premises, pointing out all the editors, presenting her around — even introducing her to the good-looking Italian intern, Dario de Monterecchi, whom Ruby had a crush on. Within three months, the editor-in-chief, Milton Berber, had hired Kathleen as a news assistant while he'd not even spoken a word to Ruby. And within ten months, Kathleen and Dario had moved in together. Over the following years, Kathleen became a hotshot reporter at the paper, a star, moving up the ranks, and finally jumping to a big-shot newspaper in Washington. Now, years later, Kathleen has returned triumphant, the boss, while Ruby — who never left, who was loyal — is a piece of dirt. "Which is exactly how they treat me." Kathleen included. "Cow." If these idiots won't fire Ruby for swearing at the publisher, she'll walk in and quit on New Year's Day. That'll be sweet. Get out of this lousy country. "Home, finally."

She takes a seat on the bus home. The irony is that she's actually good at her job. "Not that they give a shit."

The bus halts to allow New Year's tourists to flood across the intersection, then continues over the bridge toward St. Peter's, whose cupola is lit purple-yellow. As they drive past, she cranes her neck to keep the basilica in view until the last possible moment. Then it is gone.

She lives in a modern building that overlooks the Porta Portese flea market and the dog pound. The barking never ceases, so she keeps her windows closed at all times. When she was new to Rome, friends from America used to come stay with her. But each visit proved tense. It's the design of this place, like a New York railroad apartment, every room feeding into the next. These days, it's strewn with dirty clothing — tangled bustiers, oversize T-shirts, banana hair clips. The kitchen is as jumbled, with torn muffin papers, empty milk bottles, used aluminum sheets, shopping bags. No outsider has visited for years, so what's the point in tidying?

She changes into her Fordham sweatshirt, opens the refrigerator, and yawns into its white light. She cracks a Heineken and drinks it before the open fridge, her mind emptying with the can. The sharp corners of her day go smooth.

She scans the fridge: a jar of black olives, no-name ketchup, cheese slices. To eat or to sleep — the perennial night-shift conundrum. She confronts her dilemma as always, with a tub of Häagen-Dazs on the couch and Tony Bennett on the stereo, volume low. The CD came free with a magazine and has become part of her after-work routine. She has the TV on, too, with the sound off. She watches *Ballando con le Stelle* without seeing, listens to Tony Bennett without hearing, eats Vanilla Swiss Almond without tasting. Yet the mix is the most splendid she knows.

Next up, the silenced television has a documentary on the deposed Italian royal family. She changes to a news show, which is running clips of Saddam's career, from Halabja to Kuwait to the gallows. She switches back to the royals.

Explosions go off down the street: adolescents testing fireworks for tomorrow. Her feet rest on the coffee table, beside a pile of family photos she brought back from New York after her father's funeral. She drapes the edge of a blanket over the pictures to hide them from view.

She shuts her eyes, shakes her head. "Vicious place." That office. "Let them fire me." They'll do it by email: Ruby, we want to talk to you. "Performance review." Administrative probation. Fired for shouting at that idiot man-child Oliver Ott. Back to Queens. "What a relief that'd be." Seriously.

"No reason to stay here." Dario? "He's not a reason."

By 2 A.M., she is drunk. She opens her cellphone, smiling at Dario's name on the list of contacts. She'll invite him over, right now. Why not? She dials him, boozy, brassy.

He doesn't answer.

She closes the phone, wobbles over to the medicine chest. From a toilet bag, she retrieves a bottle of men's cologne, Drakkar Noir. She dabs it on her hands, breathes in, breathes out, eyes closed. She touches her palms lightly together, runs her fingers down her cheeks, around her throat, until she smells Dario all around.

A pebble of melting Häagen-Dazs remains in the container. She slurps it and cracks the last beer, drifting off in front of the TV.

The next morning, a grinding noise wakes her. A high-pitched drilling follows. Then hammer against stone. Construction? On New Year's Eve? "Must be illegal." Not that it matters here. Fucking Italians. She hides under the blanket but can't sleep. In the bathroom, she laps water from the open tap. Noise judders the apartment. She blinks murderously between the blinds at the workmen shouting over a blasting radio.

She locates a plastic bag she has been saving for an opportunity like this, teases apart the knot, and recoils at the smell. She takes out a rotten tomato, a rotten egg, and a rotten orange and opens the window. With deliberation, she aims and tosses the egg, then ducks. No one howls — she has missed. Next, the orange. Still no bull's-eye. She hurls the tomato and it lands perfectly, splattering seeds and fetid pulp. She hides under her window ledge. The workmen curse for a minute, hunting around for their attacker. They turn off their radio.

"Victory," she says.

Then the radio comes back on, they are as loud as before, and she is wide awake.

She sits on the toilet. "What kind of people are these?"

The hissing shower fills the bathroom with steam. She strips, disheartened at the sight of her naked body. "It's like I'm melting." She scrubs herself roughly under the spray, then drips sullenly around the bathroom.

She takes the bus to Piazza del Popolo and walks to the Metropolitan cinema, which is showing the latest James Bond movie, *Casino Royale.* She studies the poster outside. Is it worse to watch a movie alone in a packed theater or alone in an empty one? What if there's someone she knows? Someone from work? She recalls her tantrum at Oliver Ott. Should she go into the office and check her emails? He will have complained to Kathleen. This'll be it. They'll fire her. Imagine all she can do once freed from the paper. Only, she cannot imagine anything — she has hated this job for years, yet blanks at a future outside that newsroom.

She glances around. What if Dario saw her in front of this cinema, alone on New Year's Eve? What if he's strolling along Via del Corso with his family right now? She escapes down Via di Ripetta, cuts down side streets, emerging finally at Piazza San Salvatore in Lauro. The winter sun reaches down here, its warmth spread across the piazza like a tablecloth. She shades her brow. Traffic whooshes along Lungotevere. Pedestrians pass, quietly, respectfully. She admires the broad-shouldered church there — it looks as if it had kicked aside all those grimy cars crowding its steps. A simple crucifix hangs above the pediment, archangels under the frieze, stone columns framing the sturdy wooden door.

She walks peaceably away, gliding within tranquil thoughts, watching her shoes emerge one after the other beneath her. She crosses the Tiber and merges with the crowd entering St. Peter's. The square's curled colonnades embrace the pilgrims, the colossal basilica looms behind, a stone obelisk points to the clouds. However, the center of attention today is the Christmas tree and the Nativity scene, including a flailing baby Jesus picked out by spotlight. The throng pushes closer to the crèche, and Ruby moves, too, studying not the tableau but the surging crowd itself: dads panning camcorders across the manger, nuns contemplating the Three Wise Men, teenagers whispering rude jokes about donkeys in biblical times. As everyone else angles for a clear view, Ruby closes her eyes and leans into them, brushing strangers' hands — not for long, not so anyone would notice, but in glancing strokes.

Once home, she takes out her overnight bag, which she packed days ago, and places it by the front door. It's still too early to go to the hotel. She looks around for distraction and grabs the remote control and the blanket, inadvertently baring the family photos from New York: images of Pap, Kurt, herself. She collects them in her lap, reverse sides up.

Work crosses her mind. Dave Belling. "Such a phony," she mutters. His down-home, Southern-boy country bullshit. Her jaw tenses. Clint Oakley. "Fucking asshole." Those guys will love it when she gets fired.

"And I'll be over the goddamn moon."
Never set foot in that dump again.

She turns over the photos. The one on top is of Kurt, her brother, older by a year. He gave her the photos at Pap's funeral. "We should share them," Ruby told him at the time.

"It's okay."

"Keep *some* at least."

He said that Pap, during the last seventy-two hours, had shouted a lot.

"Saying what?"

"That he didn't want to die. Made a scene at the hospital."

"I wish you didn't tell me that, Kurt."

"But there was no point, really."

"What in?"

"In you coming back before he died."

Indeed, Ruby hadn't returned from Italy while Pap was ill — she'd been waiting for a plea. She wanted Pap to express remorse. During the last days, Ruby kept phoning Kurt, hoping to hear Pap wasn't dead, hoping to hear he was. The funeral was at St. Mary Star of the Sea Cemetery, off the Rockaway Turnpike. It was July and hot, and Ruby was afraid everyone would notice how much she sweated. Instead, everyone hugged her: cousins and nephews and kids. She was the daughter of the deceased. Kurt sat next to her, and he squeezed her hand for a few seconds during the service.

She had four days in Queens after that. Kurt took time off work and drove her around. They ate at the Astoria diner, as they had as kids, when they used to order fries and gravy and squirt on heaps of ketchup and vinegar, creating a mouth-puckering slop. As adults, they could order whatever they liked. So they ordered fries and gravy.

The whole family wanted to see her, sought her opinions and advice. "Aunt Ruby, tell Bill, the so-called great chef, what *real* Italian food is like." And: "Rube, have a word with Kelly about backpacking around Europe. I don't trust this kid she's going with."

Ruby kept hugging everyone. She stroked the little ones' chins, sat them on her knee, heard stories confided in whispers, warm on her ear. Everyone thought she was so smart and cosmopolitan. It made her scared to ever move home to Queens — if she did, they'd figure her out, see what a lie all this was, how ordinary she was.

During that trip, she spent her last day buying thank-you presents for everyone. Her gifts were acts not simply of generosity but of attention — she had listened to them all. For Kurt, it was the dashboard Global Positioning System, the only model that fit his Toyota truck; for Kelly, it was a long-coveted white Nikon Coolpix II, plus a money belt to be safe in Europe; and all the little nieces and nephews got the right video games and books and DVDs. The kids didn't want her to leave, and the adults asked when she was moving home to New York.

On the plane back to Rome, she resolved to digitize the old photos Kurt had given her and email him copies — someone in the photo department at work could show her how. She prepared an email message in her head: "Big brother, even though you don't want these now, maybe you will later. And you'll thank me! The kids will appreciate them maybe. All my love, Rube. P.S. Write back when you get this."

While Pap's funeral in New York had inflated her, the office punctured that soon enough. She returned to an avalanche of emails from the culture department (still run by Clint Oakley back then) over an edit she'd done before leaving. Clint had copied in Kathleen on all the complaints, to humiliate Ruby. Couldn't he have handled it privately, like a decent human being? Misery at work bled into her sleeping hours — she

282

woke in the dark from anger. Pap haunted her, too, in images Ruby hadn't seen in years: Pap opening the closet to show her the cup where he kept human teeth; Pap heating a spoon on the stovetop; Pap telling the priest, "Look, my girl is sprouting."

The family photos in Ruby's lap make her want to wash her hands. It has been almost six months since she left New York, and she still hasn't had them digitized.

"Can't Kurt even call?" How hard can it be? She doesn't want to nag him. But it's like he doesn't care about sticking together, wouldn't care if they vanished from each other's lives. Says he doesn't like travel. But he took his wife to London. "Could have told me." She could have met them there.

Fireworks explode outside, though it's hours before midnight. She hides the photos on a kitchen shelf. She scrubs her hands with pumice till they are raw.

The taxi drops her in front of the Nettuno, a three-star hotel just outside the Vatican walls, whose peach façade has been hidden under scaffolding for years, the owners having run out of money and ambition halfway through a blast-cleaning in 1999.

Another firecracker bangs, and she jumps with fright.

The receptionist greets her in Italian, but

she responds in English and hands him her American passport. "Hate flying during the holidays," she says. "Hate being away from my kids. But the bosses didn't want to reschedule the meeting. Which I didn't buy."

He takes a credit-card imprint.

"That's my personal card, not the company one," she tells him. "It's so I get the air miles."

He nods without interest.

She never stays at home on New Year's Eve. Every December 31, she becomes an American businesswoman stuck overseas during the holiday; each year, it's a different hotel.

The window of her room overlooks air-conditioning ducts, which suits her — less street noise. She drops her coat on the bed, takes a Peroni from the minibar, and flicks on the TV to check the pay-per-view. She watches a few minutes of a pornographic film, not aroused but dispirited. She changes to a music-video station but can't shake the feeling of pollution. "Who does that appeal to?" She fetches a Kit Kat from the minibar. "It's —" She takes a bite and stands before the mirror. "It's discouraging." She gets another beer and a packet of peanuts. "You know?" Next, she drinks a minibottle of Johnnie Walker Red, swirling it with mashed pretzels in her mouth. "No?" She has the mini of Absolut next, blended with a can of orange juice.

The guys at work are gonna celebrate when she gets fired. "And I'll be popping the champagne." She twists the cap off a half bottle of Calabrian red and rips into a packet of chocolate wafers. The combination is infelicitous, but she's too drunk to care. On the TV, Totò is impersonating a doctor. The minibar is empty. She closes her eyes, yanks the covers up. She is asleep.

A thunder of blasts — she jumps up, breathless. After a terrible instant, she orients herself: the hotel. Television, on. Outside, fireworks. She checks her watch. It's a few minutes before midnight. The paper is going to fire her.

She goes out into the hall to watch the explosions from a window that gives onto the street. The sky sparkles. The bangs are ceaseless. All around the city, choruses rise:

"Sei!"

"Cinque!"

"Quattro!"

"Tre!"

"Due!"

"UNO!"

On a rooftop across the street, teenagers scream — no one can stop them tonight.

From the roof's edge, they fling champagne flutes, which tinkle in the gutter. A distant ambulance siren whines. A man in a trench coat hurries down the sidewalk, studying the screen of his cellphone. Smoke from the fireworks rises up the street lamps like phantoms.

She knows the minibar is empty but checks it again. She tries to sleep. The noises peter out, but she can't drift off. She's wide awake. They're definitely going to fire her. Fan-fucking-tastic.

Herman Cohen said, "One more mess-up, Ruby, and it's curtains." They're looking to cut staff. Everybody knows who's next. The question is when they're going to do it.

She looks at her cellphone. She could call Kurt in Queens and wish him Happy New Year. But then he'd ask what she was doing, what sort of party she'd gone to.

From her toilet bag she fetches the Drakkar Noir, drips it on her hands, rubs it on her cheeks. She closes her eyes and inhales. It was months earlier that she bumped into Dario on Via dell'Umiltà; it had been years since they'd seen each other. He laughed that she still remembered him using Drakkar Noir. "Haven't used that in ages," he said.

She opens her mobile and brings up his number. She doesn't dial, but holds the phone to her ear. "Hello," she says to the dead air. "May I please speak with Dario? Hi, Dario, it's me. If you want to drop by, you're totally welcome." My hotel is nice. Seriously, I don't want to cause trouble. But I enjoyed getting that drink with you. "What about if you were to drop by? Just for a few minutes?" I'm pretty tired anyhow.

She calls him using the hotel phone so he won't recognize the number.

He answers. *"Pronto?"*

She doesn't respond.

"Pronto?" he repeats. *"Chi è? . . . Pronto?"* He pauses. *"Non rispondi?"* He hangs up.

She calls back.

"Chi è?" he says. *"Che vuoi?"*

"Don't scream at me," she replies in English. "It's Ruby."

He sighs. "It's the middle of the night. It's New Year's. Why are you calling me?"

She's silent.

"Fifty calls from you in the last few weeks, Ruby. Fifty."

"I'm sorry."

"Why are you calling me?"

"It's just."

"Answer me."

"Sorry."

"Stop saying 'sorry.' Answer my question. This is getting ridiculous. Fifty times. Do you have something to say?"

She can't speak.

"Ruby, I'm married. I'm not interested in finding someone. I don't want anything with you. I don't want to hear from you, I don't want to see you. I don't want to have another drink with you. I don't want you to call this number again. Please."

"Dario."

"If you call me again, I'll have to —"

But she hangs up.

She finds a nail file in her toilet bag and digs it into her thigh until she breaks the skin. She widens the wound, then stanches the blood with toilet paper and washes her hands under scalding water.

The maids wake her the next morning.

"Not yet," she mumbles, then falls back to sleep.

Front desk calls. It's past noon. She's late for checkout.

She smells Dario's cologne on her still. As she pulls on her trousers, they catch on the gash on her thigh. No time for a shower. She stuffs her possessions back into her overnight bag, looks in the mirror, tries to bring her hair to life. "My last day at the paper." It's New Year's Day; her shift starts

288

at 2 P.M. "Today is the day." This is when they fire her.

She rolls her overnight bag down the street. She could go home and shower, but instead she walks toward St. Peter's Square. The pope's Angelus speech is over, and the crowd is dispersing. She passes through tides of people, yellow Vatican kerchiefs around their necks. The basilica stands there like a throne, with humankind at its feet. She is ordered out of one vacation photo after another. "Sorry, would you mind just?" they ask. She shifts aside. "Excuse me, you're in mine now."

She is hoping that a romantic couple will ask her to take their picture. She loves that — being, for a moment, admitted into their union. But no one asks. Two young Mexicans even prefer to take the photo themselves, the man extending his disposable Kodak before himself and his new wife. He counts down and, as he reaches zero, Ruby — who stands a distance behind them — sticks her hand into the background of their shot. The camera flashes, she drops her hand, no one is the wiser. When they get home, she'll be there forever.

When she reaches the newsroom, it is empty except for Menzies. She switches on her computer, not even bothering to disinfect her workspace. They will have fired her via email. And someone has stolen her chair. Typical. She scans the room. Does this guy ever leave?

"Oh, sorry," Menzies says, jumping up as she approaches. "I'm in your chair. Here, please. Someone took mine and I thought you weren't here today. I know that's a lame excuse. It is amazingly comfortable, by the way."

"You can request one if you want. Only took me about six years."

"Here." He pushes her chair over. "We both got stuck with the crappy shift, huh."

"What's your job today?"

"I'm actually running the show. Gulp. Get ready for a bumpy ride. Kathleen and Herman both have the day off, so it's just me. I'm sort of sweating bullets," he says. "Incidentally, I have something for you that's going to redeem me on the chair theft." He rummages through his backpack and pulls out a CD. "I've been lugging this back and forth to work for days now. Keep forgetting to give it to you. Remember we were talking that time about Tony Bennett versus Frank Sinatra? I think this may settle the matter. *Live at the Sands.* You will be converted to Frank."

"Hey, thanks. When do you need it back?"

"That's for you to keep."

She touches her chest with surprise.

"You have to tell me what you think of it," he says, talking fast, unnerved by her emotion. "Some of Sinatra's lead-ins to the songs are great. I think you're gonna love it."

"That is so thoughtful of you."

"It's just a copied CD, Rube! No big deal, seriously."

Awkwardly, she hugs him.

"No problem," he says, pulling away. "No problem. By the way, did you get that email I sent you?"

"What email? Is something the matter?"

"Not at all. It's about that headline on the nuclear-arms story. You did that head, right?"

"About how everyone's freaked out over Iran and North Korea? Did I fuck it up?"

"Not at all — your headline was great: 'Kooks with Nukes.' I suck at those one-column heads."

Clearly, he doesn't know they're firing her. He must be out of the loop.

She rolls her chair back to the copydesk and looks around the newsroom. Broken venetian blinds cover the newsroom windows, the strings tangled half up, half down, casting broken grids of shadow and sunlight across the grouchy old computers, their cooling fans grumbling away. Twenty years here. "My whole career."

Her computer takes forever to load up. "Come on." She is about to lose this job. "Thank God." Almost time to celebrate.

Her computer has stopped whirring; it's ready. She can picture the email. It'll say: "Ruby, please call me at home. It's about a very serious matter. Thank you." Who will have sent it? Kathleen? Or Herman? Or Accounts Payable?

Ruby logs on. All the routine emails are there: a festive edition of the *Why?* newsletter; something about turning off the lights in the bathrooms to save money; a reminder of how much it costs per minute to be late for deadline. But her dismissal?

She checks again.

Where the hell is it?

She keeps refreshing her in-box. She can't find it. It isn't there: no email. But there must be one.

No, there simply isn't.

She rises, sits back down, then stands once more and hurries into the ladies' room. She closes herself in a stall, sits on the toilet, covering her mouth.

Her breathing increases, her insides seem to swell. A tear runs down her face, slides ticklishly under her chin. Him — that's Dario's smell. The cologne from the night before. She never washed it off, and her tears have activated the scent.

She takes out her cellphone. Swallowing, wiping her nose, she brings up his number. She reads his name aloud. She dangles the phone between her thighs and lets it fall into the toilet. It splashes and bobs in the water.

She claps her hands once.

"I get to stay," she says.

She wipes her eyes. She can't stop smiling.

"I get to stay."

1975. Ott Group Headquarters, Atlanta

Frantic calls poured in from the paper in Rome: yet another caretaker editor had quit and no one was in charge anymore. After years of neglect, Boyd had to take action.

His previous trip to the paper had been when he was still an undergraduate at Yale. Then, he'd stayed at a hotel in Rome because he lacked the stomach to visit his father's empty mansion. This time, Boyd was braver.

But from the moment he entered he fell into a dark mood. He snaked his finger along a picture frame, leaving a winding path in the dust. What are all these paintings for? A woman with a ridiculously long neck. Wine bottles and hats. A chicken in midair. A shipwreck. These things must have come with the place — Ott would never have wasted money on ornaments. Boyd called in the housekeepers and, not bothering to greet them, ordered that the mansion be scrubbed, top to bottom. "Also," he told them, "cover these paintings."

He opened the shutters. His father would have looked out from here, through the spiked fence, down the lonely lane. To think that Ott had acquired this spectacular house — not to mention the rest of the family fortune — from nothing. It was astonishing; it was humbling.

Boyd considered the living room, its soaring rococo ceiling, the worn Oriental rugs, the bookshelves, the old telephone on the wall. How grand it had been when his father marched across this room! Boyd could picture Ott striding over the carpets, up the stairs. Boyd always imagined his father like this — in perpetual motion. He could never conjure the man sitting still. Indeed, he had no sense of Ott simply living here, month after month, for years in the end.

Why had Ott stayed here so long? This place hadn't been his home. That had been in Atlanta. But buildings adjusted to Ott, not the other way around. He had deemed that the world needed the paper. So he damn well set about inventing it. He never sat still. That was how the great man had been.

Thinking of the paper's current state, Boyd went rigid with anger and shame. It was an affront to his father's memory, and Boyd himself was responsible.

The next morning, he met with all the section editors and asked them to hold tight — a new editor-in-chief was on the way. When Boyd returned to Atlanta, he employed a headhunting firm to poach a star from a top American newspaper. Someone young, bright, with spark. He got two out of three.

Milton Berber was hardly in the first bloom of youth. He'd already had a long journalistic career at a Washington paper, starting after

295

military service in World War II. He'd reported on district court, got a break covering the State Department, became deputy metro editor, then deputy national editor, then deputy assistant managing editor. But by 1975 he had to admit it: he wasn't going any higher.

This annoyed him, since he believed he'd make a fine boss. But no one had ever given him a chance, not when he was driving a jeep around Naples for the U.S. Army, nor as an editor in Washington. True, it was not exactly a dream come true to work at a second-tier international newspaper. But at least he'd be running the place.

Boyd flew out to Rome with Milton to introduce the man around. After meeting the downtrodden staff and grasping the paper's mood, Milton had doubts. But Boyd — not the most charming man, perhaps — did seem intent on turning the paper around. So Milton said yes.

He gathered the staff and told them, "Newspapers are like anything else: they're pure and incorruptible and noble — as far as they can afford to be. Starve them and they'll kneel in the muck with the rest of the bums. Rich papers can afford to be upstanding and, if you like, self-important. We don't have that luxury right now."

"So you're saying we have to kneel in

muck?" a reporter asked.

"My point is the opposite. We need to start making money here. People don't read us at the moment. We're writing stories we think we should write, but not what people actually want to read."

"Hey," an editor objected, "we know what our readers want."

"Look, I don't intend to ruffle feathers here," Milton proceeded. "I only want to be straight with you. And this is how I see the situation. The paper started out as a pamphlet."

Boyd bristled at this, interrupting to say, "It has always been more than that."

"Broad strokes, I'm using broad strokes here. Bear with me."

The staff wondered if they were witnessing a fiasco. This was Milton's first public encounter with the owner and the employees, and he was on the verge of alienating both. "Withhold your judgment," he said. "I'm going to say some lousy things. Awful things. You ready? Here goes. This publication started out as a cute pamphlet — please don't fire me on my first day, Boyd!"

Everyone laughed.

"The paper started as a terrific idea," Milton went on. "But somehow it has ended up as blotting paper. That's what it is now. That's not meant as a slight against anyone here. It certainly isn't a slight against the institution itself. I'm saying it's time to make this paper into a real paper. The way we do this is with two ingredients — the same two you need for any success: brains and hard work. I want to quit the wishy-washy approach. We don't have to match the big newspapers all the time. And we don't have to be renegades just for the sake of it. I want serious stories that are our own, on the one hand, and entertaining trifles, on the other. All the rest we run in the briefs column. And I want laughs. We're too scared of humor — so reverent all the time. Bullshit! Entertainment, folks! Look how the Brits do it. They print pretty girls, offer weekends in Brighton. And they sell a hell of a lot more copies than we do. Now, I'm not saying we turn this into a red top or a big top, let alone force anyone to go to Brighton. Heaven forbid. But we've got to acknowledge that we're entertainers of a sort. That doesn't mean phony. Doesn't mean vulgar. It means readable in the best way — so people wake up wanting us before their coffee. If we're so reverent about public service that nobody reads us, we're not doing the public any service at all. We're going to raise circulation, and make money doing it."

The staffers were right to applaud with circumspection. Milton's remarks did not bode well for everyone, particularly those who had always relied on brains and hard work *not* being requirements of the job. Boyd, for his part, was tempted to fire Milton immediately. But he knew how badly it would reflect on him. He'd chosen the man, had flown all the way over here. He would give him a year, then fire him.

Milton stood among his staff, shaking hands, memorizing names. He already knew them in a way — he understood this breed backward and had foreseen how his speech would be received. Journalists were as touchy as cabaret performers and as stubborn as factory machinists. He couldn't help smiling.

■ ■ ■ ■

"76 Die in Baghdad Bombings"

· · ·

NEWS EDITOR — CRAIG MENZIES

■ ■ ■ ■

Annika crouches before the washing machine in their apartment, unloading damp clothes. "I'm beginning to suspect that my purpose in life is laundry," she says. "All the rest is just fleeting glory."

Menzies stands behind her and touches his forefinger to the crown of her head, following the swirl of her dyed-black hair. He opens his palm across the top of her skull as if to measure it, then hooks his thumbs under the straps of her dungarees and tugs. She leans against his palm and kisses his fingers, looking up. "Seven hundred and twenty-eight socks last year," she tells him. "That's how many I washed."

"You counted?"

"Of course." She reaches into the washing machine and draws out a bedsheet that seems never to end.

He kneels beside her, hugs her around the middle. "I have the day off," he says. "Let me do something."

He gets few days off from the paper. Normally, he starts his labors at 6 A.M., logging on from home to see what has happened overnight in the United States and what is happening at that moment in Asia. He scans the websites of competing news organizations and responds to emails, typing softly so as not to wake her in the other room. By seven, he is at the bus stop on Via Marmorata, urging the No. 30 to hurry up. He's first in the office and turns on the lights: throughout the newsroom, fluorescent beams flicker on like reluctant morning eyes. He places a thermos of American coffee on his desk, turns on the TV, checks CNN and the BBC, consults the news wires, compiles a list of stories to assign. Other employees arrive: secretaries, technicians, editors, reporters. By nine, he is consulting with staff correspondents and the few stringers they have left overseas. Then Kathleen shows up, demanding a rundown of the world at that moment. She never appears to pay attention, yet absorbs it all. "Quiet day," she says. "Let's hope something happens." He shepherds the main stories through their various stages: writing, backfielding, copyediting. He consults with layout, sizes up ad space, requests photos and orders graphics — all through a blizzard of phone calls. Colleagues pester him to take a break, not because they care but to underscore that he's a sucker to toil like this. When the late edition closes, everyone else goes home and he puts the newsroom to bed: the fluorescent beams flicker back to sleep. On the bus ride home to Testaccio, he is assaulted by headlines that stream across his mind like a news ticker: "Iran test-fires 3 new missiles . . . 90% of maritime life forms extinct by 2048 . . . Evangelical leader resigns over gay hooker scandal." He takes the elevator upstairs. The news ticker continues: "Keys in right pocket, officials say . . . Unlock deadbolt, sources suggest . . . Call Annika's name, report recommends." He does so, and she arrives to kiss him on the lips. She shuttles him into the kitchen, has him tasting bubbling sauces, hearing about her day. All that mattered a minute before no longer does. The news stops.

Annika's day runs to a different schedule. She rises at ten, drains a glass of grapefruit juice over the sink, eats jam toast on the terrace, crumbs floating down to the sidewalk as she watches the neighborhood below: the bank security guard who is always on his cellphone, schoolboys kicking soccer balls, little old ladies tromping to and from the covered market. She stretches her arms above her head, emits a little squeak, licks her jam-sticky fingers. She showers with the bathroom door open, lets her hair dry while reading emails, browses the Internet, sends messages to Menzies. By 1 P.M., she emerges into the sun for a stroll up Lungotevere, along the sidewalk that overlooks the Tiber. She follows the river's snaking path from Testaccio toward the Centro Storico. The bottle-green water eddies in parts, is still in others. As with much in Rome, the river has been left to its own devices, a strip of jungle winding through the caterwauling city. Weeds clamber down the riverbanks, clasping at bogwater, snagging what litter washes downstream: plastic bottles, furniture flyers, shoeboxes, a thousand bobbing cigarette filters. The sidewalk has been abandoned, too, left to the tree roots, which seam the pavement, cracking it upward into concrete lips. Back home, she deposits her groceries on the kitchen table and flings open the shutters. Light slices across the parquet, up the white walls. She stuffs in another load of laundry, sets the dial, sits down with a book. She is trying to improve her Italian by reading short stories — Natalia Ginzburg and Alberto Moravia of late. She lunches late — 3 P.M., typically — in order to contain her appetite till his nighttime return. She watches a little idiotic Italian TV, irons, washes dishes, hangs laundry, preps dinner. By the time he arrives, she is famished and she bundles him into the kitchen. She never inquires about the day's news — news is only disappointing, and there is nothing she can do about it. After dinner, Menzies falls into bed while she watches old movies with headphones, eating homemade yogurt sweetened with rhubarb compote. When friends ask her about life in Rome, she says, "It's fine, it's good," then is out of words. She does not admit that the apartment is magnificent, the neighborhood ideal, and Menzies an endearing mess. She does not speak of the pleasure she takes in tidying him, nor that she hasn't snapped a single photo in earnest since coming to Rome, that she has no desire to, that she doesn't care about grants or galleries anymore, if indeed she ever did. Above all, she will not admit that she is happy.

"I just don't want you to get bored," he says.

"I'm not." She puts on music: Dinah Washington singing "What a Diff'rence a Day Makes." Menzies was clueless about jazz before meeting her, but she has been educating him, introducing him to Ella Fitzgerald, Nina Simone, Frank Sinatra.

"You're amazingly self-sustained," he says. "I'm just afraid you'll get sick of me. Of my socks in particular."

"There is that possibility. As long as nobody sees me cooking you dinner every night, I'm fine."

At least this life takes place overseas. She can point out that she's learning another language and that Rome is such an artistic city and that living here is itself an aesthetic education. When she does return to photography, this experience will have had a salutary effect. If she were tending house like this back in D.C. — well, she simply wouldn't. But living overseas changes the rules. As long as no one sees her. She discourages visits from friends and family, and flies home twice a year to avert them. If her mother saw this! After all those efforts to instill the importance of financial independence and a career. Or if Annika's art-school friends saw her Nikon sitting there, its case gray with dust, as her cookbook collection mounts — the domesticated horror of it! He gets the career, he gets the prestige. She? She gets to clean socks. And if anything goes wrong he has a bank account. And she?

How will she explain this gap on her résumé? How will she explain her contentment at living like a housewife?

Menzies' colleagues know little about his life with Annika. For a time, she was friendly with Hardy Benjamin and the two met for coffee most afternoons at the espresso bar downstairs from the office. But Hardy got a boyfriend, and her friendship with Annika faded. As for the others at the paper, they tend to forget that Menzies lives with someone — if they were to imagine him outside office hours, they would picture him alone, eating thin sandwiches, reading the ingredients off the bread package. For them, he exists less as a man than as a wrinkle-headed prig in a desk chair.

An office party approaches, and he considers not telling Annika. If she sees him among his colleagues, she'll gather what they think of him. "It'll just be dull news people, I warn you."

"Do you want me there?"

"I don't want *me* there."

"Maybe you need backup. Unless you don't want me to come."

"You're welcome anywhere I go."

"What should I tell them that I do out here?"

"No one'll ask that sort of thing."

"But if they do?"

As they enter the newsroom, he releases her hand, then wishes he still held it. He sees in the glances of his colleagues a thirst to know what connection he could possibly have with this much younger woman: she, in a purple frock and green-and-black striped tights, a smile so spontaneous it seems almost to surprise her; and he, in a blue oxford shirt and brown corduroys, pudgy despite the weekend sit-ups, a horse-shoe of chestnut hair around a bald dome that glistens when he is agitated, and glistens often.

Hardy catches sight of them, waves a little too exuberantly, and comes over. She and Annika chat for a few minutes and agree to sign up for yoga classes together, though both know the pledge is hollow. "Well," Hardy says, "I should probably go save my man." Her boyfriend, Rory, was last spotted with a bottle of wine in hand, trying to engage a frowning Herman in a debate on the factual accuracy of the James Bond series. Hardy trots off to the rescue.

Other staffers approach Menzies, their gazes shifting between their dreary news editor and this curvaceous young woman. "So, Menzies my man, you going to introduce us?"

Once home, he tells her, "You were very" — he pauses — "very popular with everyone."

She smiles. "Popular? What is this, ninth grade?"

"I know, it sounds ridiculous. I'm saying it in a good way, though — I'm impressed."

She kisses his eyelids and gooses his behind.

He wakes early the next morning and lies a few extra minutes in bed, alive to the softness of her back, the scent of her hair. She feels unreal: the tide of her breathing against him in the dark.

He walks to work and hesitates at a boutique window. That turquoise bracelet? What about those earrings? Are they part of a set? He can't assess jewelry, can't tell if it's pretty, if she'd like it. He needs her opinion, but that defeats the purpose. He checks the opening hours. Perhaps he can sneak back between editions. Does she need earrings? Is "need" the point? What is the point? To make a point. Which is? He doesn't know, only that there is one. He's always catching her hand, then letting it go. His every effort to make his point flops. He'll buy those earrings. But the shop is closed.

At dinner, she chats about the office party, comments on his colleagues. "Herman's adorable," she says.

"That is not the word I would have chosen."

"He's sweet," she insists. "And so insecure."

"Herman is? Herman Cohen?"

"And it was interesting talking to Kathleen. She loves you."

"Kathleen loves that I do all her work."

"She clearly has a lot of respect for you."

"Really?"

"All those interns are *so* young. Made me feel ancient. Actually, I already feel ancient."

"If you're ancient, you must think I'm prehistoric."

"Not at all — it's only age in *myself* that seems old."

"Twenty-seven is not old."

"Depends what you've done. My sister says everyone who's gonna make it is already on their way by thirty."

"That's not true; it's just the sort of thing your sister says. Anyway, you've still got three years — then we'll talk about what a failure you are. Okay? And, for the record, I hadn't achieved anything by age thirty."

"What were you doing then?"

"I was in Washington, I think. Working on the copydesk there."

"So you had made it."

"I'd hardly call that making it."

"But you had a career, a professional skill. Not something pointless like taking artsy pictures, which any loser with a digital camera and Photoshop can do nowadays," she says. "All the hours I spent in dark-rooms, inhaling fixer fumes, fiddling with stop baths and plastic trays and tongs! What a waste."

"Nothing's a waste."

"Some things are. Like, let's face it, I'm not exactly taking advantage of my time here. I'm still not even fluent in Italian. And even though I live with a hard-core news-hound, I don't know the first thing about what's going on in the world."

"Yes, you do."

"Maybe I should start reading the paper. Everybody at the party was so authoritative about stuff."

"About what stuff?"

"I don't know — parliamentary voting procedures and arms races in South Asia and U.N. tribunals in Cambodia. Then they turned to me and I'm, like, 'Hi, I used to work as a photographer's assistant, but now I hang out at Craig's place.'"

"Our place," he corrects her. "If anything, your place. And my colleagues are forced to know that stuff — it's their job."

313

"Well, exactly. I don't *have* to know anything."

"You want to restart the job hunt? I can put out feelers again."

"Do you think I should?"

"Well, you don't *need* to." This seems not to be the correct response. "But there's no harm in looking. Again, I'm happy to help. Just tell me what you'd like. Or did you want to get back into photography?"

"I don't know."

"What were you talking to Hardy about at the party — yoga classes, right? Would that be fun? I'm not saying it's the answer. I just don't want you to get sick of me, stuck in the apartment, washing socks."

Her birthday arrives and he gives her the turquoise bracelet and earrings, along with a subscription to an Italian photography magazine and a set of yoga classes.

She immediately makes friends in the class. They are all locals, artistic types who smoke too much, paint their bedrooms orange, and smell of damp wool. She is particularly sympathetic to a clumsy kid called Paolo. "I've never seen anyone more uncoordinated than this guy," she says. "Poor Paolo — can't even touch his toes. Totally incapable."

"Can *I* touch my toes?" Menzies attempts

it. He groans, straining for his shoe tips.

Annika leaps up and hugs him.

"Thank you," he says, laughing. "What's that for?"

Her yoga friends urge her to bring in her portfolio to show around. But when she considers her old photos she is ashamed; they'll think she's an amateur. So she embarks on a new series. Her subject is the graffiti blighting historical buildings around Rome. They love the pictures and urge her to exhibit them.

With Annika out shooting or with her yoga friends, Menzies often returns to an empty apartment. Oddly, the place seems louder without her: motor scooters buzzing outside, footfalls pounding across the apartment overhead, the wall clock ticking. He prepares a sandwich for dinner and descends to his basement workshop, a room he rents to conduct science projects, his hobby since boyhood. He fiddles with balsawood models, browses back issues of science-and-technology magazines, and he daydreams. It is always the same daydream: about earning a patent.

If only he'd studied sciences at college! Then again, he'd not have ended up in D.C. and not have met her. He *could* still invent something, of course. A creation so remarkable it would force MIT to admit him. He'd earn his doctorate in record time. And he'd have Annika with him. If she wanted to come. But would she? Here in Rome, he has something to offer her: a desirable place to live, the romance of Europe. If all he had was student housing in Boston and debts . . . ? But these are absurd thoughts. He's not an inventor, he doesn't have the qualifications, and he's far too old to obtain them now. He has a different life, a newsman's life, like it or not.

She's knocking at the door that leads down to his basement workshop. "I'm coming up now," he calls out. He finds her on the landing, leaning against the wall, wincing. She has done something to her back and must skip yoga for a while.

Over the next few weeks, she hangs around the apartment, drinking herbal tea, watching Italian variety shows. She is crotchety with him, then apologizes. Once healed, she resumes her photography project on graffiti but does not return to yoga.

One afternoon at the office, Menzies is reworking an awkward headline. He tries a few different versions, settling finally on the plainest, which is always his preference. "76 Die in Baghdad Bombings," he writes.

Arthur Gopal appears. He is Menzies'

only friend in the newsroom. Occasionally, they take lunch together at Corsi, a bustling trattoria on Via del Gesù. At these meals, Menzies always wants to ask how Arthur is faring without Visantha and Pickle; and Arthur wants to ask about Annika, of whom he knows little. But neither poses personal questions. Instead, the subject is work, with Arthur doing much of the talking. Between mouthfuls of bean soup, he slanders colleagues ("Kathleen misses the point," "Clint Oakley can't even do a basic obit," "Herman is living in another era") and elaborates ambitions ("This old editor friend of my father's says I should work for him in New York"). Once he has finished speaking, Arthur adopts a dissatisfied air and spoons at his soup as if hunting for a lost cuff link.

On this afternoon, however, Arthur approaches Menzies' desk with an uncommon manner. "Have you checked your email?" he asks.

"Not lately. Why? Should I?"

"You got one from someone called jojo98. I strongly advise you to read it."

Menzies prints off a copy. But the email is in Italian, which he understands poorly. The message refers to Annika, and it includes an attachment. He clicks on this and a photo fills his screen. The quality is poor, as if taken with a cellphone camera. It shows Annika — evidently unaware that she is being photographed — on their bed, undressed, looking away. In the foreground is a man's hairy thigh, presumably that of the photographer. Hurriedly, Menzies turns off his monitor. "What the hell is this?"

"I have no idea. But it went to the whole staff."

Menzies stares at his blackened screen. "Jesus."

"I'm sorry to be the one to point it out," Arthur says.

"What do I do? Call her?"

"You should probably go talk in person."

"I can't just leave work."

"You can."

Menzies takes the stairs down, hurries across Campo de' Fiori, through the Ghetto, and crosses to the narrow sidewalk that follows the Tiber. He half walks, half jogs home, gazing down at the uneven path, then up at the traffic lights on Via Marmorata, then ahead at the tall metal gate of their apartment block.

He is here and wishes he were not.

He cannot go up. Their bedroom could be occupied. He goes down to his basement workshop and takes out the printed email. With an Italian-English dictionary, he pieces together the sentences. It claims that Annika has been having sex with another man while Menzies is at work. It says she plans to leave him, and that she and her lover are buying an apartment together. "When you sleep at night, your sheets are stained with his sperm," the letter says.

Everyone in the office (he closes his eyes at the thought — they *all* got this email) would expect him to barge into the apartment, waving the letter, swearing his throat raw, demanding, "Who is the asshole that sent this, and what the hell is going on?"

But he can't. He stands before his workbench, hands on hips.

When it is late, he goes up. His mobile phone, which gets no signal in the basement, returns to life. Kathleen has phoned numerous times and Annika left three messages, asking when he'll be home, that she's getting hungry, is everything okay?

"Hey," she says, opening the front door. "What happened?"

"Hi, yeah. No, nothing — just some confusion. Sorry," he says. "You have an okay day?"

"Fine. But hang on — don't disappear. I'm still" — she pulls at her T-shirt — "still confused a bit. You got, like, a million calls from the office."

"It's no big deal." Normally, when he walks in he kisses her. He hasn't tonight, and they both notice. "They're too dependent on me." He goes into the bathroom, watches himself blandly in the mirror, returns to the arena.

She can't look at him. "He sent you that letter, right?" she says. "I can't believe that —" She says a man's name.

"Wait, wait," Menzies interrupts. "Please don't say his name. I don't want to know it. If possible."

"Okay, but I have to say some things." She is pale. "Then, after, we don't have to talk about it again. I feel like —" She shakes her head. "I feel ill. I'm really, really so sorry. I am. I have to say this, though. Paolo only sent that — I apologize, I'm not supposed to say his name." She hesitates to find the right description. "That sickening, evil, fucking letter because I wouldn't get involved in some huge thing with him. Do you mind if I get a cigarette?" She rummages through the kitchen drawer for her Camels, which she normally smokes only when she's out with her yoga friends. She has never lit one in the apartment. She does now and exhales, shaking her head. "He's trying to force me into something. That's the point of this."

320

"You're upset."

"Well, yeah." She pinches her arm. "More than. More than upset. It's, like, the only time in my life I wanted to physically harm someone. I'd like to see him hurt. Physically. Hit by a truck. You know?" Her features strain toward Menzies, as if to grasp him. "You know?"

He looks at his hands. "Okay."

"Do you see, though?"

"I think I do."

"The reason he sent that thing was to break you and me up," she says.

"So you would have a relationship with him."

She takes another drag. "Basically." She exhales. "Yeah." She stubs out the cigarette.

"Let's not talk about it. I find that —" He doesn't finish the sentence. He picks up the TV remote. "Do you know if anything happened?" He turns on CNN to learn the answer.

Arriving at work the next day, he sits at his desk staring at his thermos for a minute. "Anything happened?" he asks his computer as it loads up.

The workday passes like any other — no one even mentions his disappearance of the day before, and Kathleen doesn't seem to remember that he never returned her calls.

At newspapers, what was of the utmost importance yesterday is immaterial today.

That night, their phone rings at home and Menzies answers. It is an Italian man. He asks for Annika. Menzies hands it over. She hears the voice and immediately puts down the receiver. "Hang up next time," she tells Menzies. "Don't give it to me if it's him. Just hang up."

Paolo keeps calling. He rings late and wakes them. They change the phone number. All goes quiet for a few weeks. Then legal papers arrive — astonishingly, he's suing Annika for breach of promise, claiming that she broke a verbal contract to leave her partner and buy an apartment with him. The suit says that he carried out his part and even took on a mortgage. Now he wants compensation.

No one at work asks Menzies about the humiliating email, but they haven't forgotten it. Reporters challenge him more often. Senior editors undermine him in news meetings. Only Kathleen is unchanged: she bosses him around and takes out her moods on him, same as ever.

As for Menzies and Annika themselves, they behave almost the same as before. But the scale is off. His praise of her photo project is too intent; her queries about his

322

inventions are too assiduous. Previously, they used to try different dishes each night at dinner. Now they repeat the same few. "It's one of your favorites, I thought."

"Yes. Great. Thanks."

When they meet with the lawyer, he advises Menzies to settle, otherwise the case will drag on. Annika almost intervenes, but she shuts up. Menzies knows that she wants to fight Paolo's case — she is raging.

"I'd prefer to be done with this," Menzies tells the lawyer. "I'll happily pay for that. Well, not happily, but . . ."

They return to their apartment in silence. Later, they have a ridiculous spat: she criticizes the way he grates Parmesan. The apartment is suddenly too small for two people.

"I'm going downstairs for a bit of tinkering," he says.

And she is left alone.

She flips through their music and puts on Chet Baker's soundtrack for *Let's Get Lost,* a documentary by one of her favorite photographers, Bruce Weber. The tune is "You're My Thrill." She frowns with concentration to make out the lyrics, then loses interest. She opens her cellphone — no messages. What if she messaged him? Saying? She types into the phone keypad, erasing each snippet in turn: "this song" (delete) "idiot" (delete) "i wish" (delete) "why is it always dumb stuff?" (delete) "so stupid." She erases this, too, and writes "i miss u, can i come for visit?" She sends it. From the stereo, Chet Baker sings, "Nothing seems to matter . . . Here's my heart on a silver platter . . . Where's my will?"

Down in the workshop, Menzies flicks a rubber band, trying to hit a mark on the wall. He achieves it once, then tries for three consecutive hits. He tires of the game and turns to sketching unrealistic inventions that he will never build.

She knocks at the door. "Hi," she says uneasily. "Am I disturbing?"

"No, no. What's up?"

She takes a hop closer. "What can you show me? Some new invention that's gonna make us millions and revolutionize life as we know it?"

"I wish."

"You're not working on some evil plot against me, are you?"

"Yes, I'm going to drive you slowly mad with my diabolical cheese-grating."

She sticks out her tongue.

"We should work on a revenge invention," she says.

"For him, you mean?"

"Yeah."

"I must admit I've thought about that."

"You have to tell me."

"No, it's stupid."

"Come on."

He half smiles. "It's this: a little audio player that we'd stick in his bedroom and that would play an endless loop of a mosquito whining. But it would only activate in darkness, so every time he turned off the lights the whining would start. Then he'd turn on the lights to hunt for it and the mosquito wouldn't be there. And so on and so on, until straitjackets were required."

"That's genius! We have to do it!"

"No, no."

"Why not?"

"Well, many reasons."

"Like?"

"First of all, I'm not even sure how. Also, we'd definitely get caught. And I don't want to spend my time building a gadget for the purpose of tormenting someone. What would be the point? Making this guy's life a bit annoying? So we'd sit around at night feeling happy that someone else was irritated?"

"Okay, not your mosquito thing necessarily. But something — a bit of revenge. No?"

"I suspect revenge is one of those things

that's better in principle than in practice. I mean, there's no real satisfaction in making someone else suffer because you have."

"You are so wrong there."

"And does revenge even work? I mean, is the point to get justice — to balance out something unfair? Nothing does that. Is it to make you feel better? It wouldn't make me feel better."

"So if someone does something shitty to you, there's no way to fix it?" She looks away, as if casually.

"I don't think there is, no," he answers. "The way to get over stuff, I think, is by forgetting. But there's no way to 'fix' in the way you mean. Not in my opinion."

She shakes her head. "I hate this."

"What?"

"I feel — I don't know — out of balance. You're not a vengeful person like me. You should get pissed off."

"At him?"

"At me. You know?"

"That doesn't appeal in the least, making you suffer."

"Then I end up suffering more."

"What do you want me to do?"

"Why are you getting mad? We're just talking."

"I'm not mad. I just don't know what I'm

supposed to do." He clears his throat. "What you don't realize is that I'd be in real trouble without you. That sounded melodramatic — sorry. I just meant that, to be honest, even if you did something worse, I'm not about to reject you. I can't. Getting hurt by you only makes me need comfort more. Comfort from you. Not something I should admit. But . . ."

"It's okay."

It isn't okay. He ought to shut up. She's drifting away, more with each word of pardon he thrusts upon her. "I'm forty-one now," he says, "I live in a country whose language I don't speak, where, without you, I don't remotely fit it, where my colleagues consider me some kind of weasel."

"No, they don't."

"They do. Look, I'm Kathleen's henchman. She gives orders and I hop to it. And I don't have another option. That one day I'll come up with some great invention and get out of journalism? It's not going to happen."

"It might."

"It won't. I have no alternative to this life. Without you, I'm — you've seen me, Annika. I told you what I was before you. So I'm slightly worried. I mean, I'm terrified essentially."

"Of what?"

"I spent almost a decade alone before you."

"I know. I know that. But —" She pauses. "You can't be with someone just because you can't face being alone."

"No? Isn't that the best reason to be with someone? I'd put up with anything for that reason. I mean, look, I've never been so humiliated as I have over this situation with you. Did you know he sent that letter to everyone in my office?"

She freezes. "What?"

"I'm serious."

She covers her mouth. "You never told me that."

"And there was a photo with it. Of you. On our bed."

She goes pale.

"I'm not joking," he says. "It went to everyone."

She closes her eyes and shakes her head. "I want to die."

"It's okay," he says. "It's okay. Look, my point is that all of this, from start to finish, makes me want to, makes me want to be sick or — or, because, I don't know. Sorry, I'm sort of overwhelmed. Feel free to laugh at me. But that is how I feel about it. It doesn't matter. It's all right." He touches her cheek. "Thank you," he says, "for traveling out here to Italy with me." He kisses her. "Did you come downstairs to leave me?"

She is quiet.

"You can leave me," he says.

"I," she says, "I can't bear that I humiliated you." She can scarcely get the words out, but repeats them. "I can't bear that. I wish you would *do* something. I wish you were evil like me."

"What are you talking about?"

"I could do anything to you, then? You'd put up with anything?"

"I don't have a choice."

"Do I make *any* difference here?" Her voice wavers; she is losing control. "I mean, please — get angry with me. Give me the impression I'm involved here, that I'm not just some random girl whose job it is to make sure you don't get lonely at your new life overseas." She struggles out the words. "I don't want you to — if it's possible — to think of what I did as a humiliation to you. It was my selfishness. My acting dumb, like an idiot, for my own selfish, I don't know what, boredom. It wasn't important. I wish I could, you know, make you know that."

She calms somewhat. But there is a distance in her.

329

"Why did you come down here?" he asks. "You never come down here."

"I had something for you." She holds out an envelope.

He removes the letter and reads the opening lines. "Oh," he says with surprise. "You applied for a patent. In my name." He looks up. "And they rejected it." He laughs.

"It says why, though. You could make some changes maybe."

He reads the letter in full. She must not have realized that his infantile science projects are not nearly sophisticated enough to obtain a patent. He won't look up from the letter. If he does and she is gone, he will not make it out of this room. Of course, that is untrue — he will make it out, climb upstairs, return to work tomorrow, and the following day's paper will come out. That feels even worse.

He must keep her here. He must make his point. But what is his point? What is the point he's been trying to make all along? His impulse is to apologize, but that's wrong, too. Another apology would surely spell the end. She wants him to do something.

"Okay," he says.

"Okay what?"

"Thanks, but who said I wanted a patent?"

"Didn't you? I thought you did."

"And how did you get this stuff, anyway? I mean, did you go through my material down here? That project wasn't even finished."

"What's the problem?"

"Well, it's an intrusion is the problem. I mean, this is none of your business."

"Oh, come on. You're overreacting."

"I don't interfere with your shit."

She goes silent — he never swears. "Personally," she says, "I'd be happy if you entered my stuff in some competition."

"Oh, yeah? Really? You'd like it if I came waving a rejection letter in your face and said, 'Here, I thought I'd do you a favor'? Spare me your next favor."

"Why are you so angry about this?"

"I'm not. I just don't know what else to do," he says. "My stuff down here is mine alone. For no other reason than this dumb workshop is a pleasure for me. I spend my life at a job I hate, in a career I can't stand. I'm forty-one and my girlfriend gets screwed by some guy in her yoga class, by some little Italian kid, and has me pay the legal bills. So —" He waves the rejection letter at her.

She wipes her eyes, but her face is hard.

"So," he goes on, "you can keep your fingers out of my private business. Out of the only stuff I do that isn't a fucking disgrace."

"I'm going upstairs."

"Good." He's losing his nerve. "Good," he repeats louder. "Not upstairs, though. You can fuck off back to the States. I'll pay your ticket."

He joins her in the apartment. She's at the kitchen table, shell-shocked. He takes her suitcase from the cupboard.

"Are you kidding me?" she says.

"You need to pack."

She opens a drawer full of underwear and socks, stares at them, doing nothing for a minute.

As she fills the suitcase, he goes online and buys a ticket for her flight back to Washington, leaving the next day.

"That's three thousand bucks," she exclaims, looking at the computer screen. "Are you insane?"

"Too late. I just paid for it." He phones a hotel and books her a room for that night.

"What about my things?"

"Get them shipped. Look, don't take the flight if you don't want. But then you're paying your own way home."

He calls a taxi and carries her bags outside. He drops them beside her at the curb and goes back in, without a word. His legs tremble on the stairs up. In the apartment, he stands over the toilet, spitting bitter saliva into the bowl until his mouth is dry.

How long before she arrives at the hotel?

If he calls too soon, he'll seem insane. He must appear to have cooled down.

He sits on the cold tiles of the bathroom, his shoulder against the toilet bowl. He rereads the letter from the patent office. It was kind of her. Nothing she has done has touched him like this. And the rejection is useful: it puts an end to all these years of ridiculous daydreams. No inventor, he. That's done with, then. Good.

He waits two nauseating hours.

Has he made his point? The point he's been trying to make? But no, this isn't the point he wanted to make at all.

He picks up his cellphone and finds that she has sent him a text message: "i miss u, can i come for visit?" It was sent hours before, when he was still in the basement and she was still here. He calls her mobile, but there is no answer.

He phones the hotel. The reception desk transfers him to her room. His mouth is parched. He keeps swallowing.

"It's me," he says as the phone is answered. "My point is this. I think we both

want." He hesitates. "Don't we? Or am I
—"

But he is interrupted. It is a man's voice.
It is Paolo.

1977. *Corso Vittorio, Rome*

The paper improved under Milton Berber. It developed pluck and humor, pulled off the occasional scoop, even won a couple of awards — nothing stunning, but still unprecedented in its history.

The newsroom changed, too. In the old days, journalists were referred to as "the boys." Now many of the boys were women. Crude jokes earned fewer snorts of approval, and ethnic slurs did not fly. Milton demanded that ashtrays (and the floor is not an ashtray) be used. The filthy carpeting was changed, made pristine white again. And the cocktail bar in the east wall was replaced with a watercooler; the consequent decline in typos was extraordinary.

Typewriters disappeared next, replaced by video display terminals. Overnight, the newsroom's distinctive *clack-clack-bing* went silent. The rumbling basement presses hushed, too, with the work outsourced to modernized printing sites around the globe. No longer did vast rolls of newsprint slam into the backside of the building in the late afternoon, jolting any dozing reporter awake. No longer did delivery trucks clog Corso Vittorio at dawn as workmen loaded the papers, copies still warm.

News got cooler, quieter, cleaner.

However, the biggest change was money: the paper started making it. Not a heap, and not every month. But after decades it was profitable.

While other publications snubbed far-flung outposts, the paper targeted them, finding its niche at the fringes of the world, copies turning up on armchairs in the Diamond Dealers Club of Freetown, or at a village newsagent on the island of Gozo, or on a bar stool in Arrowtown, New Zealand. A passerby picked it up, perused a few pages and, as often as not, the paper gained a new devotee. By the early 1980s, daily circulation had neared twenty-five thousand, climbing annually.

With readers around the globe, it was impossible to produce a normal daily — yesterday in Melbourne wasn't yesterday in Guadalajara. So the paper took its own route, trusting reporters and editors to veer from the media pack, with varying success. The trick was to hire well: hungry reporters like Lloyd Burko in Paris; nitpicky wordsmiths like Herman Cohen.

The paper also gained a reputation in journalistic circles as a feeder to prestigious U.S. publications, which attracted young hotshots to Rome. Milton trained them, wrung copy from them for a few years, then hoisted them to high-profile positions elsewhere.

Those who moved away recalled him with affection and always dropped by the office when transiting through Italy, showing off their expensive jobs, boasting of bylines and babies.

Milton's reputation was enhanced by all this, and various midsize U.S. newspapers tried to lure him away. But he had no intention of leaving — this was the best job of his life.

Elsewhere in the Ott Group, matters were more bleak. The problems began when Boyd was peripherally implicated in the fraudulent bankruptcy of a Midwestern bank. He and eight others avoided criminal charges but were fined $120 million. His reputation was further sullied over a stock-fixing scandal involving several Ott Group employees. Boyd himself had no role in it, but a spate of articles conflated his bank scandal with the stock-fixing case. The ugliest blow came in the mid-1980s, when an Ott Group copper subsidiary was found to have dumped toxins into a rural water source in Zambia, causing scores of birth defects. A South African newspaper printed a ghoulish price list that Ott Group reps had used to compensate villagers: $165 for missing limbs, $40 for missing hands, and a diminishing scale from there, concluding with the curiously exact sum of $3.85 per lost toe. Ott Group headquarters claimed ignorance of this but built the villagers new houses nevertheless.

■ ■ ■ ■

"Cold War Over, Hot War Begins"

· · ·

READER — ORNELLA DE MONTERECCHI

■ ■ ■ ■

She has been dreading tomorrow ever since it happened the first time.

Ornella sits on the sofa in her living room, the paper on her lap, and picks at her lower lip. A faint ripping comes from the kitchen, where the cleaner, Marta, is tearing sheets of paper towel, which she must place between stacked pots and pans to avoid scuffing the surfaces. This is among the many rules that previous cleaners — and there have been dozens — contravened. Some were dismissed for tardiness. Some for impudence. Some stole, or were suspected of it. Others failed to learn, or didn't care to, or left dust under beds. Marta has worked here for almost two years and, so far, is almost without fault, except that she is Polish, which Ornella views as a demerit. Also, Marta has an inappropriately good figure for a cleaner, though her face is a battlefield of acne, which makes up for it.

She has a habit of looking down when confused or scolded, staring at the broom bristles and smiling. This has never struck anyone as defiance; it signals submission. Which is best with this mistress, for Ornella's home is a world where it is not possible to be good.

Holding a spray bottle of window cleaner, Marta treads cautiously into the living room in high-heeled cream pumps and nylons, a pencil skirt suit and a lace shawl — hopeless cleaning attire, but she has come directly from Mass. Ornella, who adopted her late husband's distaste for religion, insists that Marta clean every Sunday.

"How was God this morning?" Ornella asks. "Did he have anything nice to say about me?"

Marta smiles automatically, the window before her. It is not clear if she understands. Their common language is English, but Ornella's grasp of it, having used it at a thousand diplomats' dinners, is excellent, whereas Marta's is elementary. She hesitates in case her mistress plans further remarks. When none is forthcoming, she sprays the cleaning fluid in a blue mist that forms into beads on the pane; they hold briefly, then streak downward. She works faster than normal because her husband, Wojciech, is waiting downstairs, sitting on a park bench, leg hopping up and down, scratching dust with his dress shoe, dirtying the hem of his cheap gray suit, which Marta ironed that morning.

"A tribe in Rwanda killed hundreds of thousands of people belonging to another tribe in the past two weeks," Ornella says, slapping the article with the back of her hand. "How is it possible to destroy so many humans so fast? Even in practical terms, how? And why didn't the paper say anything about this when it was going on? Why only at the end?" She glances at Marta, who is wiping her way down the window. Ornella continues: "Lloyd Burko, in his piece on page one, makes the point that it's not just the Africans. The Yugoslavians are as bad, and they're Europeans. Everyone's killing everyone else. Maybe it *was* better during the Cold War. You probably don't agree, Marta — you were right in it, weren't you. Being a Pole. But at least that war was cold. Listen to this: 'Peace is a state humanity will not tolerate. Man's instinct is to commit violence.' That's from Lloyd Burko's piece. Is that true? I can't believe it is."

Marta collects the remaining cleaning rags around the apartment, rinses them, wrings them out, stashes them under the kitchen sink. For the final task of her day, she carries the stepladder into the hall and climbs to the top rung to reach the storage space, which is crammed full of copies of the paper. Editions that Ornella has read are placed to the left; unread copies are on the right. Marta reaches for tomorrow's, April 24, 1994.

"No!" Ornella cries, clamping her hands to the stepladder. "I don't *want* that one yet. I'll ask you for it when I *want* it. I'm still on April twenty-third. I'll let you know, Marta. Don't just push ahead like that, assuming."

Marta descends the ladder and takes her pay — twenty euros — her head bowed, murmuring. She hastens out of the apartment, exhaling only when she is a full flight down the stairs.

Ornella snoops around to ensure that she has not been cheated of twenty euros: hallway, bedroom, en suite bathroom, study, dining room, kitchen, terrace, guest room, guest bathroom, living room. Marta is impeccable, as usual, and this doesn't especially please Ornella.

She seats herself on the sofa and clears her throat, blinks as if to sharpen her vision, and surveys the front page of April 23, 1994, the same front page she has been stuck on for three weeks. It is a day she cannot surmount. Tomorrow — April 24, 1994 — is too hard to bear again.

She has read every copy of the paper since 1976, when her husband, Cosimo de Monterecchi, was posted to Jeddah. He, the Italian ambassador, traveled without restriction in Saudi Arabia. But she, as a woman, was effectively detained in a guarded zone for Westerners, while her two sons attended the international school all day. From boredom, she took to reading the paper, which in the late 1970s was one of the few foreign periodicals available in the kingdom. She had never learned the technique of newspaper reading, so took it in order like a book, down the columns, left to right, page after page. She read every article and refused to move on until she was done, which meant that each edition took several days to complete. Much was confusing at first. At night, she posed questions to Cosimo, initially basic ones like "Where is Upper Volta?" Later, her queries grew more complex, such as "If both the Chinese and the Russians are Communists, why do they disagree?" Until she was posing questions about the Palestinians' role in Jordanian affairs, infighting among apartheid opponents, and supply-side economics. Cosimo occasionally referred to an event that she hadn't reached yet, spoiling the surprise, so she gave him strict orders not to leak anything, even in passing. Thus began her slow drift from the present.

One year into her newspaper reading, she was six months behind. When they returned to Rome in the 1980s, she remained stranded in the late 1970s. When it was the 1990s outside, she was just getting to know President Reagan. When planes struck the Twin Towers, she was watching the Soviet Union collapse. Today, it is February 18, 2007, outside this apartment. Within, the date remains April 23, 1994.

These are her day's headlines: "Thousands Slain in Rwanda, Red Cross Fears"; "Mandela Set to Win South Africa Elections"; "After Suicide, 'Grunge' Star Cobain Viewed as Icon"; "Cold War Over, Hot War Begins." This last piece is a news analysis by the paper's Paris correspondent, Lloyd Burko, who reported on the siege of Sarajevo, and compares the slaughter in Yugoslavia to the recent massacres in Rwanda.

Ornella phones her eldest son, Dario, to complain about Marta. "She forgot to bring me down my paper for tomorrow," she tells him in Italian, which is the family language. "What am I going to do now?"

"Can't you get it yourself?"

Ornella flings up her arms, which tinkle with jewelry, and chops the air. "No," she says, "I cannot. You know I can't." What if she read a headline by mistake, something from 1996, or 2002? She doesn't ask Dario to come over, but repeats the problem until he volunteers.

She opens the front door and leans back slightly when he enters, as if to avoid a kiss, though none is offered. His six-year-old son, Massimiliano, trails in. "You're here too, Massi," she says, patting her grandson's head as if he were a rather pleasing spaniel, but a spaniel nonetheless.

Dario sets up the stepladder. She watches the tendons in his wrist flexing as he grips and shifts it into position — she wants to grab his arm and stop him. She can't look at April 24, 1994. No one but she seems to remember that day. She says softly, "Wait, wait."

He turns. "What for?"

"Shall I make us coffee first?"

"Not for me."

"What about the boy?" she says, though Massi is standing right there beside them. "Will he want something?"

"You can ask him — Massi?"

The child, instead of responding, walks away.

"Come with me to the living room," Ornella tells Dario, to delay him "I want to show you something." She hands him the paper of April 23, 1994. "This piece by Lloyd Burko. It's really worth reading."

He smiles. "I won't bother telling you that it's somewhat out of date." He turns the page. "So, what's happening today?" he says wryly, and reads out a few headlines. "God, I remember that."

She watches: Is he making fun of her? He considers me stupid. Well, I am, she thinks, burning at the insult. He looks over, about to speak, but she diverts her gaze fractionally above his sight line, as if reading the wrinkles on his forehead.

"Massi!" she calls out. "Where are you?"

He is all around the room, in the form of framed photographs. Portraits of him and Ornella's three other grandchildren stand on the table, on the mantelpiece, in the crystal cabinet. This is strange, since in person she recoils from the young — when handed a baby, she holds the child as if it were a squirming octopus. But not all the portraits are of kids. A few show her husband, Cosimo, at various postings around the world. He died more than a year ago, on November 17, 2005. Others show Ornella herself, when she was dashing, too thin and too young. (She was only sixteen at the time of her marriage to Cosimo.) She has a different face today, matted with peach foundation, orange lipstick, liner around her eyes, green mascara so thick that when she blinks one sees frog's fingers clasping. Her hair is yellow, dyed at great expense and pulled back in a bun so tight that the canvas of her face appears to be held fast by the knot at the back of her head.

"I should get rid of Marta," she says.

"Don't be mad — she forgot to bring down your paper one day. I'll get it now."

"No, no! Hang on, wait. There's no rush."

"Didn't I come over for that?"

"Yes, but I'm not sure I need it now."

"You can't fire Marta." His mobile phone rings — the digitized sound of a sheep bleating. She frowns: modern technology is not allowed in her house. "Sorry," Dario says, and takes it outside by the elevator.

Massi wanders back in, holding a white rectangular contraption studded with buttons and two unlit gray screens. He must not turn on video games at his grandmother's house.

"Let's go into the kitchen," she says. "And I don't want to see that thing you have there." If you feed children, that works. She sits this one on a chair. His legs dangle and he kicks off one of his Nikes, baring a dirty white sports sock. "What do you like?" she asks. "Are you hungry?"

"Not very."

He hardly eats, this one — Dario said something about that, didn't he? That they struggle to get Massi to finish meals. "Well, you'll have something in *my* house," she declares and searches the cupboards. "This is grown-up food, mostly." She checks the fridge. "I'll make you *pastina in brodo*."

"No thank you."

She ignores this and heats the broth. The boy watches his grandmother. Her perfume infuses the kitchen. As the broth simmers, fatty-chicken aroma overwhelms her scent. She turns to Massi, holding a wooden spoon that steams. She sweeps his bangs aside. "You can see now. But your parting is uneven," she says. "I'll fix it for you."

"No thank you."

"I'm good at it." She leans in. He leans back.

He stares at his plastic video game, a Nintendo DS Lite, which he got a few weeks ago. "Can I turn it on?"

"Your food is almost ready."

"I don't want any food."

350

Ornella doesn't speak for a moment. She switches off the stove. Crushed, she hurries into the living room. She stands motionless, watching the front door, behind which stands her eldest son, laughing into his cellphone.

He comes back inside, still smiling at the exchange that concluded his phone call. "Where's Massi? We should get going."

"I tried to make him eat something. I see what you mean — it's impossible."

Dario is puzzled. "We can't *stop* him eating."

The boy hobbles out of the kitchen, wearing only one sneaker and engrossed in his video game.

"Turn that off," his father says. The boy does not, stumbling out the front door, too engaged to say goodbye.

"Goodbye," Ornella says nonetheless.

"I meant to tell you who I saw," Dario says, nipping into the kitchen to collect his son's abandoned Nike. "Kathleen Solson." This is his former girlfriend, whom Dario met in 1987 when they were both interns at the paper. "She's back now, back from Washington."

"And how is she?"

"The same. Older."

"I don't want to know anything more."

"This has nothing to do with current events."

"It has to do with the paper. I don't want to know."

"Do you want tomorrow's or not?"

"I'm worried about tomorrow," she says, her voice dropping. "You don't remember, do you."

"Remember what?"

"Marta isn't back until Tuesday."

"And you can't wait till Tuesday to fire her?"

"You misunderstand."

She stands at the bottom of the stepladder, holding it for him. She wants to stop fretting. It's just another date — it's not as if the paper will contain an account of her own life on that day.

He climbs up and looks around the storage space. "It's not here."

"Yes, it is."

He continues searching. "It really isn't. You want to come up and look? It's missing, I promise you."

"I've collected them all," she insists. "I've never missed an edition."

"Well, you'll have to miss one now, I'm afraid. Do you want April 25, 1994? That's here."

"No, I don't. I'm not there yet."

He comes down the ladder and, leaping from the third rung, swoops beside her and kisses her fast on the cheek.

Unprepared, she smiles bashfully, then bats him aside and, catching herself, gets angry. "You could have knocked me over. It's not funny."

The paper's headquarters on Corso Vittorio are a taxi ride from Ornella's home in Parioli. She has never visited, has always been wary of that office, which contains all the world yet is itself contained in a single grubby building. But she has no choice — her storage space does not contain tomorrow, and she must find a copy.

"Che piano?" asks a man with a strong Anglophone accent.

"Not sure what floor," she answers in English. "I'm trying to find the headquarters of the paper."

"Follow me." He closes the elevator gate after them and nudges the third-floor button with his knuckle. The elevator rises.

"You work there?" she asks.

"I do."

"What's your name?"

"Arthur Gopal."

"Ah yes, I've read your obituaries. You did one on Nixon the other day."

"Nixon died ages ago," he says, confused.

353

"Anyway, I don't do obits anymore. I'm the culture editor."

"A bit too one-sided, I thought. Nixon did some good things, too."

She asks to see Kathleen Solson, and Arthur enters the newsroom to convey the request. Ornella is tempted to follow him in, to view the workings of this place herself. But, no: if you want to keep enjoying sausages, don't visit the sausage factory.

After a few minutes, Kathleen appears. "I'm seeing all the Monterecchis lately. I bumped into your son a few weeks back."

"Yes, he told me." Haltingly, Ornella leans in to hug Kathleen, regretting it the instant she has committed herself. She embraces the younger woman rigidly and fast.

They are silent in the elevator down. Ornella keeps wishing she hadn't hugged Kathleen. It was embarrassing. Was it disloyal to Dario somehow?

"Which way?"

"I can't venture too far," Kathleen says.

They walk along Corso Vittorio, the roadway a blur of buses, taxis, and droning motor scooters. Ornella must speak up to be heard. "I still read the paper religiously, you'll be glad to hear."

"What year are you up to?"

"1994. Which, as it happens, is when we

saw each other last."

"Yes — when I left."

"I even remember the date we last met —
it was at the hospital when Cosimo got sick,
April 24, 1994."

Kathleen's BlackBerry rings. It is Menzies. She issues a few orders and hangs up.

"You were rude to that person," Ornella
says.

"No time for politeness at my job, I'm
afraid."

"That can't be true." After a pause, she
adds, "You know, I sometimes wonder
whether I might not have liked to work in
journalism. In my next life, shall we say?"

"Did you ever try?"

"Don't be ridiculous."

"You could have."

"I tried to get Dario to go into it, but he
didn't take to newspapers."

"I know — we did that internship together."

"Where would I have been, had I done
something brave like you?" She glances fast
at Kathleen, then away. "I'm old now. Fifty-
eight. That's the age when a person is at the
height of their career, isn't it?"

"Can be."

"You and I are alike," Ornella says. "Don't
look so horrified. We're very different in

some ways. But in others —" She stops. Ostensibly, she came here to obtain a back issue of the paper and, secondarily, to catch up with a former acquaintance. But she finds herself tempted toward another course: she wants to say something. To talk — to confess, even. To tell this woman about tomorrow, a day in which Kathleen had a walk-on part. "Do you remember my husband at all?"

"I certainly do. I was sorry, by the way, to hear that he had passed —"

Ornella interrupts. "Terribly handsome, wasn't he."

"He was."

"And a baron, you know, though he didn't use the title. I remember when he and I met, Cosimo was so distinguished. I myself was rather a pretty young thing back then — you can see in the old photos, if you don't believe me."

"You were famous for your looks."

"I was," she says, as if only now learning the fact.

"I should get back," Kathleen says, glancing at a message on her BlackBerry. "I didn't bring a jacket."

"In a minute." She takes a corner of Kathleen's shirtsleeve and leads her across the intersection at Piazza Sant'Andrea della

356

Valle, mindless of the red light, sidestepping honking cars. "So you remember when Cosimo was hospitalized in 1994?"

"Of course — it was such a shock."

"Not really a shock. His problems started weeks before I took him in."

"I didn't realize that."

"Oh yes," Ornella says. "The first clue, I think, was when we were supposed to go on vacation and he just canceled at the last minute. I made the best of it, saying we could enjoy doing things here in the city. But he got furious. I didn't know why. Well, he was drinking, and I suppose that had something to do with it. He actually pushed me into the refrigerator!" She laughs. "The fridge door was open — I'd been getting the pitcher of ice water — and I hit into the shelves. It was strange — he kept shoving me like he was trying to stuff me in there. I knocked over all sorts of things. A jar of capers smashed. I thought, Glass inside the fridge. The cleaner will never find it all. Someone will swallow it by mistake. Such a stupid thought. Anyway, he just walked out, left. I was terrified someone would find out that he'd gone. But since we were supposed to be on vacation no one even noticed — I just stayed inside. Had lots of time to clean up the glass in the fridge."

"What a ghastly story. I'm so sorry to hear this," Kathleen says, pausing on the sidewalk. "And I'm impressed that you can share this stuff about Cosimo. But — and please don't take this the wrong way — was there a particular reason you stopped by today? Not that you need a reason. Just that I really should get back."

"It's a fair question. Normally, I don't talk about private things to anyone but my cleaner, Marta."

Kathleen laughs.

"Why is that funny?"

She takes Kathleen's shirtsleeve and leads her onward, farther still from the paper, prolonging this conversation, even if it means dragging the younger woman all the way to Piazza Venezia. "During that period in 1994 when Cosimo was gone," she proceeds, "I got a call from the bank asking about several withdrawals. They told me the amounts, which were staggering — you don't want to know. I still can't understand how he spent that much that fast. Then the police called: a man in his sixties, arrested for cocaine possession. I went to get him and he was talking nonstop. There was an Australian woman he kept mentioning. He'd picked her up during his time away and demanded that we drive around and find her. He had broken a tooth — he'd been in a fight, if you can believe it. Somehow I got us home. He kept talking and talking. He wanted to celebrate. 'Celebrate what?' I said. He poured a full glass of brandy and made me drink it. He wanted to make love. I didn't want to. But we did."

She tugs Kathleen across the tram tracks at Largo Argentina, to the pedestrian island around the Roman ruins. "Then he got angry," Ornella continues. "Said how I was ruining his job prospects. I tried to understand, to follow. He pulled me around the apartment, shouting. He was going to start a painting studio and fuck lots of girls — he told me that, said that to me, his wife. He grabbed me by the bra strap and shoved me, and it ripped. I kept trying to look him in the eyes. When I did, they were blank — it's one of the most awful things I've ever seen. And he choked me that afternoon, April 24, 1994. I remember thinking I was going to die. He choked me so long that I blacked out.

"He wasn't there when I woke up. My throat felt as if it had caved in. I splashed water on my face and tried to cry over the kitchen sink. But I couldn't get full breaths. It was a strange sort of sobbing — lots of swallowing and coughing. Then he was there, laughing at me.

"I'd been holding the handle of the kitchen cupboard to balance myself. He stuck his face close to mine, and I swung the cupboard door into his head as hard as I could. The bang shuddered the door; my hand buzzed; he fell. His hands barely stopped him, and his face hit the floor. His cheek split and blood came out. It dripped on the floor. I remember him putting his finger in the puddle."

"Jesus, this is a horror story," Kathleen interjects. "I didn't know any of this. All I remember was Cosimo being admitted to the psychiatric ward. But Dario told me it was depression."

"Well, there was depression, too. That came later." She lets go of Kathleen's sleeve, her confessional urge suddenly dissipated and replaced by a wash of guilt. "Don't tell any of this to Dario," she says. "Don't mention this if you see him. He doesn't know these details."

They turn back toward the office.

"Actually," Kathleen says, "I remember blood on your kitchen floor that night. Dario and I got there after you'd taken Cosimo to the hospital. We let your maid in. What was her name? Rina? She didn't know what to do. She didn't want to get

360

blood on the mop — she thought you'd be angry — so I wiped it up with a copy of the paper."

"I know," Ornella says. "It's the copy I'm missing. I need you to give me a new one."

"A paper from 1994? I don't know where you'd find one. We threw away our hard-copy archives years ago. It's all digitized now."

"You can't be serious."

The women walk on in silence, arriving outside the office finally.

"Do you remember our conversation at the hospital that night?" Kathleen asks. "When I said I was thinking of going to Washington but that I was undecided. You told me I should. That I should leave Rome, and Dario, and take the job."

"I never said that."

"Yes," Kathleen responds, "you did."

On Tuesday morning, Marta knocks four times and waits. She has keys, so she enters. Ornella appears in her nightgown.

"Oh, sorry," Marta says, bowing her head.

"You left me in a terrible situation Sunday without my paper," Ornella says. "Absolutely unforgivable!" She wants to retract this. Instead, she retreats into her bedroom.

She dresses and returns to the living room, shifting framed photographs as if her

361

outburst had not happened. "If I sit here," she explains to Marta, "I can see Massi when I look up from reading the paper. And if I sit over there, I can see Cosimo. Or should I put Dario here? You know, if you don't move pictures about, you stop noticing them."

Marta, who is brushing rubbish into her dustpan, nods politely.

Without another word, Ornella withdraws to her room.

"You want paper today, Signora Ornella?"

"No," she says through the closed bedroom door. "Thank you."

She hears the front door shut, and so emerges. Marta has left a note, asking for a particular brand of cleaning fluid and more paper towels. "How on earth," Ornella says, "does this girl get through so many paper towels?" She checks for dust under the sofa. While she's bent down there, snooping about, a drop of liquid plops onto the wooden floor. She touches her face; it was a teardrop. With a hard sniff, she gains control of herself. She wipes off the floor with her bare hand, dabs her eyes, stands.

Dario will come if needed, but she won't beg him. Her other son, Filippo, avoids her totally — he picked up his father's intellectual contempt for Ornella. And the grandchildren? They seem to be afraid of her.

She misses Cosimo. Their last decade together consisted of doctors and medicine, moments of hope and months of hopelessness. (She never told Dario and Filippo how their father really died, that he was discovered with a note saying, "Enough." She informed everyone that he had died of heart disease. In a corner of her mind, she knows that her sons know. It is the same corner into which she has secreted all manner of knowledge that she, at once, knows and does not know: about the existence of mobile phones, about the Internet, about what people think of her.)

She opens the stepladder below the storage space. She reaches the top and the two doors, behind which lie her papers. She has never climbed up here. She opens both doors and inhales — the storage space has a metallic smell, a scent she had vaguely considered to be that of her fingers. The space is high and deep, and filled nearly to capacity. More than ten thousand papers. Over a hundred thousand pages. A half-million articles. All those labored lines, placed up here to wait their turn.

The turn of tomorrow has come, and it has gone. Nowhere will she find a copy of

April 24, 1994. She must move on to April 25. But skipping a day has a peculiar effect: these stacks seem far less authoritative all of a sudden — less like the paper and more like plain paper. She smacks a pile on the left, the side she has read, and yanks out a few copies. She tosses them down from the storage space.

In the air, the folded pages separate; sheets float gently to the floor.

She pulls out more, a thick pile this time, and drops them. They hit the floor with a thud and splay out. She pulls out still more. She dumps newspapers until her arms ache and the floor around the ladder is heaped high.

She considers the piles still remaining in the storage space, the unread papers. She slides off the one on top, April 25, 1994, and tosses it to the floor. She hauls out a handful more, then another.

She keeps this up for almost an hour until, her hands black with ink, knees wobbling on the top rung, she is done. The storage space is empty; the floor is an ocean of black-and-white.

She climbs down, unsure how to step off. She treads on papers and, losing her footing, thrusts out her arms, jewelry tinkling, and flops gently atop the lot. She slides a little way down the heap, gasps, then comes to a halt, laughing. "Silly girl!"

A boldface headline catches her eye: ". . . Afghan Capital." She tugs out the edition, which tears slightly under her. The headline reads, "Taliban Fighters Capture Afghan Capital" (the paper of Sept. 28, 1996). She digs through the pile and picks another paper at random: "In Record, Dow Closes Above 6,000" (Oct. 15, 1996). And another: "Clinton Beats Dole to Win 2nd Term" (Nov. 6, 1996). She is lying on 1996, it seems.

She pushes these aside, digging down to 1998: "Clinton Denies Sex with Intern" (Jan. 27, 1998); "A 'Titanic' Haul as Ship Flick Sinks 11 Oscars" (March 24, 1998); "Scores Killed in Twin Attacks on U.S. Embassies in East Africa" (Aug. 8, 1998); "House Impeaches Clinton" (Dec. 20, 1998).

She reaches the new millennium: "Dow Tops 11,000" (Jan. 15, 2000); "Milosevic Quits Amid Protests" (Oct. 6, 2000); "Iraq Rejects New Inspections" (Nov. 2, 2000).

The headlines from 2002 perplex her: "Trade Center Debris Cleared from Ground Zero" (May 31, 2002); "Bomb Attack in Bali Leaves Dozens Dead" (Oct. 13, 2002); "Bush Establishes 'Homeland

Security' Agency" (Nov. 26, 2002).

She tunnels down to 2004: "Scientists Clone 30 Human Embryos" (Feb. 14, 2004); "Putin Wins Re-Election" (March 15, 2004); "U.S. Transfers Power to Iraq Interim Leaders" (June 29, 2004); "Islamic Extremist Kills Dutch Filmmaker" (Nov. 3, 2004).

She skips ahead to 2006: "In His First Veto, Bush Blocks Stem-Cell Research" (July 20, 2006); "North Korea Claims First Nuclear Test" (Oct. 10, 2006).

And then 2007: "Amid Fanfare, Apple Introduces iPhone" (Jan. 10, 2007); "Bush to Send 21,500 More Troops to Iraq" (Jan. 11, 2007); "Humans Are Cause of Climate Change, Panel Finds" (Feb. 3, 2007); "In Historic Bid, African-American Senator to Run for President" (Feb. 11, 2007).

With that, she is done. This, approximately, is the present.

She stands amid all the papers and thinks about Marta, who comes tomorrow. Ornella could clear up beforehand. Then again, Marta will be impressed — no more nonsense about old papers on one side, new papers on the other. And no more technology bans — no drama if Marta's husband calls her cellphone while she's here.

The next day, Ornella races to the door.

"I have something to show you. Come, come!" She tries to take Marta's hand, but the cleaner is still removing her coat. Ornella waits restlessly. Marta has today's paper hidden in a plastic bag, as per standing instructions. "Come!" Ornella says. But midway down the hall she pauses.

"What?" Marta asks.

"You're going to think I'm stupid." She takes the cleaner's hand. Marta doesn't grip back but allows herself to be drawn forward.

"Oh dear," Marta says, seeing the mess. "It break?"

"Did what break?"

Marta is already on her knees, tidying up this paper catastrophe.

"Nothing's broken. I did it on purpose. Nothing to worry about. I threw them down there myself," Ornella protests. "I spent all night reading. Till four in the morning. I'm still nowhere near caught up. I have all sorts of questions. You're going to have to help me."

Marta, interpreting this as a request to tidy more quickly, responds, "Yes, yes, I do it, I do it."

"Stop — listen a moment. Leave it. Tell me, where did we put today's paper?"

"Which today?"

"This today." Ornella points her finger

downward, but that only indicates several thousand todays beneath their feet. She adds, "The today you brought in. The one in the plastic bag."

Marta is hesitant to hand it over, as if this might be a test.

Ornella settles on the living-room sofa, tense with the excitement, pulse elevated. She flaps open today's paper and shifts her backside about on the cushions. She clears her throat, blinks as if to clear her view, and surveys the front page. She turns to Marta who, having been ordered to keep her mistress company, has set up the ironing board in the living room. Ornella asks, "Don't you want to read along with me?"

"No, no."

"There's a lot I'm confused about. I'm counting on your help. Like, who is this Britney Spears, and why has she shaved off all her hair?"

"I don't know," Marta responds, her answer punctuated by a hiss of steam from the iron.

"Here's one: the silly pope made nasty comments about Muslims and now they're threatening to blow up churches." Ornella looks up. "It's not dangerous for you to go to your church, is it? Marta?"

"No, no."

Ornella turns the page. "Seems like everyone is blowing themselves up. And all these computers — do you understand this computer business?"

"What business?"

But Ornella knows too little even to frame a question. "Just in general."

"Not so much."

With a rush of affection, Ornella pats the sofa cushion beside her. "Why don't you stop for a minute and join me! Let me make you some coffee! We can discuss the news. Don't you think that'd be nice for a change?"

Marta, her face strained, looks around at the apartment, at all the floors that need sweeping, all the surfaces that require wiping down. And the dust under the beds?

When Marta's work is done, Ornella walks her to the door. "See you tomorrow?"

"Yes, okay," Marta replies, looking down. "Tomorrow."

1994. *Corso Vittorio, Rome*

By the early 1990s, the success of the paper under Milton Berber was beginning to abate, reflecting declining readership across the industry. Television had been eating away at papers for years, and the rise of twenty-four-hour news channels had dealt another blow. Morning newspapers, written the afternoon before, seemed increasingly out of date. Circulation dipped back under twenty-five thousand.

Of greater concern was Milton himself. Though he remained intellectually robust, his body failed: diabetes, hypertension, weakened vision, hearing loss. In 1994, he gathered the staff.

"Why does the paper exist?" he began.

A few reporters smiled nervously. Someone whispered a wisecrack.

"Seriously," Milton went on, "I've wondered a few times. Why did Cyrus Ott come all the way out here to found this place? Why would such a rich and powerful guy bother? The story is that Ott had a righteous passion for news, and he believed that the world needed a solid publication. I don't buy that. I'm a journalist — temperamentally opposed to noble motives. The truth is, the guy came out here for the pizza."

Everyone laughed.

"As for me," Milton continued, "I can't pretend to any higher motives myself. I just love putting out a newspaper: headlines and deadlines. Nothing noble. But, folks," he concluded, "this is the end of the line for me. It's time to step down."

A few editors gasped.

Milton grinned. "Oh come on — don't act surprised. In a rumor mill like this newsroom, don't pretend you clowns didn't know."

Milton lost his voice then. The room stayed silent, awaiting his next word. He grabbed a copy of that morning's edition, raised it hurriedly, and made for his corner office. It was his final day at the paper. Three months later in Washington, he died of a stroke.

Replacing Milton was not easy. Boyd slotted in a series of middling managers, each of whom lasted a couple of years before retiring on a cushion of Ott stocks. But this did nothing to halt the slide in circulation. The staff was trimmed by attrition; the style pages closed altogether; the culture and sports sections in particular became wastelands.

The paper still filled twelve pages a day, but the proportion of original stories plummeted and wire-service copy proliferated. While other newspapers had been battling the incursions of TV news by adopting color and splashy graphics, the paper remained stolidly black-

and-white.

The next challenge was to prove even more formidable: the Internet.

At first, many publications set up websites, charging for access. But readers simply shifted to free content. So media companies slapped more and more online for nothing, expecting that Internet ads would eventually catch up with hemorrhaging print losses.

The paper, however, had an idiosyncratic response: it did nothing. The corrections editor, Herman Cohen, nixed all talk of a website. "The Internet is to news," he said, "what car horns are to music."

■ ■ ■ ■

"MARKETS CRASH OVER FEARS OF CHINA SLOWDOWN"

• • •

CHIEF FINANCIAL OFFICER —
ABBEY PINNOLA

■ ■ ■ ■

Once at the boarding gate, Abbey falls into her customary travel coma, a torpor that infuses her brain like pickling fluid during long trips. In this state, she nibbles any snack in reach, grows mesmerized by strangers' footwear, turns philosophical, ends up weepy. She gazes at the banks of seats around the departure lounge: young couples nestling, old husbands reading books about old wars, lovers sharing headphones, whispered words about duty-free and delays.

She boards the plane, praying it won't be full. The flight from Rome to Atlanta is eleven hours, and she intends to stretch out — she'll work and sleep, in that order. From the corner of her eye, she spots a man pausing at her row, consulting his ticket. She glares out the window, imploring him away. (Once, she allowed a fellow passenger to engage her in conversation and it became the longest flight of her life. He made her play Scrabble and insisted that "ug" was a word. Since then, her rule has been to never talk on planes.)

The man says, "Well, what d'ya know," and sits beside her. The plane has not even taxied and already he's attempting conversation. She twitches in his direction and offers a faint "Hmm," but does not turn from her window.

He falls silent.

The force and tilt of takeoff awaken her. She was dreaming. About what? Can't remember. She needs her files from the overhead bin, but the Fasten Seat Belts sign is still lit. She drifts back into her travel coma, staring vacantly out the window as the clouds below sink into an infinite mattress.

She studies her fingernails, worrying about Henry, who doesn't want to visit his father in London over the school holidays and is about the age where she can't force him. Is he snubbing his dad out of loyalty to her? She hopes so, and she hopes not. She'll force Henry to go until he reaches a set age. Sixteen, say?

For God's sake! Enough! She has been trying to ignore it, but if this idiot beside her doesn't cede a corner of the armrest, she'll suffocate him with the vomit bag. She makes her elbow as pointy as possible and, very gradually, digs it into his forearm. How long before he gives in?

But he doesn't seem to notice and she is disgusted to touch him, so she gives up. He is picking the skin around his thumb, working free a strand of cuticle. Repugnant. She wants to see what this guy looks like, to attach a face to her loathing, but she can't turn to him without attracting notice. So she imagines him: American, fiftysomething, a loser. Cellulite, dandruff, thyroid on the blink. Works at Office Depot selling industrial ladders. Or does tech support and plays video games after work. Fanny pack, sweat socks, high-tops. What was he doing in Rome, anyway? He'd heard it was full of culture? Had himself photographed at the Colosseum, arm around a rent-a-gladiator?

But this is ridiculous — why should *she* be uncomfortable for eleven hours because of this idiot? She launches another pointed-elbow assault on the armrest, ratcheting up the pressure on his bone.

"Here," he says, pulling away. "Let me give you some space."

"Oh, thanks," she responds, ears blushing, crimson rising from lobes upward, and she hates him more.

"Sorry," he says. "I'm bad about hogging.

Do it without realizing. Just holler if you don't get enough space. I'm kinda gangly." He jiggles his arms to make the point. "Least we got the emergency exits. You can always tell the smart people by who asks for them. Emergency exits are practically first-class — not that I sat there before, but I figure it's the same — and all for the price of cattle class."

"Listen, would you mind doing me a big favor and waking me when they serve lunch? If you're awake, obviously. Thanks." She says this with her attention fixed on the seat-back in front of her, then returns to the window and pulls down the shade. She has done something stupid, though. She doesn't want to sleep. She wants to work. Now she'll be forced to fake it. She despises him.

Seven minutes pass — all the pretend sleep she can bear. She half rises from her seat, jaw compressed in cordial smile, and reaches for the overhead bin. "Just need to grab something."

He jumps up, drops his book on his seat, and makes way.

With difficulty, she squeezes out into the aisle.

"Can I help you get something?"

It happens in two stages. First, he looks familiar. Second, she realizes that she knows him. Dear Lord. What a nightmare. "Oh my God," she says. "Hi, hi. I totally didn't recognize you." Indeed, she still can't place him.

"You didn't know it was me?"

"I'm so sorry. I was completely spaced. I get in my own little world when I fly."

"No problem at all. Can I get something down for you?"

Her brain clicks: it's Dave Belling.

She wants to die. This is copydesk Dave. Newly fired Dave. Dave, who was laid off to cut costs. Dave, whom *she* ordered fired. Eleven hours beside him. Worse still, she has been caught in travel mode, in sweatpants, hair in pigtails. (At the paper, she's all suits and boots, eyes cold as coins.) As Henry would say, *Che figura di merda.*

"I think I can reach it," she says. "Thanks, though." But she can't quite get it. Her ears boil. "It's that blue bag. No, dark blue. Yup. Yeah. That's it. Great. Thanks. Thanks so much."

He steps aside gallantly to let her retake her seat.

She does so with a light smile and lead in her stomach. "I'm sorry if I seemed rude before. I really had no idea it was you." Stop babbling. "Anyway, how are you? What's going on? Where you headed?" Where is he headed? He's on a plane to Atlanta. And how's he doing? He just got fired.

"Good, real good," he replies.

"Great, that's great."

"You?"

"Good, good. Heading to Atlanta — obviously. I have this meeting with the Ott board. Our annual reckoning."

"You're the one who has to do that?"

"Afraid so. Our benighted publisher refuses."

"So the mud pie lands on your plate."

"Yup, yup. That's my plate all right. Though I must admit," she says, "it is interesting going to headquarters. We all have this tendency in Rome to think we're the center of the Ott world. Then when I go to Atlanta it really puts everything in perspective. Just how small we are."

"Not 'we' anymore," he says good-naturedly. "Not for me, anyhow."

"Yes, yes, right. Sorry."

"There was no movement at the paper, so I figured it was time to leave."

He must not realize that she knows the truth. More important, he must not realize her role in his dismissal. "That sounds wise," she says, filling the silence. "What's that you're reading?"

He retrieves the paperback from under his

behind and shows the cover.

"Oh wow," she says. "I'm a huge Jane Austen fan."

"Oh yeah?"

"I haven't read *Persuasion,*" she says. "But *Pride and Prejudice* is probably — no, definitely — my favorite book of all time. I'm trying to get my girls to read it, but I think they're a bit young still."

"What age?"

"Ten and eleven."

"I hadn't read anything by her till a couple of months ago," he says. "But now I'm on, like, a kind of mission to read everything she ever did. Which is not all that much. This is the last on my list." He studies the cover. "This wasn't her title for it — she died before it came out. The publisher called it *Persuasion.*"

"Great title, though."

"It is, isn't it."

"What's your favorite of hers?" she asks.

"*Mansfield Park,* maybe. Maybe *Pride.* The only one that didn't do it for me was *Sense and Sensibility.*"

"I've actually only read *Pride and Prejudice.*"

"I thought she was your favorite writer."

"I know, I know. But I'm a terrible reader. Three kids. The job."

381

"Three kids?" He makes a face.

"What's that mean?"

"No, I'm impressed. You seem young to have three."

"I guess. Though I'm not that young. Anyway. Sorry, I should let you get back to your book."

"No prob, seriously — it's good getting a chance to talk. Nobody talks at that office. You notice that? Weirdest thing when I started there — I was, like, is there some kind of clique out here or do I have a real bad odor or something? It's like a veil of silence in there."

"That's the paper all right."

"You practically feel like everybody hates you."

"That's how I feel all the time there." Her colleagues don't even have the respect to use her name, referring to her as "Accounts Payable." She hates the nickname. They can't accept that she's young and a woman and above them in the food chain. But *she's* the one keeping *them* employed. Those guys — glorified stenographers, pontificating about prerogatives of the press — as if the paper were anything more than a business. Not when we're losing this kind of money. And that champion of pontificators, the insufferable Herman Cohen, constantly forwarding her articles like "How Bean Counters Are Ruining the Media." As if she were running the place into the ground. It's he who blocked the paper from starting a website. In this day and age, we still have no Web presence! But those who call her Accounts Payable don't think about this stuff. They don't think about how much money the paper drops each time they're late in closing the edition (forty-three thousand euros so far this annum). Or how much she battled against layoffs. (She got the Ott board down from sixteen to nine, with just one coming from editorial.) Without her, the staff would be on the streets in a month. And *they* slag *her* off.

"That is so sad," she continues. "It takes an intercontinental flight to actually exchange words with someone in the office."

"Although we did talk once, when I started."

"Right, my welcome-aboard chat. Was I a total cow?"

"Not a *total* one."

"Oh no! Really?"

"I'm kidding. No, you just seemed real busy."

"I am. So, so busy. The board won't pay for an assistant. And why would they, quite frankly? They're getting three employees' work out of me. It's my own fault. Sorry, I shouldn't vent. And a retroactive sorry if I was a bit of a you-know-what back at work. Just a strange atmosphere at the paper sometimes, as you know." She angles herself toward him. "So you like to read?"

He ruffles the pages of his book. "When I can." He rests the paperback facedown on his thigh.

"You shouldn't spread it out like that."

"Like what?"

"Bending your book. You're gonna break the spine."

"I don't mind."

"Sorry. I'm being bossy. I should let you read."

"Don't worry about it."

"I should probably do some work myself." She opens the tray table but hesitates. Is there anything in her files that mentions Dave? Anything he shouldn't see? She opens her binder a crack and extracts a few innocuous pages but is furtively studying him. He turns a page of his book. He seems engrossed and not remotely curious to peek at her tedious charts. What page is he on? Eighty-three. She makes a fake shuffle of her papers, a meaningless check mark, but in fact she is reading *Persuasion* over his shoulder. He turns the page. He goes faster than she does. That's sort of annoying. But it's to be expected — he already knows what's going on in the story. She makes a few more spurious shifts of her papers. He turns another page and, after perceptibly holding his breath, spreads the book wider, for both of them to see. She has been caught again. Ears burning, she turns back to her work.

"Addictive, isn't it," he says graciously.

"That's a terrible habit of mine. Sorry."

"Don't be nuts. Here. Please." He opens the book between them on the armrest. "Want me to explain what's happening?"

"No, no — it's fine, really. I should do my work."

"See, that's why they fired me," he jokes. "Everybody else is working while I'm reading damn Jane Austen!"

Fired him? That's not how he characterized it before.

"Well, you certainly have a good sense of humor about it."

"Easier when you've got a new job."

"You do? Oh, that's so good to hear."

"Thanks. Yeah, the day after I got canned I was talking to this Italian buddy of mine and he told me about this position. Guess I'm lucky."

She wonders how old Dave Belling is.

Roughly her age? Older by a bit?

"Hey, look," he says, "it's lunch number one coming down the aisle."

"Lunch number one?"

"Yeah, we get two lunches on this flight because of the time difference."

"Oh, hurrah."

"Seriously."

They eat their plastic chicken and rubber carrots and a pink confection, and make sardonic remarks about it all, as people will when faced with grim airplane food that they nonetheless consume to the crumbs.

"So why are you headed to Atlanta?" she asks.

"Just wanted to see my folks before I start the new job."

"You're from the area, then?"

"From Georgia, yeah. A little town called Ocilla."

"Nice place?"

"It's all right. Couldn't live there again. Grew up there, and that's enough for a lifetime. And you? Where you from?"

"Rochester, New York, originally."

"So you're an 'originally,' too. That means there's been a whole bunch of stops after originally."

"Not that many. I went to college in Bing-hamton, did a year abroad in Milan, which is where I met my husband. Not currently my husband. My ex. Though he wasn't that then. I never know how to say that."

"Allow my copydesk expertise to intervene: your then-pre-husband, later-to-be-post-husband in his prior-to-ex-husband status."

She laughs. "Is that how you'd phrase it in the paper?"

"Now you see why they fired me."

She smiles. "So anyway, yeah, I got involved with my whatever-he-is in Milan. He's from there. It was my first really significant romance, and I was —" She pauses.

"You were what?"

"I don't know. Stupid. Twenty-three."

"You can't complain — you got three kids out of the bargain."

"That's true. That's what I tell myself."

"I don't have any," he says. "Wanted them. But my wife — my then wife — didn't. No matter what I said, she wasn't having it. But listen to this: we get divorced in, like, '96, and she meets some guy and they go and have four kids! Guess it wasn't that she didn't want kids. She didn't want them with *me!*"

Abbey doesn't respond.

"What?" he asks.

"No, nothing. Nothing. I was just thinking," she says. "You seem very strong about
that. Very, like you don't have self-pity. I
have a lot of admiration for that."

He smiles abashedly. "Not really."

"No, seriously."

He picks at his cuticle. "I'm sure you're
the same about your divorce."

"You only say that because you haven't
heard me mouthing off about my poor ex!
Not that he's poor in any sense of the word.
Kind of a rich jerk-off, actually. Excuse my
language."

"Why's he a jerk-off?"

She twitches her head as if swooped by a
bee. "Just is. I don't know. We had this passionate love affair — I thought. Now I
suspect he just wanted to improve his English."

"Nah."

"I'm not entirely kidding. He's this terrible Anglophile. He insisted we give our
kids these traditional British names, or
names he thought were traditional."

"Like what?"

"Henry, Edith, and Hilda."

"That's like something from Victorian England."

She covers her face. "I know, I know. I'm
so embarrassed. He forced them on me! I

swear. I was young and dumb. Keep in mind that these names are also impossible for Italians to pronounce. So their own grandparents in Milan — really good people, I have to say — can't even say their own grandkids' names. It's ridiculous."

"So where's the ex-husband now?"

"London. He was so in love with it, he moved there. Supposedly to find a place big enough for all of us. I even gave in my resignation — I was an assistant in accounts back then, before I did my MBA. Then he sends me this letter about how he has 'nervous problems,' whatever that means. There was a slow, ugly end. Never told me directly about his girlfriend. He lives there now. In London. With her."

"Some proper English girl, I guess."

"Actually, to my great amusement she's from Naples."

"Well," Dave says, laughing, "if that ain't a kick in the pants."

She smiles at this funny expression. "I certainly thought so," she continues. "Ah well. How old are you, Dave, if you don't mind me asking?"

"Forty-five. You?"

"Forty. Just turned forty."

"Seriously?" he says. "You're younger than I thought."

"Oh gee, thanks a lot."

"No, no, I don't mean it that way. I mean you're young to have such an important job. And three kids and all that. Puts me to shame."

The conversation falters. She is facing him and can't inconspicuously turn away.

"Shall we read a bit?" he suggests, opening the book to where they were.

"That's nice of you, but you go ahead. I should do some work."

She glances at him now and then. They smile at each other and he waggles the book, saying, "Not tempted?"

After a stretch of work, she turns to make a joke. But he is asleep, the book flat on his chest. Jane Austen, she thinks, what guy reads Jane Austen? He's not gay, is he? Doesn't seem gay. She hasn't known many Southerners. That twang and aw-shucks about him — it's sort of exotic. Very natural.

What if he wakes and catches her scrutinizing him? So she studies him from the corner of her eye. He's not especially tall, though it's hard to tell seated. Sweatshirt, jeans, hiking shoes. A relaxed, outdoorsy look. His hand on the book is small, but angular and strong, fingernails bitten, cuticles mismanaged. More to him than meets the eye. His divorce obviously still

hurts. He's private, though — not a guy to
bleed his life over you.

He shifts in his sleep and his arm hops up
onto the rest between them, touching her
elbow. She holds still, decides to allow the
contact, resumes breathing.

An hour later, he yawns and blinks to
wakefulness. "Sorry about that."

"About what?" she whispers.

"Think I fell asleep for a minute," he
replies softly. "Hey, how come we're whispering?"

"Maybe because the lights are off." She
points toward the toilets. "Sorry, I need to
go up there for a minute."

"Oh man," he says, unbuckling his seat
belt and leaping to his feet. "Did I have you
trapped in here?"

"Not at all. Not at all." She sucks in her
tummy and squeezes out into the aisle,
retrieves her handbag from the overhead
bin, and heads for the bathroom. Safely
inside, she studies herself, hardly flattered
by the lighting. "I look fucking terrible."
She takes the roll-on deodorant from her
bag, stripes it across her underarm. She
unpacks refreshing towelettes, wipes her
face and hands, swabs on foundation to
conceal her blotchiness, adds a trace of eye-
liner, a stroke of lipstick. Or not. She kisses

it off onto a paper towel, considers the scratched metal reflection one last time, plucks an eyelash from her cheek. She adjusts her underwire, which was pinching, glances down her shirt: a tattered black bra. She peeks down her trousers: blue granny panties. Nice combo: funeral lace on top and parachute material on bottom. Don't be stupid — who cares. One more refreshing towelette. Done.

She stops at their row. "Hey."

He jumps to his feet. "Hey there."

She inhales and slides back into place.

"You take a shower in there?"

"Why? Because I took so long?"

"Because you look, like, so awake and stuff. I don't know how you girls manage that. When I travel, I look like a pair of old boots."

"We ladies have our secrets," she declares with pride.

"Well," he responds enthusiastically, "I'm all for that."

Not gay, she thinks. "Listen, it's only plane travel," she says, touching his arm. "Nobody expects anyone to look their best."

"You're sure doing pretty good," he says, voice subsiding at the baldness of the compliment. "Anyhow," he picks up, "I reckon I'll go freshen up a bit myself. Even if I'm not working with so much."

"Oh stop it."

He returns, slapping damp hands against his cheeks. "Better." He drops into his seat. "Better."

"So," she says. "Anyway."

A moment of silence.

"So," she attempts again, "do you like living in Rome? Do you have millions of friends and everything?"

"Sort of. I mean not millions. I didn't speak any Italian at the get-go, which held me back."

"Still, I bet you had tons of girls chasing you, right? The single American journalist and all that."

"Not so much. For a while, I dated this girl from New Zealand that worked at this pub near my place."

"And where's that?"

"My place? In Monti. Via dei Serpenti."

"Cool area."

"Small apartment, but yeah. You know, one thing I learned in Rome is that the Italians are real friendly and stuff, but they got their cliques. You know? They hang out their whole lives with the same people they met in first grade. And if you weren't at that school, well, you're never getting a dinner invite. You know what I mean?"

"Absolutely. That's so Italian."

"Kind of hard to break into. For an American. Easier, I guess, for girls. Those slick Italian guys and so forth."

"You haven't bought into that Latin-lover myth, have you? Let me tell you a secret: Italian guys — and I know, I married one — are prima donnas, not studs. And I refuse to fall for a guy whose wardrobe is better than mine. A lot of these Italians, they're like little boys. My son, Henry, is way more mature and he's thirteen. A lot of them are still having Mama do their laundry, turn up their jeans, fix them mortadella sandwiches for lunch. They never quite get over it." She wiggles her nose. "What, me bitter? Sorry — no more tirades, I swear."

"It's kind of good to hear this, actually. I spent the last couple of years feeling like one big pile of American slob."

"Listen." She touches his arm confidentially. "You've seriously got nothing to worry about."

"Keep it coming. This is good for my ego after, like, two years of seeing Italian guys in pink sweaters and orange pants and, like, pulling it off. You know what I'm saying?"

She laughs.

"To tell the truth," he goes on, "the past six months or so, I've sort of given up on all that. On getting to know some Italian woman. Like, lost a bit of patience."

"How do you mean?"

"I guess I'm tired of getting burned. I know that sounds cynical. And, if you talked to me in my twenties and thirties, I used to be the most romantic guy. You should've seen me at my wedding. I was the one who pushed for a big ceremony. My ex wanted it all restrained. But I'm crazy that way. Over the top that way. Life'd be easier if I weren't a dumb romantic. But that's me. So."

"It's not a bad thing."

"Maybe. Makes life complicated, though."

"Anything that's worth anything is complicated. Don't you think? Or is that stupid?"

"No, no. You're probably right."

"My problem is the amount of time I spend on my job — honestly, I wonder if I'd even have time for a proper relationship anymore. And I'm way too embarrassed to admit when my last one was."

"Oh, come on."

"I'm not telling. Seriously. You don't want to know. Henry says I'm substituting work for love. That's Henry, thirteen going on thirty. I think another problem is — and I don't want this to sound conceited — is that a lot of guys can be intimidated by me. I think I can come off as too driven, too career-oriented. I don't know. Not mean-hearted, I hope. That's completely *not* who I am. But you can't be weak in the job I have. You have to be tough or everybody walks all over you. That's how it goes. People think I'm some kind of storm trooper. But I actually don't have a lot of confidence; I'm pretty shy. I know I don't come off that way. But —" She checks his response. "Way too much information, right? Sorry, I'm blabbing."

"Not at all. I get you. I believe every person on this planet needs human contact to be normal, to be sane. Simple as that. And, I'll admit, I'm no exception."

She hadn't been brave enough to say it so directly, didn't want to appear the pathetic single mother. "Maybe you have a point," she says. "I mean, it's probably just normal."

"More than normal."

She crosses her legs tightly — she's dying to pee. She was too busy prettifying herself before to remember to use the toilet. She doesn't want to seem like she has a bladder problem, but she can't hold it much longer. "I'm going to stretch my legs a second," she says. Instead of using the toilet at the front of the plane, she saunters toward the tail. Out of his sight, she sidesteps into the bathroom. She sits in there after she's done, thinking.

She smells her forearm, which touched his. He has a particular scent — kind of nice, actually. What is it? Manly. Skin smell. Wonder what his place in Via dei Serpenti is like. Empty wine bottles, half-burnt candles, wax stains in the rug. A small place, he said, which suggests that he's there alone. She couldn't invite him to her place in Rome, with the kids. Well, eventually, maybe. For the next few days, she's got a four-star hotel room in Atlanta. She gets a tingle. Forget it, you freak. But it would be nice to hang out a bit. Talk. He's cute, no? Surprisingly. Totally natural. Nice to have a bit of company. A proper grown-up. Having a man around again. Forgotten what that's like. This hotel they always put her in — wouldn't it be cool if . . . Hang on. Stop. This is the travel coma speaking: getting all weird and flirty. The Ott board meeting. Think about that. Should get this guy's number, though. Find out when he gets back to Rome. Meet up there.

The in-flight movie is starting when she gets back. He has her headphones ready. It's a comedy. She keeps the volume low so she can still hear herself — she doesn't want to giggle too loudly or too stupidly or not enough. He has a nice chuckle. Wry, honest. When he laughs, he turns to her, twinkling. "We need popcorn."

"You're so right!"

The stewardess trundles a trolley down the aisle, delivering the second meal.

Abbey checks her watch. "Which is this? Lunch number two? Feels like dinner."

"Sort of a dinner-lunch," Dave says.

"What would you call that? A dlunch?"

"Or a linner."

"Unless it's a mix of lunch and supper. Then you've got slupper," she says. "Or slunch."

"Slunch. I like that. We should trademark that."

We? Hmm. Interesting.

"Hey, listen, Dave," she says. "We should get together sometime in Rome. Don't you think? Get a coffee or a drink or something? When you get back."

"Yeah, totally. That's a good idea."

"You should give me your number."

"My number in Rome?"

"Yeah."

"I don't have one there."

She frowns. "What do you mean?"

"Well, I don't live there anymore."

Each of them is puzzled by the other.

"I don't live there anymore," he repeats. "Can't afford two rents."

"Two? Where's the other?"

"In San Jose."

"I'm totally lost here."

"My new job. In San Jose, California."

"Oh, oh, oh," she says, faking a smile. "I'm so stupid. I thought you meant — when you said before you'd got a new job — I stupidly assumed you meant in Rome."

"No, no, I don't have papers to work in Europe anymore. And, anyhow, I was ready to get back to the States."

"So what is your new job?" she asks hurriedly, as if the location were insignificant.

"Some Web thing. Helping edit this music-mag start-up. A Web-based magazine, basically."

"Okay. I'm beginning to get it," she says. "But . . ."

"What?"

"No, nothing."

"Your ears are all red," he says. "You okay?"

Can't believe he just said that. What an assholish thing to say — to point that out. "Yeah, I'm fine," she replies sharply.

The food arrives. He takes chicken. It's the last one. She wanted chicken. She takes fish. Kind of rude not to have asked her.

"How's yours?" he asks.

"Fine." After a minute, she adds, "Would

have preferred chicken. But, whatever."

"You want to switch?"

"No, no. No big deal." She puts down her cutlery, opens a binder, and resumes work. Rather, she glowers at the page. What an idiotic thing for him to say. To point out to somebody: Hey there, by the way, you're blushing. Is he five years old? And how is she supposed to know he's moving to California? He says it like it's obvious, like the whole world has been following his life.

He opens *Persuasion* again but remains on the same page, picking at the skin around his cuticles.

Disgusting. And is he really reading that book at all? Is this some kind of show? To be fair, this isn't the brightest guy on earth. Good ol' boy from wherever. Some podunk town in Georgia. This is a guy who couldn't hack it at the paper, who was outclassed by those Thorazine-addled cretins on the copy-desk. When she wanted to ax a job from the editorial side, Dave Belling was the most expendable — a real accomplishment among a group of such disposable losers. (In fairness, Abbey's first choice had been Ruby Zaga, but Kathleen interceded to protect her.)

"Excuse me," Abbey says, rising without explanation. She walks down their aisle, up the other, then back again. She spies the crown of Dave's head from behind. Going bald. What is wrong with guys? Half are molting; half are nothing but undergrowth. Is there some link between baldness and assholishness? Or hairiness and being dumb? It wasn't by chance that she got Dave fired. Kathleen had wanted all nine layoffs to come from the technical staff. But Abbey insisted that at least one come from editorial — time to teach the newsroom a lesson. She checked that Dave's performance evaluations were impeccably mediocre and that he had no insurmountable allies — i.e., Kathleen or Herman — then filed the paperwork for dismissal. Thank God, too. Imagine if she had to see this jerk every day at work now.

She goes over her files until they arrive in Atlanta. The plane taxis toward the gate, the seat-belt sign turns off, the economy-class detainees unfold themselves, arms shooting for the overhead bins. By contrast, Dave stretches casually and yawns. "Can I get your bag for you?"

"No, please just leave it. I have some fragile stuff in there."

The front exit opens and the crowd inches toward it, disembarking to the plodding rhythm of the cabin crew's "Bye now . . .

bye now . . . bye now."

Dave waits for her to gather her belongings.

"Please — go ahead," she says.

"It's no problem."

She stalls for as long as possible. "No need to wait for me. Seriously."

"It's fine."

In the terminal, he veers toward the baggage carousel.

"Well, take care then," she says.

"You only had carry-on?"

"Always."

"Where you staying, by the way?"

"I forget. Some hotel."

"Which one?"

"Can't remember. The Intercontinental, possibly."

"Maybe we could share a cab."

"Don't you have to get going to wherever it is you have to go? Your hometown? Anyway, I'm expensing the ride, so I'll get my own. Otherwise, the receipts get too complicated."

"Oh," he says. "Well, hey."

"Yup. Take care."

He leans in to kiss her cheek.

She pulls back. "Don't want to give you my cold." She shakes his hand.

At the Intercontinental, she lays out her

work on the desk. She wasted too much time yakking to that idiot. She keeps yawning. She needs to stay up, to adjust to the time difference immediately — it's the only way. She checks the clock. Too late to call the kids. But how can you not mention that your new job is in San Jose? Whatever. When's the first meeting tomorrow morning? A breakfast thing. Welcome back to the land of bad coffee and doughnuts the size of toilet seats. What was the point of him flirting the whole time if he lives in another city? Her desk in the hotel room is backed by a mirror. She catches sight of herself. She'd kill to have a chat with Henry. Travel coma is making her weepy.

A ringing. She opens her eyes, disoriented. It's dark. What time is it? The alarm is blinking. Has she missed the meeting? Fuck! That ringing. It's not the alarm, though. She reaches for the phone. "Hello?"

"Finally, I get you!"

"Hello?" she repeats.

"It's Dave Belling. I'm downstairs. I'm being real rude here. Taking a chance. But I decided, you know, my folks can wait a few hours. I didn't want us to not see each other again. I was all the way down at the bus station. Then I was, like, this is too dumb. So I came over here. I hope you weren't sleeping. And listen, if this is an imposition at all, please just say so and I'll be on my merry way, no problem. But if it isn't, I was figuring on maybe buying you a drink or something. Even some dlunch. Or a spot of slupper."

She laughs, rubbing her eyes. She flicks on the desk lamp, blinking. "What time is it?"

"Slupper time."

"I think I dozed off. I thought it was tomorrow."

"If this isn't good for you, I can get going. No problem."

"Hang on, hang on, wait. Can you stay there a minute? I'll come right down. Don't come up. Where are you?"

She hasn't got time for a shower, so she freshens up as best she can in the bathroom, working in the skin moisturizer as if kneading dough. She should be preparing for the board meeting. She should be getting an early night.

"Hey," she says, tapping his shoulder from behind.

He is by the concierge desk, flipping through a magazine. "Hey there," he says, his face lighting up. "Sure I'm not imposing?"

"Of course not."

"What do you feel like? A drink? Something to eat?"

"After that pink mystery cake on the plane, I'm off food until October."

"I hear that. A drink it is."

They take a booth at the hotel bar. A television mounted on the wall is showing CNBC, with a headline that reads, "Markets Crash Over Fears of China Slowdown."

"It'll go fine tomorrow," he tells her. "You're obviously going to be the smartest girl in the room, so don't sweat it."

They talk and talk, him about his divorce, her about hers. After three Bacardi Breezers, she tells him: "It's like you were saying on the plane. I'm too romantic for my own good. And okay, you get kicked in the butt sometimes. But, frankly, I'd rather have, you know — actual sentiments. Than. You know? You know what I mean?"

"I hear that."

"Well, hey," she says.

"Hey," he says.

They laugh.

He says, more softly, "Come here," and leans across the table. He kisses her. He sits back slowly, as if he hadn't been expecting to do that.

"Well," she says.

"Well then," he says.

"No kidding."

They go up to her room. She rushes into the bathroom, mouthing at her reflection: "You're nuts."

When she emerges, he reaches out for her. She moves into his embrace, expecting a kiss but he only hugs her, tightening, then slackening as he breathes out serenely. He leans back, looks into her eyes.

"Mmm," she says. "I needed that."

"*I* needed that," he says.

She kisses him, tenderly, then with passion. Lips locked, they lumber to the bed, tripping, giggling. She flops onto the mattress and hits the remote control, turning on the television. "Oh God, I'm sorry!" she exclaims, suddenly serious.

He turns it off, tosses aside the remote. He unbuttons her top and pulls it off. He unzips her trousers, tugs them down and off. She's wearing only the funereal black bra and the blue granny panties. She folds her arms to cover her chest and crosses her legs. "Can we turn off a light?"

"Let's leave it on a second," he says.

"But aren't you getting undressed?"

"Hey, don't cover yourself."

"It's kinda bright in here."

"I want to look at you," he says.

"But you're still dressed. And I'm in my,

406

in my, in this bra and these." She laughs uncertainly.

"Wait, wait, hang on. Don't pull up the covers."

"How come? Can't I?"

"One point of order first." His tone changes. His voice goes cold. "One small thing." His eyes track down her body. He proceeds, "Tell me this, Accounts Payable."

She freezes at the name.

"Why," he says, "why of all the people there, Accounts Payable, did you go and get *me* fired?" He stands at the foot of the bed, staring. "So?" he says. "Explain me that."

2004. Ott Group Headquarters, Atlanta
Newspapers were spiraling downward.

Competing entertainments abounded, from cellphones to video games, from social-networking sites to online porn. Technology was not merely luring readers; it was changing them. Full printed pages didn't fit onto monitors, so portion size shrank, dicing news into ever-smaller morsels. Instant updates on the Internet bred contempt for day-old headlines in ink. Even the habit of exchanging money for information dwindled — online, payment was merely an option.

As readership plummeted, advertisers fled and losses mounted. But, doggedly, the pay-per-view papers kept at it. They made their daily judgments, produced their digests of the world, laid them out across pages, printed tonight and delivered tomorrow, to be flapped open before bleary breakfast eyes. Fewer eyes, each day.

Despite all this, Boyd was not about to let his father's paper go under. He had rescued it once before, when he'd hired Milton Berber. The trick was to find the right leader. This time, he chose Kathleen Solson, a former protégée of Milton's. Kathleen had risen through the ranks in Rome, then jumped to Milton's old newspaper in Washington, progressing fast. She covered a suburban beat, joined the

Pentagon team, became national reporter for the Southwest and then national editor, all in less than a decade.

But at that level in the Washington hierarchy, competition stiffened. To climb the masthead, she'd need to play politics for years. Or she could gamble, jump to the top job at a smaller newspaper, and use it as a proving ground. She flew to Rome to meet with the current crop of senior editors, a sparse breed by then, their numbers diminished by years of attrition.

If she was to take the job, she told Boyd, much would have to change. The paper needed to fill those empty cubicles, buy new computers, bulk up its coverage abroad: a Chinese speaker for Shanghai, an Arabic speaker for the Middle East, and so forth. This was too critical a time in history — the war on terror, the rise of Asia, climate change — to be reporting about the fat folds of celebrities at the beach. "We can leave that to the Internet," she said.

Boyd agreed, and she made the move back to Rome, bringing along her deputy from the Washington national desk, Craig Menzies.

Soon she had cause for concern. The Ott Group — despite Boyd's promises — proved reluctant to fund her plans. She found herself hamstrung by increasingly restrictive budgets and Boyd himself ignored her, leaving everything to underlings — above all to the swinging ax of the paper's chief financial officer, Abbey Pinnola. First, Abbey ordered yet another hiring freeze. Then she abolished merit raises. Then she demanded layoffs.

Kathleen appealed for color pages and for a website, and she hammered on about hiring more correspondents overseas. The Ott board rejected every request. It was only when she sought to contact Boyd through private channels that she learned how ill he was.

It was cancer, the same that had killed Ott. When Boyd heard his diagnosis, he experienced something close to pride: he and his father were allied in this. But as Boyd's symptoms worsened, any such fancy abandoned him. He seethed at those around him, those who would outlive him, who did not deserve to — his grown children, typing asinine messages into mobile phones, idiots who understood nothing. Eventually, even fury failed him, giving way to dark days. His life had been wasted, second-rate beside his father's. No time to fix it.

As chairman, Boyd had transformed the Ott Group. But he had not enriched it. At the time of his death, the company was worth one-third as much as when he had taken it over.

Not one of his four children was an obvious successor. His eldest son, Vaughn, was widely disliked; his two daughters were intelligent but wild; and the youngest boy, Oliver, was so weak-willed as to have recused himself from the Ott board.

That didn't mean Oliver had been left alone. It was he who had cared for Boyd during the illness, and his siblings felt uncomfortably indebted. They intended to discharge their obligation and sought a role for him. The Ott Group holdings were varied enough to offer something. How about this paper they owned in Rome? No one in the new generation could explain why their grandfather had founded this money-losing operation. He must have lost his touch. But now, at least, the paper would come in handy. It would be ideal for Oliver: no pressure, since it could scarcely do worse. Plus, Europe was artsy, which would appeal to him. And he could live in Grandpa's empty old mansion in Rome. Perhaps he would even stun them and turn the paper around.

Oliver himself had no such illusions. He opposed the appointment, reminding his brother and sisters that he knew nothing about business and had scarcely read a newspaper in his life, except to check the arts listings. Vaughn said a business is a business.

"But I don't know anything about *any* business," Oliver replied.

"You'll learn."

411

On his arrival, the paper was in an uproar. Kathleen and Abbey leaped at Oliver like polar bears on a walrus — he was an actual, live Ott, and they had him in their midst. Their demands, boiled down, were this: money. Chippy staffers beset him, too, protesting the wage freeze, the threat of layoffs, the filthy carpeting (unwashed since 1977, they said). He rushed off to phone Vaughn.

"Not gonna happen," Vaughn said. "You know how much the paper is losing?"

"Not exactly."

"Well, they're lucky we're still paying their salaries."

Oliver avoided the office after that, dropping by only after hours to sign documents and pick up mail. Otherwise, he hid out at the mansion, his sole daily excursion to walk his basset hound, Schopenhauer.

■ ■ ■ ■

"Gunman Kills 32 in Campus Rampage"

• • •

PUBLISHER — OLIVER OTT

■ ■ ■ ■

The phone rings in the living room. He knows who it is, so he puts on his coat, summons Schopenhauer, and leads the dog outside for a walk.

Oliver is a lanky man, not quite thirty but already hunched, his head dangling forward as if from a coat hook rather than mounted upon a spine. An oily blond fringe curtains his blemished forehead and pale blue eyes, while a turnip nose bobs between strands of hair as he walks. His lips bear nibbled indents, and his chin wavers as he mumbles to his dog. He gazes fixedly down the line of the leash, witnessing the world from Schopenhauer's vantage point — life at sniff level.

A scent catches the basset hound's attention and he jumps toward a urine-drizzled tussock of grass. He pulls this way, wrenches that, braiding Oliver into ever more intricate tangles. "I'm beginning to think," Oliver

415

says, "that the leash is here largely for irony."

Their walks take them all around the city. To the Botanical Gardens on the slopes of the Janiculum. To the Valle dei Cani in Villa Borghese. To the parched turf of the Circus Maximus, where tourists trudge the ancient chariot circuit, chugging bottled water. On the hottest days, Oliver and Schopenhauer cross the Tiber, making for the shaded alleys of Trastevere. Or they stroll up Via Giulia, whose resolutely tall buildings stand up to the sun. Or they saunter through the Protestant Cemetery in Testaccio, where Oliver's grandfather is buried.

The headstone is an uninspiring affair — "Cyrus Ott. Born 1899. Died 1960" — so Oliver proceeds to more diverting tombs, reading under his breath the inscribed names: "Gertrude Parsons Marcella . . . Lieutenant Colonel Harris Arthur McCormack . . . Wolfgang Rappaport. Dead at age four." He tells the dog, "Michael James Lamont Hosgood died at fifteen. That's him, beside his mother. But she died twenty years later in Kent. She must have asked to be buried back here, alongside her son. Don't you think, Schop?" The tomb of Devereux Plantagenet Cockburn is adorned with a life-size statue of the deceased, a young fop reclining with a cocker spaniel in his lap and his thumb inserted in a book, as if every visitor to the grave were a pleasant interruption from his studies. Oliver reads the lengthy inscription, which concludes: "He was beloved by all who knew him, and most precious to his parents and family, who had sought his health in many foreign climes. He departed this life in Rome, on the 3rd of May 1850, aged 21 years."

The sun resigns its position in the sky and the mosquitoes assume theirs, so Oliver and Schopenhauer head back to the Aventine Hill. Their home is a sixteenth-century mansion that Cyrus Ott bought cheap in the early 1950s. Oliver punches in the digital code and the mechanized steel gate parts squeakily. Inside, the telephone rings.

Oliver releases Schopenhauer, winds up the leash, and enters the living room. The ceiling is even higher than in the entrance hall, paneled with rococo reliefs, with starbursts and peach cherubim gamboling around the corners. The oil paintings on the walls are too poorly lit for their subjects to be immediately discernible — from a distance, all appear to depict woods at night; only the gilt frames glint. Into the Oriental rugs, deep paths have been worn from pedestrian traffic: to the kitchen, to the shuttered windows, to the bookshelves, to the tête-à-tête settee, to the old telephone whose antiquated bell at this moment rattles against the wallpaper. The answering machine kicks in.

"Hi, it's me again," Kathleen says. "I'm at the office. Please give me a call. Thanks."

Oliver plucks a paperback Agatha Christie from a stack on the floor and settles himself and the dog (lured with a chocolate cookie) on the settee. At 7 P.M., the housekeepers announce dinner. It's some sort of stew. Too much rosemary and too little salt, but perfectly edible. Schopenhauer sniffs the meat-scented air beseechingly, his droopy eyes bloodshot, spittle on his chops. Oliver fetches that day's paper — the subscription department insists on sending it, though he never reads the thing. He spreads it across the table and places his plate of leftovers on top. He pulls up a chair for Schopenhauer, who leaps up and shoots his snout across the table. The dog turns his muzzle to one side to snap up meat and carrots, then jerks his head back, flinging the food down his throat.

"A knife and fork would be preferable," Oliver says. "But there's no teaching you."

Once the plate is clean, Oliver scrunches up the paper, specked with gravy and gobbets of gristle. He disposes of the mess in the kitchen as Schopenhauer drinks from his bowl, tongue and ears slapping the water.

The phone in the living room rings again. And, again, the machine gets it. "I'm headed home now," Kathleen says wearily. "You can get me on my cell. Appreciate if you'd call tonight. Kinda urgent. Thanks."

Schopenhauer noses open the door and wanders off, padding upstairs.

"Time alone is good for any relationship," Oliver comments as if the dog were still in the room to hear it. Oliver lies on his belly on the floor, piles of books ranged around him like tall grass: *Miss Marple's Final Cases*, a Taschen monograph on Turner, Sotheby's twentieth-century British art-auction listing, *The Penguin Complete Father Brown*, a catalog from *Caravaggio: The Final Years* at the National Gallery, and *The Case-Book of Sherlock Holmes*. "Where have you gone?" he asks the absent dog. He checks in the kitchen. "Schop?" He peers into the dining room. "Where in the devil's name are you?"

He climbs the darkened staircase with a flashlight. (Oliver inhabits only the ground floor; the rest of the mansion is all darkness, covered by tarpaulins.) The beam of his torch sweeps across the second-floor landing. "Schopenhauer, where are you?"

Oliver is swallowed into the black belly of the house; a chandelier twinkles; the telephone in the living room rings. The answering machine beeps, its message number flashing permanently at "99" because the display lacks a third digit.

"Where are you, you fool?" Oliver calls into the darkened ballroom. He shines the flashlight about and exclaims, "Ah!" — reflective eyes under the piano. "Sorry, I'm blinding you." He turns off the flashlight and the basset hound trots over, his overlong nails clacking on the hardwood floor. Oliver kneels to greet his friend. "What were you doing under the piano? Sleeping?" He strokes Schopenhauer's long, damp ear. "I hope I didn't wake you."

They fumble through the dark to the study, which contains documents from his grandfather's time in Rome. Oliver clicks on the lamp and, snooping like a whodunit detective, peeks into the drawers. He finds a letter pad containing Ott's notes of fifty years before — references to newsprint rolls, the price of Linotype machines, telex rates. There is an unfinished letter from Ott to his wife and son: "Dear Jeanne and Boyd, the important thing to realize, and I need to make this clear." It ends there.

Oliver turns the page and finds another of

Ott's letters. "I want you to have all the paintings — we bought them together and I feel they should be yours," it begins. "Take this to my lawyers and they will do as I say." The next line is illegible. Then: "I long to see you, but I will not telephone. Nothing pleasant about this illness. Nothing anybody needs to see. But you should know that I regret certain things," the letter says. "I regret that I left you in New York. But I made that decision and I must live with it. I married, then you married. I was not going to interfere after that. I was an honorable man, I believed, and did not know how to stop being one. To think of that now, it seems outright madness. But I got myself into a tangle. I tied myself in knots. I built and I built — heaven knows I have done that well. Those skyscrapers, full of tenants, floor after floor, and not a single room containing you. You asked why I came here to Rome. I never cared about the news. I came to be in the same room as you, even if I had to build that room, fill it with people, with typewriters, the rest. I only hope you understand that the paper was for you."

A blue ink stain follows, as if the tip of the pen rested here for some time. The handwriting resumes, tiny now: "Can't send this . . . Damn well must . . . Too late now . . . Don't be a fool — just send her this."

He never did.

Oliver places the pad back in the drawer. "You fat beast," he tells Schopenhauer, as he carries him down the stairs. "You're so much heavier than I think — I always forget that." He puts the dog down in the living room, as if lowering a table to its feet. The table scampers away. "Asleep under the piano!" he remarks, smacking his hands together. "Now I'm all covered in dust."

The phone rattles the wallpaper. "I pretend it's not ringing," Oliver says, "and it pretends I'm not here."

The machine beeps. "Oliver, this is Abbey. I'm happy to brief you on my meetings in Atlanta. Anyway, I'm back now. So call me. Thanks."

Oliver coaxes Schopenhauer back onto the settee. "Stop staring at me," he tells the dog. "I'm trying to read."

Schopenhauer burps.

"You disgusting contrarian," Oliver says. But he is unable to resist for long and strokes the dog's ears. Schopenhauer rumbles contentedly, leaning into Oliver's hip. "My dear friend," Oliver says. "I'm so lucky." He adds, suddenly self-conscious, "If anyone heard me talking to you! But it's not like I'm talking to myself. You're listening because —" He stops there, to see if it prompts a response.

The dog yawns.

"See, I have to get to the end of my sentence. You won't have it otherwise."

The dog's eyelids sink shut.

Over the coming weeks, the phone calls increase.

"Money, money, money," Oliver tells Schopenhauer. "What am I supposed to do? I don't run the Ott Group."

Kathleen is talking into the machine: ". . . and I'm going to need you at that staff meeting. I've told everyone you'll be there, so I'd appreciate it if you'd call me back."

At the Valle dei Cani, Oliver switches Schopenhauer to the extendable leash, which allows the animal to play with the dogs but not to run away. The other owners watch Oliver with amusement: he retreats to the edge of the grassy bowl, behind a tree, with a detective novel pressed to his nose, unwilling to engage human eyes as he clings to the world's longest and most unmanageable leash. Every few minutes, he must rush over to Schopenhauer and remove the cord from an animal or a person. Oliver never speaks on these occasions, even if spoken to. He unties his friend, hurries back to his tree, resumes reading — or, rather, resumes pretending to read.

He has no friends in Rome except Schopenhauer. He has no friends anywhere except Schopenhauer, unless his companion from school days, the pensioner Mr. Deveen, is still alive. But Mr. Deveen must be dead by now. How old would he be? He'd not have reached the twenty-first century, not with all those cigarettes. Dear man. Can't condemn him. He must have been lonely. That's the best way to explain it.

Dinner that evening is *bigoli al tartufo nero,* and Schopenhauer makes an ungodly mess of it again. Long pasta is not his strong point. "They warned me that you bayed," Oliver says, "but never about your table manners."

The two best friends embark on another expedition to the darkened upper floors. Oliver steals through the rooms, peeking at the paintings under tarpaulin: Modigliani's portrait of a Gypsy; Léger's green bottles and black bowler hats; Chagall's blue chickens leaping over the moon; the English country landscape as seen by Pissarro.

Oliver stands before the Turner: a disintegrating ship and the spray of the sea; the way Turner captured water, the sloshing bulk of it. He could stare at it for hours —

and Turner is not particularly his thing. What is his thing, then? At Yale, his thesis (aborted when Boyd fell ill) was "Wreck in the Moonlight: Caspar David Friedrich and the Nineteenth-Century German Landscape." But it's preposterous to speak of "his thing" when it comes to art.

As he admires the Turner, his gaze flits from one aspect to another on the canvas, impatient for the pleasure of the next detail, rapt by the process of looking. "Beauty," he tells Schopenhauer, "is all I care about." Only the drowning figures in the foreground are a disappointment: visual noise within an otherwise impeccable panorama. Turner flubbed it, not simply because his human forms were inept but because the human form can never be rendered beautiful. A face is the opposite of beauty, lurching as it will from laughter to brutality. "How," Oliver asks, "can people be attracted to each other?"

His ear twitches at the incessant ringing downstairs. It's after midnight. "Can they not leave me alone?" From the answering machine comes the drone of his eldest brother, Vaughn, calling from Atlanta. Presumably to ask if Oliver has an Italian girlfriend yet. The family fears he is gay. They don't like gays. Or Communists. What about art historians? Same difference. He's not, though. Not what? An art historian. He's an art fancier. An appreciator of beauty. Only, not of faces. "You would have liked Mr. Deveen," he tells Schopenhauer. "But I would have been afraid to bring you two together — what if you hadn't gotten along? Still, I think you would have. You know, I was assigned to Mr. Deveen; I didn't pick him. It was luck. You see, there was this adopt-a-pensioner scheme at my school. Everyone had to do it." Unlike his three siblings, Oliver was sent to a boarding school in England, his father not wanting such an irritating little boy mincing around the house. "I went every Saturday to Mr. Deveen's house," Oliver tells Schopenhauer. "Made him tea, did the chores, the shopping, which in his case meant cigarettes and Irish whiskey — what brand was it? And the *New Statesman.* You wouldn't know that, Schop — it's a magazine for leftists and art historians. And actors, I imagine, which is what he'd been. In healthier days, he virtually lived at the galleries. He had the most amazing catalogs. I can fairly say, Schop, that Mr. Deveen introduced me to art. What an education! He could talk about absolutely any period, and in such a captivating way. Though he didn't fancy contemporary art — he had a bee in his bonnet about Pollock and just about everyone who came after that. I used to ask him about artists, and he'd respond with the exhibition, as in, 'Mr. Deveen, what do you think of Klee?' To which I'd get: 'The Collections of Sir Edward and Lady Hulton at the Tate in 1957 — top shelf.' I'd bring down the catalog and he'd flip through, explaining it all, sipping his Irish whiskey with milk, which I had to keep warming on the stove. (It's harder heating milk than you think, Schop — it keeps sticking to the bloody pot.) That smell, though — I'll never forget it. And the same chipped mug. He used to say, 'Don't destroy it, I beg you!' Had the finest baritone voice, too. Did radio plays for BBC Manchester in his day, and you could hear why. Ah, well," Oliver says. "It was the whiskey, I think. Not anything else. He wasn't. It wasn't. I mean, I don't condemn him. He was alone and . . . Yes, and the whiskey. Not his fault. Well, anyway, enough fussing."

Oliver asks the housekeepers to make *involtini di vitello* for dinner. He isn't crazy about the dish, but his wagging companion is an avid consumer. Schopenhauer eats almost all of it — too much, it turns out, for he suffers an upset stomach. Oliver plays nursemaid for the next twenty-four hours, cleaning up puddles of dog vomit.

Once the worst is over, he reads aloud from *The Hound of the Baskervilles* as the Hound of the Aventine dozes at his hip. Oliver knows this book so well that "reading" is hardly the word — he wanders about in it, renews old acquaintances, allows Dr. Watson's lank thread to reel him gently forward. This evening, however, the pages remain dry and yellow. He raises Schopenhauer's chin.

"You must get well!" he says. "You must be better soon!" He pulls Schopenhauer nearer. "I've spent too much time as a nursemaid already." He strokes the dog. "And I'm awful at it. When I nursed Boyd, I was constantly bothering him. I tried not to, but I couldn't help it. He used to tell me, 'You must be thrilled that I'm sick — you can use me as an excuse to drop out of Yale. You'll never have to graduate now.' But I thought *he'd* wanted me home to look after him. I mean, I thought so. I sometimes wonder if he called me back home to test me — to see if I'd comply. And, being such a softie, I did, of course, and he hated that. He used to say, 'Women comply, men defy.' Ah, well," Oliver says. "And, I mean, was I really going to end up as an academic? Me, lecturing? Can't see it. I hope I was useful to him. He certainly adored you, my little friend! Do you remember my father? He liked to throw that squeaky rubber rat of yours. Do you remember him throwing it down the lawn for you in Atlanta? And you'd just sit there, doing nothing, staring at the thing with such disdain." Oliver smiles. "Oh, come on — you know exactly the look I'm talking about. And my father — hardly a man to fetch objects — going down the garden with his cane, picking up your silly rat, throwing it again. And you sitting there, yawning!"

The phone rings, and Kathleen leaves another message: she has set a date for the staff meeting and Oliver must address the employees about the Ott Group's plans.

"What plans?" Oliver asks Schopenhauer.

Vaughn calls that evening, and Oliver picks up this time — if there are plans, perhaps he should be apprised.

"So," Vaughn asks, "are we going to sell that house?"

"Which house?"

"The house you're living in."

"Grandpa's? What for?"

"Well, you are coming back, I assume."

"What are you talking about, Vaughn?"

"Ollie, you do know we're putting the

paper out of its misery, right? Abbey recommended that we shut it. How can you not know this, Ollie? What are you doing out there?"

"But why close it?"

"Money, basically. Maybe if we'd got more layoffs a few months back we could've dragged it out. But they fought us on everything — all they agreed to in the end was one job cut from editorial. And they're expecting capital infusions after that? It's crazy. We kept Kathleen going for a while, dangling the possibility of fresh investment. But what's the point? You guys don't even have a website. How can you expect revenue without a Web presence? We could have ditched Kathleen, I guess. But let's be honest: the paper is a lemon. Time to move on."

"Don't we have enough money to keep it going?"

"Sure we do," Vaughn responds. "We have enough money *because* we make a habit of not keeping shit going that's a lemon."

"Oh."

"I want you at that staff meeting. Kathleen is adamant about it. And we need to keep her happy for now — we don't want bad publicity, okay?"

"What do they want *me* there for?"

"We need an Ott rep on-site. No way out

of this one, Ollie."

The morning of the meeting, Oliver asks Schopenhauer, "If they come at me as a mob, will you bite them?" He tickles the dog. "You wouldn't, would you — you'd be useless. Come on."

They walk all the way there, up Via del Teatro di Marcello, through Piazza Campitelli, along Corso Vittorio, Oliver muttering to Schopenhauer as they go: "I mean, we all know that I don't understand this sort of thing. The rest of the family does. But I seem to be missing it somehow. Missing the chromosome for it. The cleverness gene. I'm faulty. So here's my question, Schop: can I be blamed for my defects? I mean, are my faults my fault?" The dog glances up at him. "Don't give me that condescending look," Oliver says. "What have you ever done with your life that's so spectacular?"

They arrive at the scribble-gray building that has housed the paper for a half century. Employees smoke industriously before the towering oak door. Oliver hurries past them all, through the hinged portal, down the frayed burgundy runner to the elevator cage. Upstairs, he learns that Kathleen and Abbey have gone out. Thankfully, most of the editorial staffers are occupied piecing together copy on a shooting at Virginia

Tech. But a few employees attempt to buttonhole Oliver about "the big announcement" they have been promised. Is it good news? Sinkingly, he realizes that they don't know yet. He touches his cold hands to Schopenhauer's coat for warmth. The dog licks them.

Kathleen returns, escorts him to her office, and says he will have to run the meeting alone. Abbey joins them and seconds Kathleen's position: he will get no help.

"But I don't know anyone here," he says.

"I'll introduce you," Kathleen replies.

"And I don't know anything about the media industry."

"Maybe you should have learned something," she says. "You've been here two years."

They check the clock: a few minutes until the meeting.

"I'm really sorry," he says, "about this."

Kathleen scoffs. "Sorry? Come on — you could have averted this. You've been totally indifferent."

"No, no, I'm not."

"Oh, come on — you've made no effort here. The paper has been going all these years, and it's ending with you in charge. Your grandfather started this place. Doesn't that bother you? He wanted to build a newspaper for the world. Now you're closing it."

"But I'm totally useless at this sort of thing — they shouldn't have given me the job in the first place."

"Yeah, but they did, Oliver. They did. You were it."

"But I'm — I'm faulty, if you know what I mean. I don't work right." He laughs nervously, sweeping hair from his spotty forehead, still staring down at Schopenhauer, not once looking up at the women. "I lack the right chromosome or something."

"Cut it out."

"We should probably go in there," Abbey says.

Oliver moves toward the door, but Kathleen halts him with her forefinger. "You're not bringing the dog in."

"For moral support, I thought."

"Absolutely not. Show some respect."

Oliver ties Schopenhauer's leash around a leg of Kathleen's desk and strokes his friend quickly. "Wish me luck." He closes the door after himself and follows Kathleen and Abbey into the newsroom.

They lead him to a central position and retreat several paces. The staffers gather before him. How dirty the carpeting is, he notes. Whispers emanate from the crowd. He fills a plastic cup from the watercooler.

"We should probably start," Kathleen says. He offers a wobbly smile.

"You know everybody here?" Kathleen asks.

"I think some faces might be familiar," he says, looking at none. He leans in to shake hands, murmuring, "Thank you . . . thanks . . . hi . . . thanks for coming."

Most of the paper's employees have worked here for years. They married based on their earning prospects, took out mortgages because of this place, started families knowing that the paper would fund their children's lives. If this place folds, they're ruined. All these years, they have vilified the paper, but now it's threatening to quit them, they're desperately in love with it again.

"Everyone here?" Oliver asks. He speaks extemporaneously for a minute, then loses his nerve and grabs for a copy of the Ott board's confidential report on the paper. As he scans its pages, he glances imploringly in Kathleen's direction. She looks away. He clears his throat and locates a relevant passage. He reads it aloud, adding, "That's what the board decided." He clears his throat again. "I'm really sorry."

The room is silent.

"I don't know what else to say."

A question rips from the back of the room.

434

The crowd turns, makes a gap. The questioner is the head technician, a broad-shouldered American who appears even taller because he happens to be wearing Rollerblades that day. "What the fuck is this?" he says. "In plain English, tell us what's happening."

Oliver stammers out a few words, but the man interrupts: "Stop bullshitting us, man."

"I'm not. I'm trying to be clear. I think that —"

Ruby Zaga breaks in: "So, the Ott Group is pulling the plug? Is that what you're saying?"

"I'm afraid that's how I read it," Oliver answers. "I'm incredibly, incredibly sorry. I know that's inadequate. I do feel terrible about this, if that makes you feel any better."

"No, it doesn't actually," the head technician says. "And what the hell do you mean, 'That's how I read it'? Read what? You guys *wrote* it. Don't give me that, man. Don't give me that."

"I didn't write it. The board wrote it."

"Aren't you part of the board?"

"Yes, but I wasn't at this meeting."

"Well, why didn't you go?"

Someone else mutters, "Who appointed this guy publisher?"

"The report says," Oliver continues, "that . . . that it's a question of the business environment. It's not solely the paper — it's the whole of the media. I think. I mean. All I know is what's written in the report."

"Bullshit."

Oliver turns to Kathleen and Abbey.

"Wait a second," Herman Cohen says. "Before we all fly off the handle here, is there something that can be worked out? I'd like to know how final this decision is."

The head technician ignores this and clomps in his Rollerblades closer to Oliver. "You're an asshole, man."

The situation teeters on the edge of violence.

Oliver steps back. "I . . . I don't know what to say."

The technician storms out, taking a dozen furious employees with him.

"My kids are at private school," Clint Oakley says. "How am I supposed to pay the fees now? What are they supposed to do?"

"Is the Ott Group offering buyouts?" Hardy Benjamin asks.

"I don't know," Oliver says.

"Not to be blunt," Arthur Gopal interjects, "but what's the purpose of this meeting if you're not able to tell us anything?"

"Would it be possible to talk to someone who can give us a bit more information?" Craig Menzies asks. "Kathleen? Abbey?"

Abbey steps forward. "Mr. Ott is the only person authorized to speak on behalf of the Ott Group." She steps back.

More enraged employees walk out.

"How long have you known this was coming?" someone asks.

"I just found out," Oliver answers.

Several staffers roar with incredulity.

"Total waste of time," someone says.

More people leave.

"Maybe if the Ott Group had tried investing in the paper at some point instead of running this place into the ground, we wouldn't be in this mess."

Oliver leans toward Kathleen. "What do I do?" he whispers. "I think this is getting out of hand. Should we end the meeting?"

"That's your call."

He turns back to the crowd, though it's not much of a crowd any longer. Only a few people stand before him. In various corners of the newsroom, employees commiserate, make unauthorized long-distance calls, put on their coats to leave.

"I'm incredibly sorry," Oliver says. "I keep repeating that, but I don't know what else to say. I'm going to try to get answers to all your questions."

"Could you bring in someone who actually knows something?"

"Yes," he says, nodding at the floor. "Yes. I'll try to get a proper person to come and talk to you."

Even Kathleen and Abbey have gone. It is him alone now, before the last few bewildered staffers. "Uhm, bye," he says.

He is lost for a moment, then stumbles toward Kathleen's office. But midway there he pauses. He turns his head, sweeps the hair from over his ears.

A noise is coming from down there.

Oliver hurries into her office. Abbey and Kathleen are kneeling on the floor.

Between the two women is Schopenhauer, looking not at Oliver but at the wall, in the direction that someone has twisted his neck.

The dog wheezes, his jaw hangs limply, he emits a curious sound. He cannot seem to draw a breath: his lungs expand partly, he winces, his chest falls. He is still lashed to the leg of the desk and Kathleen yanks at the leash. "Damn it!" She pulls the knot apart finally, but to no useful end: Schopenhauer has stopped moving. "Damn it," she repeats. She slaps the leg of the desk. "Damn."

"What happened?" Oliver asks. "I don't

understand what happened."

"Someone came in, I think," Kathleen says, "while we all were out there."

But Oliver didn't mean that — he meant, What just happened? He meant, Why is Schopenhauer so quiet?

"This is sick," Abbey says. "Completely sick. And it was someone who works here. Did you notice who left the meeting early?"

"Almost everyone left early," Kathleen replies.

Abbey says, "I'm really sorry, Oliver."

"Extremely sorry," Kathleen says.

"Is he badly hurt?" Oliver asks.

Neither woman responds.

"We have to call the police," Abbey says.

"Don't, please," Oliver says.

"We have to find who did this."

"I'm going to take him now. Let's not," he says, "let's not blame people. I don't want to know who did it. They were all angry with me."

"That doesn't make it okay. This is disgusting."

"It's not anybody's fault," he says.

"Yes, it is," Kathleen insists.

Oliver slides his arms under Schopenhauer's limp body and, with a grunt, lifts the animal. "He always weighs more than I think."

He carries the dog across the newsroom, tugs open the elevator cage with his baby finger and enters, straining for the ground-floor button. But he cannot reach it and must put Schopenhauer down. "Good boy," he says, lowering his friend to the floor. "Good boy." He presses the button and stares up at the ceiling. The elevator rattles for a moment, then descends.

2007. *Corso Vittorio, Rome*

The final days of the paper were fraught. Some employees stopped turning up. Others looted computer equipment in lieu of future wages. A few drank openly, missed deadlines, even scuffled in the newsroom. Then the last day arrived, ended, and they were all, abruptly, free.

Some had jobs lined up, but many did not. A few planned to take time off. Others aimed to get out of journalism altogether. Maybe this is a blessing in disguise, they said, though it was hard to say how.

In Paris, Lloyd Burko was blissfully unaware of the commotion. He hadn't read the paper, or any other news, for months. He and his son, Jérôme, lived together, scrimping and getting by, just. Each man believed he was looking after the other. Lloyd cooked with gusto, if badly, for Jérôme and his skinny friends, a pleasant bunch of bohemians. They always invited the old man to join in their activities. Lloyd smiled thankfully at their offers but retreated graciously to his room.

To everyone's surprise, it was Arthur Gopal who got the most prestigious job, moving to New York as a reporter for a major newspaper. This was quite a change: doorstepping gunshot victims, getting yelled at by cops, feeding color to rewrite hacks who said things like

"Yeah, we know the shooting took place in a soup factory, but what kind of soup?" A year earlier, Arthur had a wife and daughter. It was strange to think of that now, so he did not.

Hardy Benjamin found work in London, reporting on technology for a business news-wire. Her Irish boyfriend, Rory, didn't have a job, so she paid the rent for their flat on Tower Hill. She bristled at those who suggested that he was living off her — in this regard alone, she refused to see matters in terms of business.

Kathleen Solson was rehired at her old newspaper in Washington, but to a lower-ranking position. Ultimately, the interlude in Rome hadn't served her career. She and her husband, Nigel, returned to their former apartment near Dupont Circle. She had a few days left before her new job started, so she caught up on the news online, took her books out of boxes, hung the oversize black-and-white photographs. Mostly, though, she wished this liberty were over.

Herman Cohen retired to write a history of the paper. He and his wife, Miriam, bought a house outside Philadelphia, and he told her, This is the last time I move. In the end, he never did start his book — it was so pleasant simply to be near the grandkids. When the little ones visited, he was in heaven, and no matter how much they abused the English language he never corrected their grammar.

Winston Cheung, after a period of sleeping in his parents' basement, found work at an exotic-animal refuge in Minnesota. He adored the job overall but disliked lining the monkey cages with newspaper — even the sight of headlines made him panicky these days. However, this was not to bother him for long: the local paper folded, and he switched to sawdust. Soon, even the monkeys forgot the comforts of newspaper.

Ruby Zaga could finally return home to Queens. And it was the last thing she wanted. Rome gave her solace. She had saved money and, in theory, could stay for years without working. The notion petrified her, then excited her. Her family — the beloved nieces, nephews, her brother — could come stay. She'd give them the grand tour. She had spent half her life in Rome. Half her life at the paper. She exhaled: she was free.

Craig Menzies left journalism to work at a lobbying firm in Brussels. He could afford to rent an entire house now and set up a science workshop in the garage. He even toyed with the idea of compiling a proper patent application. Often, he thought of contacting Annika in Rome, where she still lived. He had something to say to her, a point yet to make.

Abbey Pinnola was offered a position at Ott headquarters in Atlanta, but she refused it. She wouldn't uproot her kids, or put an ocean between them and her ex-husband in London, no matter how much she disliked the man. Her next job, she decided, would be in an industry that would never betray her. So she settled on international finance and found a post at the Milan offices of Lehman Brothers.

As for Oliver Ott, he did take a job at headquarters, where he was expected to do nothing, and he did so. He stared out his window over steamy Atlanta, wishing each day to be over. His siblings encouraged him to buy another dog at least.

He attended all the board meetings, voting however everyone demanded, even acceding to the sale of the mansion in Rome and all the paintings inside. At auction, the Modigliani went to an art dealer in New York, the Léger to a private collector in Toronto, the Chagall to a foundation in Tel Aviv, the Pissarro to a gallery in London, and the Turner to a shipping company in Hong Kong, which mounted it behind the receptionist's desk.

As Oliver's siblings debated in the boardroom, he contemplated the portrait of their grandfather. Nobody in that room had met the late patriarch. They knew only the legends: that Ott had fought in World War I and been shot, which took him out of the fighting and probably saved his life. That he'd turned a bankrupt sugar refinery into an empire. Much more was unknown. Why, for example, had Ott gone to Europe and never come back? There had been a woman at the paper, Betty, and some said Ott had had an affair with her. Was that true? She had died in 1979, and the paper's other founding partner, Leo, had passed away in 1990. Who was left to say?

Overnight, the paper disappeared from newsstands, taking with it the front-page banner, the characteristic fonts, the sports pages and the news, the business section and culture, Puzzle-Wuzzle and the obits.

The paper's most loyal reader, Ornella de Monterecchi, trooped down to headquarters to demand that closure be reconsidered. But she had arrived too late. The doorman was kind enough to unlock the vacated newsroom. He turned on the flickering fluorescent beams and left her to wander.

The place was ghostly: abandoned desks and cables leading nowhere, broken computer printers, crippled rolling chairs. She stepped haltingly across the filthy carpeting and paused at the copydesk, still covered with defaced proofs and old editions. This room once contained all the world. Today, it contained only litter.

The paper — that daily report on the idiocy and the brilliance of the species — had never before missed an appointment. Now it was gone.

ACKNOWLEDGMENTS

To begin, I wish to record those who cannot read this. My marvelous battling grandfather Robert Philips (1912–2007) and my dear bookish grandmother Monica Roberts (1911–1996). With them, Charles Dominic Philips (1940–1955), whose memory I intend to store in this book; Nick's birthday was February 10. My uncle and childhood hero, Bernard Rachman (1931–1987). And my uncle Lionel Rachman (1928–2008), one of the most remarkable men ever to stroll into a used bookshop or a racetrack.

Next, those whom I have the fortune to thank directly. My family: wonderful parents, Clare and Jack, who have been so generous, who always surrounded me with books and ideas and such kindness. My sister Emily, the most brilliant advocate, whose astute suggestions, selfless help, and unstoppable enthusiasm have boosted me countless times. My eldest sister, Carla, a

447

splendid ally, providing me with friendship and access to her sublime mind, full of wit and thoughtfulness. My brother, Gideon, endlessly amusing and generous, as well as my favorite columnist, wine purveyor, and Chelsea attacking midfielder. Also, Joel Salzmann, and my nieces Talia and Laura; Olivia Stewart, and my niece Tasha and my nephews, Joe, Adam, and Nat. My cousin and friend Jack Slier, as well as his father, Lionel Slier, another cousin and friend. Also, my warm thanks to Paula, Hayley, and Alicia. In London, Sandra Rachman and Mike Catsis. In Israel, Aviva Rachman and Omri Dan. And in Vancouver, Alice Philips and Greg Oryall.

Now, my friends. Ian Martin, whose humanity, mind, and uppercut have rescued me more than once. His father, Paul Martin (1938–2007), one of my favorite readers — how I'd have loved to have handed him a copy. Hetty Martin, for cups of tea, kosher duck, and other Welsh specialties. From Toronto days, Suzanne Brandreth and Stephen Yach. From New York, Ian Mader, Mareike Schomerus, and Hien Thu Dao. From Vancouver, Valerie Juniper. From Paris, Paul Geitner, Chuck Jackson, and Maureen Brown. From Ankara, Selcan Hacaoglu. From Rome, Jason Horowitz, Daniele Sobrini, Aidan Lewis, and the delightful Rizzo family: Aldo, Margherita, and Benedetta.

Finally, this book would be incomplete without the inclusion of my favorite short story, Alessandra Rizzo, whose patience, support, and affection kept me afloat while I wrote.

Thanks also to my agent, Susan Golomb, for fishing my manuscript from across the pond and doing such marvels with it. Also, Terra Chalberg and Casey Panell of the Susan Golomb Agency. And my editor, Susan Kamil of the Dial Press and Random House, whose wisdom and deft touch helped make *The Imperfectionists* that much less imperfect. My thanks also to Noah Eaker, Carol Anderson, and all those who worked on the book at Dial and Random House.

ABOUT THE AUTHOR

Born in London and raised in Vancouver, **Tom Rachman** is a graduate of the University of Toronto and the Columbia School of Journalism. He has been a foreign correspondent for the Associated Press stationed in Rome, with assignments that have taken him to Japan, South Korea, Turkey, and Egypt, among other places. From 2006 to 2008, he worked as an editor at the *International Herald Tribune* in Paris. He lives in Rome.